UNAPOLOGETIC FOR MY
FLAWS AND ALL

CHARLENA JACKSON,
B.S., M.S., M.H.A.

BOOKS BY CHARLENA E. JACKSON, B.S., M.S., M.H.A

No Cross, No Crown: Trust God Through the Battle

I'm Speaking Up but You're Not Listening

Teachers Just Don't Understand Bullying Hurts

A Woman's Love Is Never Good Enough

To my lovely daughter, Sarah you are my precious pearl. Know your worth and never sell yourself short to make someone feel good about themselves. You are my sweet Love Bug! You fill my heart with so much peace, happiness, and joy! Thank you for all you do. I am proud of you and keep up the amazing work! I will love you for eternity!

To my amazing one of a kind mother Mae Jackson. You are one of the most courageous women I know. Your strength gives to courage to always put my best foot forward. One thing for sure, I learned from the best, thank you! I love you to the moon and back!

To my nieces, Shanny, Raven, Imani, Maya, Nyla, and Reese. My girls, Janan and Rania. Embrace who you are and know you deserve the best and nothing but the best! I love you all dearly!

* * *

In memory of Dr. Deloss Brubaker (1948-2018)

Printed in the United States of America

1st edition, February, 2019

ISBN 13: 978-1-73356-666-7

CHAPTERS

CHAPTER ONE

THE ALARM GOES OFF AND I DON'T WANT TO MOVE. I KEEP MY EYES closed, thinking about my confused life as I reach over and hit the button. I feel like every day I am on a roller coaster going up, down, in a circle, upside down, and sometimes I am going backwards without a break. It's never-ending. There are times when I am ready to get off the ride, but if I do, I know my life will change tremendously. Maybe, change will not be a bad thing.

People say that I am the "most popular" girl in school. I do not know how I became most popular. The best person I can be is myself. My friends, classmates, some of my teachers, and people who know me, act like my shit don't stink. I am human and I try my best to stay humble. I guess I am the most popular person in school because I am not afraid to be myself.

It has never been my mission to keep up with the latest style. I do not have a preferred style; however, I love to dress neatly.

Most importantly, I love to dress comfortably, according to my mood. Goodwill is my favorite store. Nothing is ever the same, there is always something new or gently used. It is not like a typical store that will have the "norm" that you expect. It has some of everything, and sometimes things that you least expect–I might add, for a reasonable price. Honestly, I love the Goodwill store! Every time I walk in, I know that I am going to have a field day! It's a one-stop-shop convenience store. I buy all my books from Goodwill. I literally live in the book section. I bought a white desk there that was in great condition, and it had a matching chair. It fits perfectly in my room. Their clothes are used, but the ones I pick are quality and gently used. At times, I find 'affirmation' decorations to hang on my wall. I make sure I have time on my hands when I am shopping at Goodwill because I never know what I might find.

I always love to get my hair, toes, and nails done. They're always on point. However, my friends and other people fail to realize that most of the time I do my own hair, nails, and toes. YouTube is my best friend! People are always coming up to me asking where I get my hair done, or what color I'm wearing on my toes and nails; they even ask me what kind of toothpaste I use to brush my teeth, because my teeth are always white. I tell them, I floss and brush my teeth with regular toothpaste like everyone else. For some people, it must be stressful being someone that you're not. However, I do not know about that, because I am unapologetic for my flaws and all. I love me for me. There's no reason for me to change to fit in. I am perfectly fine fitting into my own world. I love the woman who I am becoming. I wish other females would jump on board and know they are beautiful just the way they are.

It is strange how people follow me on social media and pay close attention to who I follow. Before I follow other people,

I make sure I read their profile. If I do not know them, I do not follow them at all. I tend to follow meditation, affirmation and earth picture bloggers. I am not a goody two shoes, but I am cautious because the world is crazy. Well, technically the world isn't crazy; it's the people that are in it.

The other day, my best friend asked me why do I follow this person or that person. I told her, because I want too. She really gave me a speech on why I shouldn't follow certain people. She thinks most of the people I follow are "lame". I couldn't entertain her, because that is the problem with so many people; they care too much about what other people think.

She really told me I cannot follow everyone who follows me on social media. That is forbidden if I want to keep my A-1 status. She went on to say, it is a must that I have more followers than my "so-called friends" (who copy my every move.) Honestly, I totally ignored her.

Ugh. It is annoying seeing people who break their necks trying to keep up with me. Sometimes I cannot keep up with myself because there is so much going on. Everyone is telling me about their problems; they really wait for me to give them advice. I tell them to take a number because I cannot help everybody at the same time. Shoot, half the time, I cannot help myself, let alone everyone else.

Not to mention, my number one problem is my boyfriend. I will talk about him later. If I let him consume my mind right now I will never ever get out of bed.

My personal problems are seeds that I've planted. They do not sprout when they are supposed to, and they tend to grow when I least expect it. That is when most of my problems occur. I have to work on planting my seeds at the right time so they can sprout during the right season.

As my eyes are stilled closed, I have a good laugh. The problem isn't planting my seeds at the right time; it's also ensuring they get enough sunshine, rain and a lot of love. Most of the time I let them wither and die because I tend to take on too much at one time. When will I ever learn? Well, what can I say, I can only do what I can, and let the rest fall into place.

My classes are not challenging because I love learning. Keeping my grades up is a must! I am a senior at Jackson-Miles High. I completed my high school courses in tenth grade. Since eleventh grade, I've been participating in the Early College Program. I am working hard to earn more than enough credits to graduate with an Associate Degree during my high school years. I work part-time at a coffee shop because I love the smell of coffee. I know that's silly. Although I do not drink coffee, the smell of coffee is so vibrant. It changes my mood from being confused and overwhelmed to calm and relaxed. I participate in extra activities at school, and sometimes they are a hassle.

My goal is to stay focused because I need to make sure I have more than enough extra activities on my college applications. That way, they will see that I know to multitask.

I am the captain of the cheerleading team. Honestly, I never cared about being captain but it would look good on my college applications as well. I've been cheering since I was six years old and I invested in cheerleading as a hobby. My mom was captain on her squad; and prom queen. Consequently, my mom was really popular and she loved it! As for me, as I stated earlier, I really do not care for it, as being 'most popular' now will soon be forgotten.

My mom loves to "see" and "know" that I am popular. I never understood why my mother wanted me to always be the "it" girl in everything I do. When I was on the track team in ninth grade, she asked me was I the "it" girl? When I joined the debate club in tenth grade she seriously asked me, was I the "it" girl? I was like ugh, gross, Mom – the "it" girl in the debate club? The debate club isn't focused on how "popular" we are. We are focused on executing the debate. Being very popular is the only thing my mom cares about. Sadly, my mom was never ever at one cheerleading game, she never cheered me on during my track and field meets, and she never warmed a seat in the debate tournaments. Little does she know, it would be nice to have her support.

My friends think I have it made. I am a long way from having it made. They seriously think my family is perfect. They are so wrong. They only see material things: my house is a reasonable size. We have six bedrooms; eight bathrooms, a mini movie theater, the additional rooms we have are my parent's offices because they own their own businesses and work from home.

We have a nice-sized back yard with a fire pit and a gazebo (which is my favorite); therefore, my friends think my parents are rich because my father is an architect, an engineer and a contractor, and my mother is an accountant and stockbroker. My father always tells us, their money isn't our money, because they worked hard to get where they are; and we have to do the same. That is why I work so hard; because I want to live life comfortably.

I am so sick and tired of hearing what my friends think. They really think my mother and I are extremely close but we are becoming more and more distant. My mother thinks the definition of love is spending money. If I have a problem and I need my mother's advice, she would say, "Breana, let's go on a shopping spree to release your problems." Shopping never ever cured my problems. It actually caused more problems because new problems build up on top of current problems.

I am lost in so many ways. It is hard for me to trust, because my parents are always busy. Most of the time, my daddy spends time with me; and he does give me great advice, but it is hard to gain my mother's attention. I am not the type of girl who acts out in the worst way for attention. I keep a lot of things deep down inside; which isn't healthy. Nobody really knows my deepest thoughts and feelings. I let people know exactly what I want them to know. Other than that, I keep most of it in.

Sadly, people have made me into who they "think" I am in their eyes. To them, I am "most popular". However, as I get to know more about me, the real me is plain old Breana (Bree-un-na).

I only can relate to the real me. I wonder if I would be liked as much as "the me I know" rather than the most popular girl in school. My mother doesn't even see the "real" me. It bothers me most of the time; because people only see what they want to see, and hear what they want to hear.

I heard a knock on my door. I didn't respond. Another knock. I turned over and pretended I was sleep. I heard the door open. "I know you're up, bird brain!" a tiny high-pitched voice yelled. Oh, did I forget to mention that I have a little sister who really gets on my last nerve? Summer is a handful, but she's smart to be in the seventh grade. I try to be there for her as much as I can because I do not want her to feel neglected. I do not want her to feel just as I do when it comes to my mother. However, I do not think she notices. Maybe she doesn't notice because I pick up my mother's slack. At least Summer can say her big sister was always there for her. I let her know she can always lean on me and come to me about anything.

"Summer, please lower your voice," I said in a groggy voice. "Get up, bird brain!" she yelled. As I threw the covers off, books and papers fell on the floor. I answered her, laughing, "Just yesterday I was brilliant in your eyes and today I have a bird brain!" She was leaning on the door, brushing her hair, and with a blue toothbrush in her mouth. Her hair wasn't completely done, as one side was neatly tied in a bow with a bright orange ribbon. She had on black leggings, an orange shirt with black letters that spelled out "Go Tigers!" with a tiger on it looking like he is ready for a feast. "Goodness gracious, Bree-Bree, you should be ashamed of yourself. Look at your room—what in the world?" As she moved her fingers from side to side real fast, "You know you need to do something with all of this," she scolded. "How do you sleep with all that stuff on your bed?" she asked. "Good grief, Bree-Bree, that is disgusting," she added.

Shaking my head, I ignored her comments. "How are you brushing your hair and brushing your teeth at the same time? That is gross. Ugh. You are going to have your nasty bacteria-filled morning saliva on my floor. I would appreciate it if you would dismiss yourself, please," I said as I rolled over onto the scattered paper on the other side of the bed.

"For your information, I can do anything I put my mind to. As a matter of fact, you were the one who told me that. But if you must know, I was brushing my teeth when Mommy asked me to come and see if you were up. I figured if I have to wake up my sister, who I might add has two alarm clocks (Summer shook her head) and still can't manage to wake herself up. What a pity. Anyway, I figured I could brush my hair as I took my time walking down the hall, up the stairs to your room to wake you up. With that being said, Bree-Bree, unlike you, I manage my time wisely, thank you very much. And you're more than welcome for my services. Therefore, I will be more than happy to dismiss myself from your messy room," Summer responded.

I wanted to stir the pot a little bit more, "Well, you look like a tall, skinny bumblebee. I guess waving your fingers as fast as they can go represents your wings." I laughed and was about to say something else, but Summer abruptly cut me off. Summer yelled, "Clueless Bree-dumb-ana, I am not dressed up as a bumblebee. I am wearing orange and black. Bumblebees are yellow and black. Duh. Clearly, you can see the tiger on my shirt. Today is Spirit Week. I need for you to wash your face, brush your teeth, drink some tea, meditate or whatever you do to get yourself together. Right now, you look and sound stupid; and nothing else in between, just straight stupid!"

Did I mention that my sister has an explanation for everything? Most of the time she has her facts lined up. It's better to say okay and keep it moving, or she will go back and forward with you all day. "Summer, thank you for your inspirational speech," I said. "You're more than welcome, Breana." Summer closed my door and yelled from the top of the steps, "Mommy, your oldest daughter is still lying in her bed, but she is awake." My sister can be a headache sometimes, but I love her to death. I heard her marching back into my room.

"Bree! Oh, I forget to tell you to look up! she said with excitement. I looked up at the ceiling. I blinked my eyes a couple of times, thinking I was dreaming. I muttered slowly, in my groggy voice, "What in the world???" My sister had a good laugh, "Ms. Queen of Jackson-Miles High! Do you like it?" I lay there for a moment and slowly said, "Wait. Summer, how and when did you put my prom campaign poster on my ceiling?" "Yesterday, around nine. You were knocked out asleep. Mommy and I were about to kill ourselves with all this mess on your bed and floor. We figured you'd like it! What do you think?" Summer said, giggling and excited at the same time. "Yes. I love it." I replied as I stretched, trying to understand why they put it on the ceiling. "You do? I thought you would!" Summer said, smiling. She added, "I am going to run for prom queen too. I am going to follow in your and Mommy's footsteps." She looked up at the ceiling and said, "I love your peach puffy dress. You look like a princess with your hair pinned up with a sparkly diamond crown. You're so beautiful in this picture. Too bad you do not look the same when you wake up. Bree, you look like ugh. Ugh. Just ugh."

"Bye, Summer," I replied dryly. "You don't have to tell me a second time, Ms. Grinch of Jackson-Miles High!" Summer cried, as she got a kick out of her lame joke. She was about to close the door. "Summer," I said quickly. "Yes, Mean Queen?" She asked, smirking. "Come here." She walked over and I gave her a big hug. "Thank you, baby sis! I love the effort, and you are the best sister in the world and I appreciate you!" Summer said, "May I remind you, I am your only sister, Bree. Give me a break with all the lovey-dovey stuff," Summer laughed as she tried to pull away. I held her tight and kissed her with my wet stinky-breath lips. She ran out of my room as fast as she could. I yelled, still laughing, "I love you, Summer!" As she ran down the steps she yelled, "Although you have spoiled trashy breath, Bree-Bree, I love you too."

I laughed and shook my head as I reach over to check my phone. I don't remember dozing off last night. Brian called me three times. I hope everything is okay. Or maybe he was calling to argue over nothing like always.

I scrolled down and saw seven text messages.

Text: Monday, 7:46 p.m.
"Breana, are you up?"
"Bree, call me back."
"Bree. Stop playing. Hit me back."

Text: Monday, 8:37 p.m.
"Okay, play your games. I'm done!"

Text: Monday, 9:14 p.m.
"Bree, I know you see me texting you."

Text: Monday, 9:53 p.m.
"So, it's like that now?"
"Cool. Whatever."

Here we go again. I am so over his ass. I need to break up with him. Every time I think about breaking up with him I feel like I am going to miss out on something. In all honesty, my mind is playing tricks on me because I do not want him to be with anyone else. I put in a lot of work, love and time. Maybe my work is done. Maybe my time has run out. And just maybe my love has run its course because there's nothing left to do but to let go. We've been a couple for over two years now and it has been hell since day one.

Well, I wouldn't say it's been all hell, but most of it has been very challenging. We have our good days, but those are very rare. I always make up excuses as I tell myself, we all have our ups and downs, things are not always going to be easy, and if we want something to work we have to put in the work, time, love, and dedication. When I face reality, it's different. It's more work, more stress, and love doesn't conquer our relationship.

I am a smart girl. My daddy always says when being in a relationship you cannot be blind and ignore the signs. I've seen so many signs, and guess what? I ignore them every single time.

Brian and I got into an argument the other day. He thinks I have so much time on my hands, but I don't. I have a lot of responsibilities, and most of the time I am last on my list – or not even *on* my list. He acts like he cannot understand that I have to submit my college applications, I have tons of classes, work, and I am in different clubs and activities around campus. He is very busy too, but I do not nag the shit out of him.

Last Saturday, I called off work to make time for our relationship. I thought a lot about what I wanted to do. I wanted to make it special. I packed a lunch for us and laid out a blanket in the park. We had a nice peaceful picnic as we sat on the grass, swung on the swing, and enjoyed the city view. We stayed there all day until after the sun fully set.

Just last Wednesday, we went skating. We had a good time. After skating, we went out to eat and topped it off with ice cream from Baskin Robbins.

Brian transferred to our school three years ago. He tried out for varsity football and the basketball team. I am captain of both the basketball and football cheerleading teams. We had our eyes on each other for a while, and he made his first move on the bus on an away football game. I was cold and he put his jacket around my shoulder to warm me up. He was so sweet as he put his sweater on my legs to cover me up after seeing me shiver. Needless to say, it took off from there.

As I lay in the bed I start to smile because he is so hand-some. His dark luscious chocolate skin makes me have butterflies. His smile is ridiculously cute. He has straight pearly white teeth. His dimples are to die for. He is always groomed from his low top fade and his sick hairline that is always so crisp and straight. He is very stylish and looks like an athlete with his hot-ass body. Can you say six-pack, toned arms, and ripped muscles on his back? I can look at him all day during practice. Ahh, now I see why I haven't broken up with him. He is too fine to let go. I can't help but smile when I think about...

Ring. Ring. (Trey Songz *I'm Already Taken* is my ringtone for Brian)

(Dry tone) "Hello, Brian."

His voice sounds relieved, "Bree, are you up?"

"Of course, I am up, Brian. I answered the phone," I say, trying not to sound sarcastic.

His voice deepens and rises at the same time with madness, "Bree, it was messed up that you didn't text me back last night."

"Good morning to you too, Brian," I say calmly as I rolled my eyes.

His voice got louder, "Bree, I swear, you be tripping."

Once again, I said in a calm voice, "Good morning to you too, Brian."

He started to yell, "Why didn't you answer the phone last night? I called you over and over again. No answer! I was looking like a damn fool texting after I called!"

"Good morning to you too, Brian," I said again in a firm voice, thinking to myself, *I am not going through this shit today. It is too early.*

He paused, took a deep breath, "I am not playing games this morning, Bree."

I put my longest finger on the red button on my phone – basically saying without words, fuck you, Brian, as I said, "Goodbye, Brian."

When I was about to hang up, I heard him yell, "Bree! Wait! Don't hang up, Bree!"

"I said good morning to you three times. I am not going through this shit again today." I told him in an 'I-don't-give-a shit' tone.

He yelled, "Good morning, Breana! Are you happy now?"

"No, I am not. I will talk to you later, Brian," I answered. As I put the bird finger on the red button all I heard was him yelling my name, "Bree! Bree! Bree!"

I hung up on Brian. It was too early to be going through this nonsense. Before I answered the phone then, I was going to say I can't help but smile when I think about his outward appearance. ...Wish I could say the same about his personality. He just killed my vibe. All I can think of is—why do I let him do this to me?

Most of the time when I talk to him, I can never get out of bed on the right foot without having any drama.

I should stay in bed and call it a day.

I have one foot hanging off my bed as I pulled the covers back over my face (more stuff falls off my bed) for one minute to regroup.

Ring. Ring. (Google Duo from Chloe) Ugh. Forget it. Today, no such thing as regrouping.

Chloe is my best friend. She and I have known each other since third grade. Sometimes she really gets on my last nerve too, but she's like a sister. We have our ups and downs; break up to make up. I wouldn't ever want to lose her as a friend. I believe she is the only true friend I have. Chloe has that 'I don't give a shit attitude'. She be playing these boys like a deck of cards. One thing for sure, she makes it known, loud and clear that she is the queen and a fearless boss. I don't know how she does it, but these boys be eating out the palm of her hands.

I love her personality, she's thick, and she be making it do what it does! She is the type of person that prefers all or nothing. Her energy is so carefree, outgoing, bold, and she doesn't take anything for granted. Her motto is: "Everything happens for a reason." Chloe is my better half, she is my other "me". She is my girl! We always tell people, we might not have the same parents, but we were in the same womb in another life. We are like twins, but opposite, yet the same in many ways. We call ourselves the Yin/Yang Twins. As the saying goes, opposites attract.

Her face looks so huge on the screen. "Hey, Girl! What you doing? Are you still in bed? How about Brian called me last night looking for you? Where were you? Whaaatt..."

I am looking confused. I can't take all these questions so I cut her off. "Oh, my gosh, Chloe, it is too early in the morning to be asking me a trillion questions. And why is your face so huge on the screen, please back up or something, you are making my head hurt."

"Oh, my bad girl. Let me adjust my phone. Is that better?"

"Yes, it is so much better," I answered.

I let Chloe tell it as she said, "Girl, you look bad. Are you sick or something? Eww, your lips are so crusty and dry. Girl, you really look a hot damn mess."

I laughed, "Really, a hot damn mess?"

She looked really serious when she said, "Bree, look, call me back and get yourself together; your hair looks like you just got electrocuted. Your lips need some serious treatment. Vaseline lip therapy with aloe will most definitely do the trick and put moisture back into your lips. Are you staying home today?"

I laughed, "Funny how everyone has jokes this morning."

"Who says, I am joking? Girl, you need to do something with all that," she says as she's chewing gum and filing her nails.

"Look who's talking! When you wake up in the morning you look like a rusty bag of rocks," I said.

She laughed, "Maybe, but not today. Sweetie."

She put her clear lip gloss on, "Girl, don't act like you don't know. The bag might be rusty, but the rocks are beautiful in all shapes and sizes. I prefer the healthy rocks that's full of life, that's me all day. I am big boned and the bomb! I am the shit and loving it! Girl, I am flawless in my sleep. All day and every day. You better act like you know."

Chloe is funny. Her confidence is through the roof. You cannot tell her she isn't looking her best. I love that she is sure of herself and conformable in her skin. I must say, I love her boldness, it inspires me.

I laughed, "Yeah, yeah, I know. Let me not go there, because you will be talking about yourself all day."

As she focused hard on painting her toes and chewing the hell out of her gum, she said, "And you know it! Anyway, are you staying home today?"

I took a deep breath, "No, I am going to school. I got up later than expected and my first class is later this morning."

Her dimples were so deep and cute as she continued to chew the hell out of her gum, she said, as she focused on her pinky toe, "Damn, Girl, my pinky toe always give me a hard time. So, girl, where were you last night?"

I laughed and smiled at the same time with a smirk on my face, "What? What you mean, where was I last night? I was in my bed."

Chloe rolled her eyes. "Yeah, right. You went to bed at. ... what time? Five in the afternoon."

"No. I went on a phone fast." I said.

"You and your fasting. Food fast. Phone fast. Fast. Fast. Fast. Only Bree does all this extra stuff." (I admire fasting. It is a way for me to stay grounded. I fast from everything that could be a distraction. When I fast, I focus on my mental state of being, I enjoy nature, I focus on what I need instead of want, my short-comings are more visible, and fasting helps me to execute my goals. Fasting helps me a lot.)

I laughed. "I have to stay grounded. Fasting helps me gain inner peace."

Chloe smiled, "Yeah. Yeah. Yeah. I know. Please spare me the details. I know. I know. Oh, good grief do I know."

Looking serious, I said, "Anyway, I have a lot going on. I have to send off the last bit of college applications and I have a list of things I have to do. Time is ticking and it is ticking fast. You know I am not a last-minute type of girl. I have to get my shit done before time."

Chloe, blowing her toes, said, "Girl, what was I thinking? My fan is on the other side of my room. Ugh, it is going to take forever for me to dry my toes by blowing on them. ...Oh yeah, that's right, Ms. Perfect. Ms. Organizer. One day, you have to let go and live life as it comes. Loosen up, girl. As long as I've known you, you have always been a neat freak."

I was about to comment on her question about what she was thinking, but she said, "Bree, you've already been accepted into I do not know how many colleges already. Why send off more applications? I do not understand, you are doing too much, and you put too much pressure on yourself."

She added, "You know Bree, you are your worse critic. You have to live life, love it, and as you say, stay grounded, but let the Universe take its course. You've done all you can do, now it is time to let the Universe do its part. Bree, have you ever thought, that sometimes you might be in the way of your own blessings? Honestly, chill out. Take a breather, and relax."

"Thank you for the encouraging words. Sometimes, I feel like I am hard on myself, but I have to get it done. I cannot leave anything unfinished. When I complete everything and know I have done everything to the best of my ability, with hopes my hard work will be overflowing with blessings and the Universe favors my dedication. Hopefully." I say.

Chloe started to breathe hard and said, "Okay, Ms. Run Yourself in the Ground."

I lowered my voice and humbly replied, "Call it whatever you want too. I set goals that I have to accomplish, and I cannot accomplish them running under my girls or running after a boy."

Chloe, all of a sudden came back to life, "Ahhh, speaking of boys. Your man was blowing up my phone last night looking for you. And how about Keith's ass was tripping, talking about it is about that time? I was like, boy, bye."

"About that time? What time?" I asked.

Chloe had that 'are you fucking kidding me' look on her face as she said, "Bree, are you awake? Are you listening? Sometimes I swear you..."

"I am listening and you clearly see that I am wide awake. You are the one talking in code. Time…Time for what? If you want me to crack the code you'd better explain. The only time I can think of is time for… What, sex?" I answered.

She shrugged her shoulders, "What else is it going to be, Bree? Time for marriage? Ugh, hell no. Time for a baby? Ugh, most definitely, hell to the no. Gosh, Bree. Sometimes you… Never mind."

"Sometimes I what?" I asked, smirking.

"Never mind, Bree," she said.

I said slowly, "Well, technically, Chloe, if you have sex there is a possibility you will get pregnant."

Chloe rolled her eyes again, "You know what? I am not going there with you today. Let me know when you're on campus. I will see you then."

I made a boo-boo face, "Chloe, eww, you are in such a badass mood this morning. Why turn sour all of a sudden?"

"Bree. I will talk to you later," she said.

My facial expression changed to serious, "Chloe. I was just kidding."

Her voice changed as well, "Bree, I was serious. He wants to have sex and I am not ready for all of that. I felt like you were being a smartass with your smartass comment. I am very much aware of getting pregnant, Bree. I didn't need to hear that from you."

"Chloe, I didn't mean it that way, I thought we were kidding around. My apology." I told her sincerely.

She slightly closed her eyes and smiled, "I accept your apology. I apologize too. Damn, I *did* flip the script."

"Yeah, you did. But it's okay, I see that it bothered you," I said.

"Yes, it did," Chloe answered.

"Well, you know, my Yang, my twin, nobody can make us do something we do not want to do. Talk to him about it; and if he doesn't respect your decision then, he got to go. There is no compromising on anything you do not feel comfortable with. Like we always say, will it be worth it? Ugh, no. Remember, Brian tried to pressure me to have sex, and I told him, no, and if he wants to have sex that bad, he needs to beat his meat, or break up with me and find a girl to fulfill his needs, because I am not the one. I refused to give up my virginity to someone I know for a fact we will not have a future together. Not only that, you know, we want it to be special, not just a fling thingy and move on. We will regret our decision if we do it. Shoot, all the girls I know of that had sex said it wasn't even worth it. They were in pain, and it was only a couple of minutes. They cannot get their pureness back. I am keeping my pureness until I am ready. Plus, we will be the ones who use protection and still get pregnant or an STD, because we know better."

Chloe laughed, "Yeah, that is so true. We could be cautious and prevent all of the above and still get caught up. Nope, I'll pass."

I smiled, "Me too. I'll pass for sure."

Chloe gave me an air hug through the phone, "Thank you, my Yin, you are so right. Sometimes, I feel like I want to do it, but then I ask myself, is it worth it? I see these girls walking around school pregnant and the dudes go around saying, "It's not my baby."

Chloe had a high-pitched voice (that's her gossip tone) as she said, "Girl, how about Shay is thirteen weeks pregnant! Did you know that?

My mouth dropped, "Shay? I know you are not talking about Shay Tucker."

Chloe's tone got higher, "Yes, girl, Shay Tucker. She is pregnant with nobody knows whose baby."

I squinted my eyes and said, "Wait. What? With what? Nobody knows whose baby? Chloe, you are not making any sense."

"Oh, yes, I am. Nobody's claiming her baby. Shay is walking around looking crazy. They are calling her all kinds of names. They saying its Tony's baby, then Tony says, "Hell, fuck, nah, it's Brad's baby." Brad's going around saying, "That ain't my kid, it is Marcus'". Marcus says in front of the whole cafeteria, "That bastard ain't mines," Chloe replied, going nonstop as if she couldn't catch her breath because she didn't want to forget a thing.

My mouth opened as I asked, "What? See, girl, we need to keep the lock on our pocketbooks and throw away the key. We can always call Lock Smith to replace the key."

Chloe laughed so loud, "What? Called Lock Smith to replace the key? I was keeping up with you and agreed until you start talking about Lock Smith. Girl, you are crazy! Hey, my pocketbook's on lockdown for sure. I feel so bad for Shay."

I said sadly, "Yeah, me too, but I want to know who is the baby's father."

"I wonder, are they willing to get a DNA test?" Chloe asked.

"Damn, I know she wasn't having sex with all of them. They are making her look like a sloppy-second ho. I am more than sure she didn't have sex with all those boys," I said in a distasteful way.

"Boys ain't shit," I added in an angry tone.

"They want to get between your legs and call it a day after they get it. Then talk shit about it like they are a fucking hero. See, girls go through a lot with these useless boys." I added, still filled with anger.

"You are so right, Yin," Chloe said.

"We as girls, young girls, and women, have the power to say no. We hold the power; all of it. We give dudes too much power. Yang, keep your legs closed and if Keith don't understand, that means he never gave a rat's ass. That is when you tell his ass to go kick rocks. If he says he understands, it could be a setup to warm you up."

Chloe laughed, "What? A setup to warm me up?"

"Yeah, a setup to warm you up. Meaning he going to be like. ...Yeah, I am going to stir the stew in the pot, sauté it and make it sound good and look tasty; then he is going to go in for the emotional mind games. He is going to make you feel like you are the one playing games because he is going to be like; Chloe, you had me waiting all this time and we still not having sex. Then he thinks you are going to give in because he is going to play with your emotions to make him seem like the victim so you can give in," I said.

Chloe said slowly, "Girl, that is deep. I didn't think about it that way."

"Girl, yeah, they want us to seem like the bad one. They want us to feel bad. So they try to blind us with their manipulations. We cannot fall for that shit. No way in hell we are going to get caught up. Hell, no," I said, arching my eyebrows.

"Hell, nah, we are not getting caught up. Then they will be moving on, living their lives and we stuck with problems and a baby. Shoot, twins run on both sides of my family. Most definitely, I'll pass. Thank you, Bree-Bree for listening, being here and knocking some sense into my head," Chloe said.

I laughed, "It was knowledge knocking some sense in both of our heads. Shay's situation knocked the wind out of both of us. When we think about having sex, we need to think about what Shay's going through. And you are more than welcome! Girl, we have to keep each other grounded."

"Yes, we do, and no problem. That's what sisters are for! And, yeah, I wish the best for Shay. Well, I'll see you at school later," Chloe, said as she waved her hand.

I waved my hand too, "Yeah, I need to get out of bed and get myself together. I will see you in a couple of hours when I go to cheerleading practice. In the meantime, do not do anything I wouldn't do."

Chloe smirked, "Oh gosh, if that was the case I would have a really boring life. I have to have a little excitement. See you soon."

Chloe blew a couple of kisses.

"Ciao, Bree-Bree."

"See you soon."

I stretched my entire body. It felt so good as I literally rolled out of bed and landed on top of everything that was piled on the floor.

I squinted my eyes to look at the calendar. Time goes by so fast. This past July my brother Luke moved out early for college. Wow, now it's the last week in August. Goodness! My parents are putting the finishing touch on my room. I'm loving it so far! It is in the attic and I will have my own privacy. Since Summer will be moving up there after me when she starts high school, she and I had to compromise on the layout. I didn't care, but she wanted a bay window. I must admit it's kind of cute. I can't wait because I will be moving in in a couple of weeks!

Ouch! I stepped on my lip gloss top. Dang it, I just got sticky dark red plum lip gloss all over my carpet. I have to try to get it up before my mom sees it.

Knock. Knock. "Breana," Mom said.

As I was rubbing my foot I told her, "Come in."

Smelling like a bed of flowers my mom said, "Good morning, sweetie."

My mommy looks beautiful, like always. She's dressed in a navy blue pants suit with a pretty pink blouse and looking like the boss. I love to see my mommy's hair fall in her face when she talks and she looks so innocent when she brushes it back. Her skin is so dark-toned and moist she looks like she bathes in shea butter lotion.

Still rubbing my foot, I said, "Good morning, Mommy."

My mom looked curious and asked, "What are you doing?"

As I was rubbing my foot with one hand and trying to get the lip gloss up with the other, I said, "I made a mistake and stepped on my lip gloss and it stained the carpet. I'm trying to get it up."

As she looked down and dusted herself off she said, "Oh honey, don't worry about that. Your dad and I are going to take up the carpet when you move out. We're turning your room into a guest room with wood floors."

"Oh, okay. Pretty cool," I replied.

My phone started to ring. *I'm Already Taken.*

My mother rolled her eyes and asked, "Is that that boy Brian calling?"

I slightly smiled, "Yes, ma'am"

She took a deep breath and told me, "You know your daddy and I do not care for that boy. He is nothing but trouble. He is no good for you."

"Mommy, I know," I said, trying not to make eye contact.

When my daddy and mother met Brian for the first time it didn't go so well. He looked decent and was well put together on the outside, but it was the words that came out of his mouth that didn't sit well with my parents and my brother Luke. Long story short, Daddy asked Brian, since he was in high school, what were his future goals? Brian told my parents he takes it one day at a time and lets everything fall into place.

22

My daddy said, "Okay, I understand that. However, everyone must have a goal. Are you going to college, vocational school, heading straight to the workforce, or what? Brian looked at my daddy, "Honestly, sir, I haven't thought about none of it. College isn't for me. I am tired of school." My mom looked at my daddy, then she looked at me. Lastly, she looked at Brian and asked, "Well, Brian. What do you like to do?" He replied, "Play basketball and football. My goal is to make it to the pros."

My mom and daddy looked at each other again. My mother curled her lip. I knew exactly what she was saying to herself, *another young boy without a plan, yet wants to get drafted into the NFL or NBA.*

My daddy raised his eyebrows, "Okay, how long have you been playing sports?"

Brian smiled, "Well... I always loved basketball. I've been playing since middle school. As for football, I am just now learning the sport. It's not my thing, but it keeps me busy."

As I looked at my mother's face I could tell she wasn't too happy. She broke her silence and asked, "Are scouts out looking at you?"

Brian looked confused and repeated, "Scouts?"

"Yes, scouts. Recruiters from colleges. Do they have their eyes on you and are they discussing the possibility of a full ride or partial scholarship?" my mom asked.

Brian looked at her as he laughed lightly and said, "Oh no, I just play for fun. It would be nice to be drafted, but who knows."

My parents looked at each other again with concern.

My mother knew Brian didn't have a clue about what he wanted to do with his life. She then asked, "How are your parents doing?"

"My mother walked out on my pops and me. My pop is a self-taught mechanic. To answer your question, sir, I might follow in my pop's footsteps."

My daddy looked at me and I could only imagine what he was saying to himself.

He said, "You know Breana is going to off to college. Right?"

Brian answered, "Yes. Bree and I talked about this already. We are going to have a long-distance relationship."

My brother Luke started laughing and asked, "Is that right? Do you to think that's going to work?" Brian looked at Luke, "Yeah, man, I know it's going to work. We have everything planned out. I am going to visit and that's how it's going to go." Luke looked at Brian and said, "Don't you think that's wishful thinking?" Brian paused for a minute, "No."

The conversation was about to get heated until my mother said, "Brian we are about to have dinner. You can stay and have dinner with us if you like."

Brian said, "Thank you, but if you don't mind, I would like to have a plate, and if it's possible, can my pops have a plate too?"

My mother replied, "Sure."

Daddy told him, "You are welcome to eat at the table with us. We are not a "to-go or takeout" restaurant."

My mother cleared her throat, "Luke Senior, let me talk to you in the kitchen for a minute."

I overheard my daddy say, "What the hell does he think this is? There is such a thing as hospitality and being ungrateful. He doesn't want to sit with us but his ass wants two to-go plates. Hell, no."

I knew then my family didn't care for him.

Brian left without saying goodbye to my parents. I walked him to the door and that was that.

My daddy came back into the family room and asked, "Your friend left?"

I said, "Yes, because you made him feel uncomfortable and unwelcome. Not to mention, you embarrassed me"

He told me to get my act and tone together and to remember who I was talking to.

I ran up to my room and he told me to get my butt back down the stairs and eat dinner.

We sat at the dinner table in complete silence.

Daddy broke the silence and said, "That boy is going to be hell on wheels."

I said, "Daddy, you don't even know him."

He replied, "I don't have to know him. I saw all I needed to see, and I most definitely heard all I needed to hear. He doesn't have any goals or plans. If you get involved with that boy it is a disaster waiting to happen."

I looked at my mom and said, "Mom."

She looked at me. "I agree with your father. Baby, he is going to be a load to carry with so much baggage. Sweetie, you do not want that."

I cried, "Mommy, when you met Daddy, Grandma and Grandpa didn't like him, either, but they gave him a chance."

Daddy said, "The difference is, Breana, I had goals. I had a plan. Whether your grandparents liked me or not I knew what I wanted to do in life. That boy's walking blind and don't give a damn about anything or anyone."

I looked at Luke and said, "Help me."

As Luke pierced his peas with the fork he said, "Bree, I don't like him."

He looked at me, "Momma and Dad are protecting you from getting hurt. That dude is going to put a hurting on you. You just don't see it."

I asked to be excused.

From that day forth I made it official with Brian.

The phone started to ring again. *I'm Already Taken*

My mom rolled her eyes again, but she didn't say anything.

My phone was going off and a couple of text messages came through back-to-back. I didn't look at it, but my mom rolled her eyes and said, "Good God, what does he want?"

My mom looked around as she turned up her nose, "Your room is a huge mess. All those boxes everywhere." Then she smiled and said, "Can you believe it, next year you will be packing up again, heading off to college? I am so proud of you."

I took a deep breath as I looked at the boxes, "I can't believe it either. Thanks, Mommy. It hasn't been easy."

I started moving things out of the way as I walked into my bathroom.

"Well, I am going to get out the way and let you get ready. What time is your first class today?" she asked.

"I have Psychology at 11 a.m., then Anatomy at 1 p.m. Later, I have to go up to the high school to talk to my advisor. Then I have cheerleading practice." I replied.

"I see you have a full schedule," she said.

"Yes, I do. Every single day," I replied.

"Well, my love, I am going to head off to a meeting. Have a wonderful and blessed day. Mommy loves you," she said in a high voice.

"Have a blessed day too, Mommy. I love you too. I am going to meditate, shower and head out the door. Be safe."

"Okay, you be safe too. Let me know when you make it," she said.

"I will," I replied.

* * *

26

My favorite meditation smooth relaxing CD is the Holiday Soundtrack. The tracks I love the most are *Maestro, Kiss Goodbye, It's Complicated*, the "Cowch", *Three Musketeers, Iris and Jasper, Christmas Surprise*, and *If I wanted to Call You*. I have them on repeat every morning and sometimes at night when I am reading and winding down.

As I walked out of the bathroom and gathering my thoughts for my meditation, my mother caught me off guard. "Oh. Breana. I forgot to tell you the affirmation for today is: "I deserve the best of the best!"

I smiled and told her, "Good one, Mommy! I love that!"

As my mom walked off, I paused and said, "Mommy?"

She turned around, "Yes."

I said, "You deserve the best of the best too!"

She smiled, gave me a hug, swinging me side-to-side as she looked me in the eyes and said, "My sweet baby, you always deserve the best of the best!"

She tapped her index finger on my nose, "Make sure you remember that."

I walked into my personal sanctuary. Over and over I said softly, *I deserve the best of the best. Breana, you deserve the best of the best.*

The sun is so bright and loving. My sanctuary looks naked since I took down my crystals for positive energy to prepare to move upstairs. I always wear my citrine stone around my neck, and I never leave the house without my chakra bracelets. I called on my Higher Self and the Great Divines (I considered the Great Divines to be God, my Higher Self, Angels, Mother Nature, High Vibration and Frequency) to join me. I sat down and closed my eyes to clear my chakras as I prepared my mind for today.

Thirty minutes passed.

I felt so calm, relaxed and energized.

Since it's eighty-one degrees and the sun is beaming some extra love in late August, I decided to wear a yellow sundress, painted my toenails with cotton candy polish, put on some flip-flops, and pulled out my favorite blue jean jacket. I brushed my hair with a wide tooth comb to part it as I braided my hair into two goddess braids, put on my chakra bracelets and went downstairs to prepare a veggie/fruit smoothie, grab my keys and head out the door.

Wow, it is such a beautiful day! It is a wonderful thing to hear the birds singing. The sun is bright, and the breeze is perfect as the leaves gently move, playing a melody.

Today is going to be a great day because I deserve the best of the best!

CHAPTER TWO

MY DADDY CALLED ME AS I GATHERED MY THINGS FOR my psychology class, "Good morning, sweet baby girl!"

"Good morning, Daddy!" I said with excitement.

"I had to leave early this morning to meet up with a couple of contractors, but I wanted to call before your first class to tell you to have a wonderful and blessed day!" he said.

"Daddy, thank you! Have a wonderful and blessed day too!"

"Love you, baby girl!" Daddy said.

I smiled, "Have a great day, Daddy, and I love you too!"

I walked into my psychology class thinking I was going to get a good seat. Boy, was I wrong! I looked at my watch and noticed that I was ten minutes early. It is always a hassle trying to find a seat since I am near-sighted and have to sit in the back. Sitting in middle does not bother me too much, but if I sit in the front I feel like everything is magnified, and my head starts to hurt. Dr. Wright's class has stadium seats and it is a huge class. It reminds me of people who attend church once a year on Easter Sunday.

I looked around for a while before I was going to settle in the corner on the floor. A classmate of mine, T'eo, waved me down as he pointed to an empty seat. Thank God for T'eo. People were irritated because I had to cross over.

"Excuse me," I said, trying to get by.

"Oh, my bad, excuse me," I said as I tried to walk sideways, and not fall. I held on to their stuff so their books and papers wouldn't fall.

One guy was waiting for me to pass him. I saw him watching, itching and waiting to say something before T'eo waved me down. "Dang, you about to knock over my papers, books, and my instrument. Watch where you are going!" he said in a voice when you know someone wants to complain and say something just because and for no reason.

He was such a jackass with a bad attitude. I was going to let his comment ride, but I had to say something, "You know I have to get by, and I said excuse me. Who brings an instrument to class anyway? You're acting like you are at home with all this mess on your desk. You need to clean it up. I feel bad for the people beside you and for the ones who are in front of you too."

He squinted his eyes as he looked at me. I looked back at him and sucked my teeth, letting him know he didn't scare me.

Oh, I forget to mention that I'm very outspoken. I am a Sagittarius; and as they say, Saggies do not have a filter and we are bold; which we are. However, we are mindful when necessary; but most of the time, some people deserve to hear our blunt facts because they need to be put in their place. Other than that, I try to be humble.

"T'eo, thank you," I said with relief.

"No problem, I saved the seat for you because I noticed you weren't here."

"That was very nice of you," I said,

T'eo is a sophomore in college. He is very mature and handsome. He is not an athlete like Brian. His smile is cute, but his teeth are not pearly white. When I look at him, I try not to look at his uneven tooth in the front. You can't hardly tell, but I notice it. His heritage is mixed. I do not know for sure, but he looks like he is mixed with white, black and Italian. I never asked. His hair is very curly. Sometimes he cuts it short, but it grows back quickly. He is really handsome when he wears a cap. His nose is a little pointy, his lips are thin and attractive. I love his eyes, they change color when the seasons change. I thought they were contacts, but nope, they are green during the fall, hazel brown during the summer, strangely blue in the winter and gray in the spring. Dressing or keeping up with the latest fashion isn't on his agenda. He always wears shorts or pants, with a sweater or maybe a short-sleeved shirt (which, most of the time is faded) with flip-flops. Today, he has on tennis shoes. I am surprised. I wonder what the occasion is.

We are associates. I met him in the library last semester. We were sitting at the same table studying for our exams. I remember that day clearly. He was studying Statistics and I was studying Math 101. For some reason, he knew I was struggling and asked me if I needed help. Come to find out, he's a math major: his major is Economics and his minor is Accounting.

As for me, I am still up in the air. I love Economics too, but I have an itch for something in the biology field. I've taken Biology 101, 102 and I decided to take Anatomy this semester.

Later that day, after studying all morning long, we took a break and ate at the Student Café. (I wouldn't say we are close because there are a lot of things we don't know about each other. I am the type of person who, if you don't ask, I won't tell.) Ever since then, we will chat here and there, but we never talked about our personal lives. Just school stuff.

He smirked, "I try."

(I had never seen him smirk before. It was kind of cute)

I smirked back, "What's up with the tennis shoes today?"

He smiled and said, "Ah, you noticed."

I arched my eyebrows and asked, "What do you mean... I noticed?"

As he continued to smile, he said, "I mean... you noticed something about me."

I begin playing with my pencil, "I notice something about everybody. I'm an observer."

T'eo cleared his throat, "But... I am not "everybody".

I opened my folder and said, "Oooo... kay..."

Dr. Wright walked in the classroom saying, "Actions. Actions speak louder than words."

Everyone nodded their heads.

Today, Dr. Wright is wearing light brown penny loafers with a shiny bronze penny in them. He has on a wool checked jacket with a black and gold Malcolm X t-shirt underneath and green jeans. This is the norm for Dr. Wright. Sometimes I wonder, *does he get dressed in the dark?* He yelled, "Does it? Or is that just a figure of speech?"

"Actions speak louder than words," answered a girl with an amazing body and a lilac headband on her head.

"Why is that?" Dr. Wright asked.

"Words are just that, words. Actions show and tell," she answered.

"You think so?" Dr. Wright asked.

"Yes," she replied.

Another opinion please?" Dr. Wright suggested.

I raised my hand and said, "Words are powerful. They produce ideas, and what you believe in. Words are actions, because if you don't speak or think it, how else will actions be applied? Most people's actions come from what they see and what other people do. Most of the time their actions are an image of what I call "copycat" because people do what they see. Now, on the other hand, words are powerful because you have to think in order to achieve."

Dr. Wright interrupted, "I'm loving it, you are getting somewhere here. Go on."

"Well, as I stated, actions are seen and can be copied. Words can be heard, but only if you want them to be heard. Therefore, if you keep your thoughts to yourself people will not be able to copy you. They can "assume" it is something you will do… They only will know by your words. To answer your question. Actions do speak louder than words because words cannot be heard unless you are willing to listen. And if you are listening, then a person will take in sometimes what they want to hear. With that being said, we all have to be very careful with what and how we say things. The reason for that is, it might be taken out of proportion."

Dr. Wright was engaged. He asked, "Taken the wrong way? How?"

I answered, looking serious, "It can be taken the wrong way by a person's tone, facial expression, and body language. At times, it can be taken the wrong way because a person can assume the wrong things."

I paused, and continued, "Let me get back to what I was saying about actions. Actions are just that—actions. The question is, Dr. Wright, are actions true? Loyal? Real? Or just figments of people's imagination? People can show us anything. Most of the time, people only show you what want to see. And words are powerful because sometimes people never follow through with what they say. If you say it, you must put actions behind it. Therefore, words are the stamp of approval, and actions follow. That's just my opinion."

Silence in the room.

Dr. Wright looked at me and smiled, "Ms. Breana, do you have a boyfriend?"

I hesitated to answer that question. I wondered, *why is he asking me about my personal life?*

"Dr. Wright, you caught me off guard," I replied.

"I asked because when or if he sends you flowers and roses, do his actions tell you he cares or is sorry?"

I felt uncomfortable answering that question. He could have given another example. Maybe I am overthinking the questions.

Inside I was feeling uncomfortable, but I didn't show it and said, "Sending flowers is cute. The words on the card are just that: words on a card. I am the type of person who listens to what people say and I take it at face value. Flowers don't faze me. They are sweet, but I am not a materialist kind of girl. I mean, it's okay to be thoughtful. It's wonderful to know that someone is thinking of me... but I prefer him to express his feeling and that we talk face to face. Speaking the words are more valuable to me. The symbol of words to me is communication. Communication is key. Listening follows, then action."

"A hard to please lady," Dr. Wright replied.

I said to myself, *Ugh. He is one of those types of men.* I said in a sharp tone with meaning, "No. I am not hard to please. I am a realist. With all due respect, Dr. Wright, if I was a man saying this, would you say that I am hard to please?"

He looked down on the floor then looked directly at me. "Men go with the flow. Women dissect everything," he replied.

"Dr. Wright, that was a biased comment," I added.

"I wouldn't call it biased. It's the way of the world. Just like you said, that's the reality." Dr. Wright replied.

I paused as I stood up, "Your comment was biased, and in my opinion, sexual discrimination. Just because I wouldn't take flowers that were given for whatever reason, I am hard to please. If it was given to me out of love I'd appreciate it. If it was given to me after an argument, well it didn't solve the issue. Either way, I prefer to express my feelings verbally and I expect the same from my partner. That doesn't have anything to do with being hard to please."

Before I sat down, I said, "If you believe women dissect things, maybe it's because we think before we get ourselves in hot water. We, as women, are cautious and wise. With all due respect, it's men like you who cause us to dissect everything before we take the leap. It's called 'been there and done that.' Affirmation for today, when a woman is "dissecting" something or a man, maybe you all need to prepare yourself to be dis-missed. Just a thought."

"Ms. Breana, you are a smart and intelligent young lady. You will need to date an older man because a younger man wouldn't be on your level," Dr. Wright said, and he smiled.

He continued, "Breana, great conversation and participation."

He looked at me, winked his eye, and smiled.

Weird. I felt so uncomfortable.

He continued, "Actions speak louder than words. Let Ms. Breana tell it, words are powerful without actions and actions are powerful without words. Write a five-page essay and tell me your thoughts. Class dismissed."

I gathered my belongings.

"Wow. Woman of steel," T'eo said as he laughed.

"No, I am a woman who won't back down from what I believe in. I don't care what anyone says, Dr. Wright was being biased in the worst way," I said as I put my book in my backpack.

"Yeah... He was being biased, but you handled it well." T'eo said.

"Yep. I know I did," I replied quickly.

I started walking. I stopped in my tracks, "Wait. Did you just say you thought he was being biased too?"

T'eo moved his eyes from left to right, "Uh. Yeah."

I put my hand on my hip and said, "If that's what you were thinking, why didn't you say anything?"

He bit his lip, "Well, I didn't think it was my place to say anything. From the looks of it, you had it covered all on your own. I wasn't the only one keeping quiet. You shut the classroom down. I know one thing, nobody is going to battle you," he added. "You didn't back down. I'm proud of you."

I rolled my eyes, "Whatever, T'eo. I think that's what's wrong with the world today. Not enough people are standing up for what they believe in. They'd rather let one person stand alone. How is that fair?"

T'eo didn't say anything.

I said, "Everyone is proud of me. People do not understand, it takes courage to be me."

I was in a daze.

T'eo changed the subject, "You asked me why am I wearing tennis shoes."

I was still in a daze and asked, "What?"

T'eo clapped his hands, "Snap out of it, Breana. Are you there? Are you there? Earth to Breana."

I blinked my eyes and asked, "What did you say?"

T'eo snapped his fingers, "Earth to Breana?"

I laughed, "I heard that part."

T'eo looked at me, "I said, you asked me why I'm wearing tennis shoes?"

I said, "Oh, yeah."

He answered, "It's because I am going to do just that... play tennis."

I laughed, "Oh... okay, that makes perfectly good sense."

We walked outside and sat on the bench in a slightly shaded area for a short while. I took off my backpack, crossed my legs, closed my eyes and enjoyed the rays of the sun.

T'eo looked at me and asked, "Breana, what are you doing for the rest of today?"

"I have another class. Then I have to talk to my counselor; then cheerleading practice." I replied.

He looked confused, "Cheerleading practice? I didn't know you were on the cheerleading team?"

I looked at him and smiled, "Yeah. I am."

He was still looking confused when he said, "Really? I never saw you at any of the games."

I widened my eyes and said, "Oh, no. I am not on the cheerleading team here at Brubaker State University. I am captain on my cheerleading team at Jackson-Miles High school. I am a senior. Class of 2019."

T'eo hopped up and said, "High school? Wait... How old are you?"

I told him, "I am seventeen years old. I will be eighteen on December 1st."

He took a deep breath and laughed, "So... you are seventeen years old?"

I arched my eyebrows as I said, "Yes. Is it illegal for you to talk to me or something?" He held his hand out, "Let me see your driver's license."

I looked at him and said, "Hold up. Let me see your ID. Dang, you're acting like we hooked up and you are going to jail or something."

He pulled out his license.

I looked over and said, "You were born on July 1st."

I took his license out of his hand and said, "Wait, you just turned eighteen this year. Did you graduate high school early?" As I pulled out my driver's license from my purse, he answered my question, "Yes. I graduated high school a year early and started college nearly a year early too."

I showed him my license.

He was speaking to himself out loud while reading my ID saying, "Breana Anderson, born December 1st."

I snatched my ID and said, "Ugh. That's all you need to know."

He smiled, "Okay. Well... so, you are in high school and attending college."

I smiled with pride and confidence, "That's right!"

He bumped my shoulder with his and said, "I see you. You are a S.P.Y.T."

My eyebrows arched as I asked, "Huh? What? What is S.P.Y.T?"

"Smart Pretty Young Thing," he said.

I looked at him, "Ugh. No. I am a Smart Pretty Young Lady."

T'eo laughed, "Yes, you are. Bold and so wise. I agree with Mr. Wright, if you date, you need an older man. Are you dating?"

My expression changed because he made me think about my issues with Brian, "Yes. I have a boyfriend. His name is Brian."

T'eo said, "Really? Okay. Well, I guess we can be friends. Right?

I gave him a fist bump, "Of course. Why not? We are taking it up a notch from associates to being friends—I don't see any harm in that."

CHAPTER THREE

TODAY IS SUCH A BEAUTIFUL DAY! IT'S NEARLY FALL BUT it is hot in Atlanta. Thanksgiving is around the corner in a few months and it is still in the low- and mid-eighties. One thing's for sure, traffic is beyond crazy. I cannot get to point A or to point B without being in traffic. I hate putting on the AC because it burns up my gas. I like to conserve my money, but it is too damn hot.

Incoming call from Brian. I asked Google to answer his call.

"Bree, are you on your way to school?" Brian asked without giving me time to say hello. As a matter of fact, he didn't say hello.

I replied in a dry tone, "Brian, I will be there in about ten minutes."

He said, "Cool, can you bring me a $5 pizza?"

I said to myself, *What?* I looked at the phone and said, "No, I cannot. I have an appointment with Mrs. Morgan at three."

Brian slightly raised his voice, "Breana, it's down the street."

I told him, "Brian, if it's only down the street, then you shouldn't have a problem getting it yourself. Don't you have practice today?"

He yelled, "Bree, I don't need you to be my mother! You know what? I don't have time for this. I am done with you. We are through!"

The phone hung up.

This relationship is stressful. He says he doesn't want me to be his mother. Really? After all these years, I feel like I've been his mother. Every time I turn around, I am listening to his dysfunctional life and all of his trillion problems. I am always there to bail him out of shit, and he never ever appreciates it. This is an unhealthy relationship. Regardless of how good he looks, I have to let it go sooner or later. Maybe later than sooner, because he needs me.

As I drive into the parking lot, I see a couple of posters on the gate with my picture on them, saying, *Vote for Brenna Anderson for Queen of Jackson-Miles High*. The marching band was doing their thing, and the majorettes shaking their tails, getting down. As I sat in the car I started to dance to the beat. I got out of the car and joined the majorette line, shaking my behind and moving to the beat of the drum. The band was on fire! "Go, Bree, do your thing, girl!" a saxophone player yelled. I don't know his name, but I know his face.

I broke it down and start doing the old-school electric slide. The band changed the beat and followed my lead. We were all breaking down the electric slide and we added in the Janet Jackson move, added the Bankhead bounce to put a little modern version to it, and finished it off with a smooth slow motion nae nae. As I was dancing, my hair fell in my face because the braid came apart. When I am whipping my hair as I dance, nobody can tell me anything! I laughed and said, "It was fun breaking it down with you ladies and gentlemen!"

I wanted to stay and dance. Instead, I got out of the line because I had to make my appointment on time. The band was still jamming. I smiled and said, "See ya'll in a minute. Thank you for the fun!" I was looking at my phone and scrolled down to a rude-ass text from Brian, saying, "So you were in a rush to shake your ass. I thought you had an appointment. I'm done with you, Bree." Once again, he's done with me. How many times can a person break up with someone in one day? I didn't reply because I knew if I did, I would be late. That's the shit I'm talking about. If I have a nanosecond, Brian wants that too.

As I was walking up the steps, I heard a lot of people saying, "Hey Bree!" or "Hey Breana!"

I waved and said hey to everyone.

Someone yelled, "Bree, Girl, you know you got my vote!" "Thank you!" I replied as I looked up and waved.

"Hey, Breana. You got my vote too!" said a girl with red hair as she gave me a high-five. I gave her a high-five in return, "Thank you. I truly appreciate it!"

As I walked in the door a girl on the JV team said, "Hey, Girl! I love your nails!" I replied, "Really? Thanks! Girl, it took me all day." She looked at them again, "I can't tell you did the damn thing yourself!" I said, "Thank you, Girl!"

She walked with me down the hall and said, "Bree, I know you are a senior and captain on the Varsity team. I was wondering, could you put in a good word for me? I am going to try out for the Varsity team and I really been working my butt off to earn a spot."

She kept up with me because I was in a rush. I said, "I apologize, but what is your name?" "Faith," she replied. I stopped walking and said, "It's nice to meet you, Faith." As I reached to shake her hand I asked, "Faith, what grade are you in?" "Tenth," she replied. I pulled out a piece of paper from my back pocket and said, "Okay, write your name and number down. I will call you before the week is out." Faith was so excited as she wrote on the paper. She said, "Really? Thank you, Bree!" I gave her a hug, "Faith, you're more than welcome!"

Someone else came up to me. "Hey, Bree. Girl, I like your shoes." I smiled, "Thank you, I like yours too!" I didn't even look at her shoes, but I do not like it when someone compliments me without me giving a compliment back. I wasn't lying, but I'm sure there was something about her shoes that I would like.

As we were going in opposite directions, towards the end of the hallway she yelled, "Bree, by the way, you got my vote!" I laughed and yelled back, "Thank you, Girl!"

I ran up the steps to the third floor. When I opened the door the cheerleader squad were cheering in the hallway. I gave some of them a hug as I said, "Hey, y'all!" They were all happy as they said, "Hey, Bree! Bree! Bree!" "Hey y'all! Get ready and warm up. I'll be there shortly. Nicole, take over until I get there," I said.

Nicole is co-captain. She is always doing her thing! She's in the eleventh grade and she is running for Ms. Eleventh Grade. She answered, "Okay, Girl. No problem." "I appreciate it," I replied. I added, "Nicole, you look so cute today! You are glow-ing." She started laughing and said, "Bree, girl, how am I glow-ing?" I touched her hair and said, "Your skin looks so healthy. It looks like Werther's caramel candy! It's so shiny and healthy! Your hair's full of volume and so bouncy." "Okay, Bree," she said, smiling from ear to ear. I smiled back, "I am glad you are smiling. See, I told you your braces look good on you!" "Yeah, I am get-ting used to them now. Thanks, Bree!" she replied.

Walking down to the basement, I run into Brian. Damn. I do not need this crap right now. He walked along with me at a fast pace, saying, "Bree, we need to talk." I kept walking and said, "No, we don't. You just broke up with me for the I-don't-know-how-many times today, Brian." He said softly as he touched my elbow, "Bree, you know I was just playing." I kept walking and told him, "Whatever, Brian. I am so over all this bullshit you put me through." He pleaded, "Slow down, Bree, damn. I'm just saying. I was mad."

I started to walk faster and faster without making eye contact and said, "Every time you don't get your way you want to break up with me. Do what you have to do, Brian. One thing I do know is that I am going to be okay. With or without you." Brian grabbed my arm hard and yelled at me, "Oh, is that right? Okay. Well. We are done. For real this time."

I jerked my arm back. I looked at him and said, "Brian, I am tired of you pulling on me." He moved closer and said in a harsh tone, "At least I don't beat your ass like most guys I know who beat their girls." I walked up a little closer to make sure he heard me clearly. I curled my lip as I said, "If you ever think about putting your hands on me again you will regret it for the rest of your life."

He looked me in the eyes, smiled sarcastically, and replied, "Fuck you, Bree. Don't you know how many girls want me? I can do better than you." As I walked away, I put my hands up and said, "So it's 'fuck me' now? Wow, you are so disrespectful on so many levels. You have no loyalty whatsoever. It's all about what I can do for you." He followed me and said, "Yeah, you heard me right. Fuck your ass; I can do so much better than you."

I shrugged my shoulders, "Brian, can you?" He laughed, "I am going to make sure my boys don't vote for your ass, and I am not voting for you either." I ignored him. His words stabbed me in the chest and my heart was on fire. I know I shouldn't expect much from him, but damn, I didn't think he would be so cut-throat. He was so heartless.

I walked into the girl's restroom. I checked each stall to make sure they were empty. Once the coast was clear, I looked in the mirror and asked myself, *how did I get here?* I cried because Brian's words and actions were the same; they both hurt. It reminded me of my open floor discussion in class today. I acted like I didn't care around Brian. I couldn't show him my weakness because then he would have surely taken advantage. I had to stay strong for my dignity. The tears were flowing because I never thought someone could be so cruel. If I would have gotten him a pizza this would never have occurred. It was always his way or no way. I did this to myself because I allowed him to do this shit to me.

Brian has taught me a valuable lesson—we teach people how to treat us. I cannot stop crying because I am hurting deeply. I would have thought he would have shown me some kind of respect because I've always been there for him. He throws all that out the window when he feels like he is the victim. How can a person feel like they are the victim when they are the one who hurts people? He is so selfish because he is an "all his way" kind of person. I am late for my appointment. I always let him mess things up for me because I always put him first. I put him before my needs and wants all the time. Again, it's my fault. My face is puffy, my eyes are swollen, and I look a damn mess.

I walked down the hall as fast as I could because I didn't want to be late for my appointment. I stopped and took a deep breath. My head started to hurt and I became dizzy. I tried my best to get myself together before I knocked on my counsel-or's door.

"Breana, are you okay?" she asked, looking concerned. "Yes, Mrs. Morgan, I am fine. Thank you for asking." I replied, sounding angry, frustrated and sad as I held back my tears. I went on to say, "Mrs. Morgan, I need to make sure I am on point with all my classes and BSU classes. I sent off about a dozen college applications a couple months ago. I'll be sending off a couple more before the weekend is out. Then I will be done filling out the applications. With hopes to hear from the rest of them soon."

Mrs. Morgan didn't want to show her concern as she said, "You are on it, Breana." "I am trying to stay on top of things. How about my GPA? I took the SAT's and ACT's twice this year and I am going to take them one more time next year to see if I can get a higher score. Mrs. Morgan, do I have enough credit to graduate with an Associate degree?" I asked. Mrs. Morgan flipped through tons of paper, "Let me see. Well, your SAT scores are high enough, what are you trying to get? Your ACT is almost at the top of the charts as well. Breana, do not be too hard on yourself."

My legs were shaking and I bit my lip as I told her, "I am not hard on myself. I like to challenge myself. I like to know I have options and I work hard because I deserve the best of the best." Mrs. Morgan said in a normal voice, trying not to ask what was wrong again, "Well, as of now, you are still valedictorian."

"As of now. I am going to be Jackson-Miles valedictorian. No ifs, ands, or buts about it. How do my credits look for early college?" I asked in a firm voice. I looked at the time. Goodness. Time was flying by. Mrs. Morgan replied with joy in her voice, "Breana, you need nine more credits in order to graduate with an Associate degree."

That changed my mood! "Okay, great! I will take Economics, Anatomy II, and Sociology next semester. That way, I will have all of my electives out of the way when I start college in the fall." Mrs. Morgan smiled, "Seems like you have it all figured out. Breana, we need more students like you. You are going to be alright, girl!" "Thank you, Mrs. Morgan. I have to run down to cheerleading practice and I have to study for my exams that are coming up," I replied. "Okay, slow down and make sure you take time out for yourself," Mrs. Morgan said. As I gathered my papers I said, "Thank you, Mrs. Morgan. I will keep that in mind."

I opened the door. As I was about to take off and run down to practice, Mrs. Morgan said, "Breana, off the record, I heard you and Brian arguing. You are such a sweet young lady. You have carried Brian since he arrived at this school." I nodded my head as if I was ashamed and admitted, "Yes. We were arguing." I shrugged my shoulders, "He broke up with me again, so I don't have to worry about carrying him anymore."

Mrs. Morgan walked up to me and said in a concerned voice, "I am not telling you what to do... but he is not your problem. Do not let him stop you from your blessings and what you worked so hard for." I needed to hear that. I gave Ms. Morgan a hug, "Mrs. Morgan, thank you for the advice. As matter of fact, thank you for always being here for me. Over the course of the years, you've always been like a mother to me. I truly appreciate it."

Mrs. Morgan smiled as she hugged me back, "You're more than welcome."

* * *

As I walked down the hallway. I was beginning to think. Mrs. Morgan is so right. Every time I turn around I am saving Brian from something. When he and his dad got into it I sneaked out of the house to meet up with him to talk. I got caught and was punished for a month. I didn't have my phone or my car. My parents picked me up and dropped me off at school and work.

Nothing more and nothing less. And the only thing he said was, "Bree, I am sorry."

Hell yeah, he is sorry. A sorry excuse for a man. Just damn right sorry. When he didn't have enough money for basketball and football camp, I worked overtime and gave him the money to participate and I never got a dime back. Not one red cent. And I didn't have anything to show for it. Damn, I am so stupid. Ugh, Summer is right, I am Bree-dumb-una.

He got into a bad accident a couple of months ago. It wasn't too serious, but I was there to make sure he had what he needed. I made sure he had a way home from his doctor's appointment, and food. Did he appreciate it? No, he didn't and still doesn't appreciate anything I do.

Early this year, he had surgery because he had a stomach ulcer. I was there at the hospital every single day before and after school. I was there on the weekends too. When they discharged him, I was at his house around the clock. I was his after-school nurse, and I nursed him back to good health.

It was me! I did it all! Talking about 'he does not need me to be his momma.' What the hell? I've been acting like his momma and his damn daddy too. His dad is a junkie and his mom left him. He stays with his next-door neighbor who he says raised him. He calls her his Momma. I have done too much for him to let him to treat me this way. It's my fault because I allow it. I feel like I can make him a better person, but I can't. I pity him, and I shouldn't.

I hear my girls cheering their hearts out, "Go! Go! Go! Eagles! Go!"

I ran in clapping and yelled, "Soar! Eagles! Soar!" As if nothing had happened.

I looked over to the right, and Brian was hugged up on Angel on the bleachers in the corner. She was giggling, "Brian, you are going to be in big trouble," she said as she touched his lips with the tip of her index finger. His hands were placed on her inner thigh and they kept moving in the direction of her private area. She put her hand on his hand as she gave him permission to keep moving forward. He is so in the zone of his lust the whole time that he doesn't even see me. My eyes are tearing up. I am standing here looking like a damn fool.

He closed his eyes as his voiced deepened and softened, "Babe, come here and give me those sweet lips." Softly, in a sexual tone, Angel asked, "How do you know they are sweet?"

I couldn't believe my eyes nor could I believe what I was hearing. I was frozen. I couldn't move or speak. I was in a state of shock. I put my hand on my heart.

Brian put both of his hands-on Angel's ass and pulled her up closer as he murmured, "Come here, baby. Bring your ass here. Why are you so far away?" Angel laughed. They begin to kiss.

I was in a daze. My heart was hurting and beating fast. My head was spinning. I felt sick. I ran out of the gym to the locker room. "Bree! Bree!" I heard someone say. I couldn't believe what I just saw. I fell on the locker room floor. I rolled up into a ball.

Simone asked in a calm concerned voice, "Bree! Are you sick? Are you pregnant or something?" Simone is a shit starter. I do not trust her. If it was up to me, she wouldn't be on the team. To be honest, nobody likes her. We just put up with her because she is on the team. I remember when she shitted all over me, telling the cheerleading committee that I was on drugs so she could take my place as captain. I have asthma, and when I am in the red zone I am given steroids to clear the airway in my lungs so I can breathe. I was upset with the committee because I gave them my physical, therefore they knew in advance. That wasn't enough. I was embarrassed. They made me take a drug test, which I passed. I was on probation and had to produce a year of my medical records from my primary caregiver and the physicians at the hospital so they could approve it. All of this because Simone lied because she wanted to be captain. After all was said and done, I was clean and clear to participate on the team. Simone didn't suffer the consequences of the lies she told.

I couldn't catch my breath. I couldn't talk.

Simone yelled, "Call 911!!" Her dark long thick hair brushed across my face as I tried to catch my breath. Her dark brown eyes looked me dead in the eye as she asked, "Bree, what is wrong? Are you cramping or something? What is it?"

Emma brought me a brown paper bag and said quickly, "Here, Bree, breathe in the bag." Emma ran out of the locker room and ran back in quickly with my purse. She was throwing everything out, and finally gave up as she poured all my stuff on the floor, "Bree, here, open your mouth. I have your asthma pump."

Emma is an associate of Chloe and me. She isn't a part of the Yin Yang, but she's a good person. Sometimes, I do not understand her ways. I do not think she means any harm, but sometimes she makes racist remarks, and it's towards her own race. I wonder if she says what she says to "fit in" or maybe she means what she says. Either way, it makes me feel uncomfortable. One day we were in the car and she said she hates white people. I said, "Emma, you know you are white. Right?" She replied, "So that doesn't mean I have to like it. I can get away with being white or Hispanic. My mother told me to use both to my advantage."

My face turned sour as I said, "What... use what to your advantage?"

"I have a choice to be white or Hispanic. It depends where I am and who I am around. I'm going to take my Momma's advice and use it to my advantage," Emma replied.

I asked, "Emma, you're not comfortable in the skin you're in?"

Her eyes got bigger and bigger as she flipped her hair, "Bree, I am comfortable in my skin. I'm just saying since I am white and look Hispanic, I am going to take advantage of both."

I wasn't going to go back for forth with Emma so I left that conversation alone. Everything she said I left right there and kept it moving.

I wasn't comprehending, because I was hyperventilating. What made matters worse, I felt like the entire school was watching me on the floor.

Emma cradled me in her arms as if I was an infant. She rocked me back and forth with one arm holding me slightly. She put the bag over my mouth and yelled with a shaky voice, "Breathe in the bag, Bree! Breathe! I got you! Breathe!" I started to breathe in the bag. I was breathing so fast and was so scared because I felt like I was losing my mind. Emma asked me to open my mouth as she gave me my asthma pump. I inhaled two puffs.

Emma began to hold me tightly, and with a soft loving voice, she said, "Bree, breathe slowly. I love you, Bree. Think about the beach as we clean your chakras. Let's start from your higher chakras. There's a bright light over your head, beaming down on your crown chakra. It is traveling through your third eye. As it cleans your crown and third eye, it is washing all the negative energy from your throat chakra."

I start to breathe slowly as I allowed my chakra to be cleansed.

Emma continued in a calm voice, "Bree, I know your heart chakra is hurting, but the white and golden light are balancing your energy and clearing out the negative vibration."

I started crying and I stayed calm.

Emma kept going, "As it cleans your heart chakra it is traveling down to your solar plexus and sacral chakras as it lifts your vibration. The golden light has cleansed your heart, solar and sacral chakras as it reaches your root chakra. The Great Divine has officially cut all the negative cords. He is walking and talking with you as He cleanses your root chakra. As He sends the bright white light back up to the highest vibration your chakras are balanced. You are on a higher vibration and frequency."

As Emma helped me clear my chakras I felt so much better. I then begin to breathe normally.

I lay back on Emma for a couple minutes and said, "Thank you so much. Thank you."

"What happened?" Simone asked as she looked confused. Right before I opened my mouth to speak two first responders in all blue with sky blue gloves on came in with a gurney, an AED and all kinds of equipment, hurrying and saying, "Coming through!"

"Clear out!"

"Everyone, clear out!"

"Clear out!"

"Is everything okay?"

I looked down and said to myself, *this is so embarrassing,* "Yes, I am okay. Thank you."

"I am Rachel. I will be helping you today. I see you are alert," she said as she shone a small light in my face. She was so close to my face I could smell her breath. It smelled like coffee and something fruity. She had clusters of freckles on her right cheek and her arms. Her eyes were ocean blue and her hair was carrot red.

"Okay, everything's fine there," she added as she cut off the bright light.

"Yes. I had an episode of hyperventilation. I've been stressed all day," I replied

"Hello. I am Niles and I am going to check your blood pressure," he said as he pulled out a stethoscope. Niles' fingers were super long and his nails were super clean. They looked like he had clear fingernail polish on them. His hair looked like fluffy curly light brown clouds. I wanted to ask him how did he get so much bounce in his hair. Every time he moved it would move from side to side, I loved the volume in his curly afro. I wondered what product he used. He was very handsome. When he talked, his teeth were straight, his smile was like a ray of sunshine, his eyes were hazel light brown. He had on a dog tag that said, Courage. Boldness. Wisdom.

Rachel pulled out a needle. I pulled back. "Wait. What is that? I am okay." I said, starting to breathe hard again. "Don't move, I am trying to take your blood pressure," Niles said as he was trying to focus on the scope. I tried to stay still as I told him in a scared voice, "I hate needles. What are you doing?" "It is okay. I am going to check your blood sugar to make sure your blood level is okay." "I don't have diabetes," I said, frightened. "We just want to make sure your blood sugar isn't too high or too low. It will be a little prick. That's all."

News travels fast.

Chloe ran into the locker room in a rush, asking questions, "What is going on with my sister?"

Rachel said to Chloe, "Please let us do what we have to do to make sure your sister is okay." In a scary tone and high-pitched voice, Chloe said, "Tell me what is going on! Breana is my sister." "Ma'am, your sister is okay. Please step aside." Rachel told her in a frustrated tone.

Brian ran in the locker room but he didn't say anything. Rachel looked up as she shook her head, rolled her eyes and said, "All done. Your blood sugar is normal." I hadn't noticed the prick because Brian changed my whole mood. "Her blood pressure is normal too," Niles added. They started to gather their things and left the locker room.

"How dare you bring your ass in here!" I told Brian. He had an ugly smirk in his face. Everyone was looking as if I was losing my mind. Nicole's mouth was open, anxious to hear what I was going to say next. Simone was gathering the paper bags. As she walked to throw them away, she was shaking her head as if she knew what I was about to say. I wonder, did she see Brian and Angel touching each other and kissing?

Chloe had her hands on her hips as she tapped her foot a million miles an hour. As she moved side to side, popping her gum, with her eyebrows arched, ready to snap as if fire was coming out of her nose and ears. She couldn't hold it in any longer and said with an attitude, "Brian, what did you do?"

He raised his voice, "What you mean? What did I do? Why you blaming me? Shit, I am here to see what is going on." Chloe raised her voice, "Don't come at me like that. I know your no-good, got-nothing ass did something. All of this is your doing! Nobody else but Brian, pity party, victim-ass."

He looked at Chloe as he waved her off and said, "What the fuck ever, I am not going to feed into your fat ass today."

I sat there in a rage. I started to breathe hard as I jumped up off the floor and wanted to punch him in the face. I yelled, "Brian, you think I am fucking stupid!" Before I knew it, I lost my temper and slapped the shit out of Brian, "Chloe is right! I'm in this condition because of you. I am always feeling this way because of your ass. Where is that skanky diseased bitch? If she is what you want, she can have your damaged ass! I'm done!"

He said, "What you..."

I cut him off, "Don't play dumb with me, asshole. I saw you and Angel hiding in the corner of the bleachers. Hugging, touching and kissing. I saw it all! I saw you touching her STD's skanky cat, I saw you kissing her and I heard what you said. I leaned forward, punched him in the chest and tried to punch him in the face, but he caught my hand and moved his head back as he struggled and yelled, "Bree! Stop! Stop, Bree!"

Everyone was crowded around us and holding me back. I tried to break lose to get to him, but there were too many people. I was so angry and never knew this side of myself. I always tried to be the bigger person. I couldn't take it anymore. I am tired of being the "good girl". I am so tired of always being the one people can call on when they need something. I am so tired of this shit. I tried to get my hands on him. I yelled and I tried to run up on him again, "Get the fuck out of here, you low-down dirty piece of shit. You ain't shit! It is officially over."

After trying for so long, I wore myself out.

He looked at me with a nasty, dirty smile, "You act liked you didn't give a shit. I don't see you shrugging your shoulders now." He continued as he walked away, turned around and said, "I told you I could find someone better than you. Angel was more than happy to take your place." He straightened up his face, "Look at you. You can't live without me."

Chloe ran up to him, "You are a punk bitch and a fucking coward. You can have nasty STD Angel. She's a thirsty nasty skank ho who will open her herpes legs up to anybody. I hope you get blisters all over your lips and dick. You will get your day, Brian."

Brian laughed, "Damn, Chloe do you have herpes? You know you have the side effects down to a tee!" Chloe looked at him as she squinted her eyes, "I pay attention in class, dummy!"

He walked off looking satisfied and said, "Yeah, we all will have our day."

I was sweaty and tired. I sat on the bench, laid my head on my knees and let it out all as I cried and cried. I felt so stupid. I couldn't believe I let myself be played. I felt like a used fool. I gave him so much of me; and the only thing I got out of this dysfunctional relationship was hurt and pain.

I saw Simone's shoes in front of me. She sat down beside me on the bench, rubbed my back and said, "Bree. I am so sorry. I saw them talking, smiling, and very friendly with each other. I saw them being touchy before you walked in, but I was going to tell you after practice. I apologize. I should have said something before-hand."

"It doesn't matter," I mumbled.

Emma, sat beside me on the bench, hugged me and said, "Bree, let it all out. Do not hold it in. Let it go. You don't have to say anything. Sometimes saying nothing at all is best."

Chloe rubbed my back and added, "My Yin Yang, shake it off. One thing's for sure, they better be lucky I wasn't here, because I would have busted their ass out! No offense, Simone, but you should have said something. How could you see what was going on and not interrupt their lowest-of-the-low shitty connection? That was wrong of you not to say anything at all. That is what I do not like about you, you're always quiet when you need to speak up."

Simone looked at Chloe and said, "Well, it wasn't my story to tell."

Emma looked as if she had a bitter taste in her mouth and said, "Back up, you just told Bree you were going to tell her, but now it's not your story to tell. What sense does that make? Either you were going to tell her or it wasn't your story to tell. Which one is it?

With tears, all over my face, I told them, "It doesn't matter. What happened, happened."

Emma and Chloe said at the same time, "Bree, it *does* matter."

Chloe rolled her eyes, balled up her fist and said, "I really should beat your ass right now. How can you call yourself Bree's friend? Bree, see I told you Simone is a tacky, sneaky, selfish bitch, and looks out only for herself."

Simone turned around, laughed, and said, "Tacky bitch? This tacky bitch is about to get up in your ass."

Chloe ran up to Simone, got in her face and said, "Yeah, you heard me right You are a tacky, sloppy bitch that has no loyalty. I want to see you beat my ass."

Chloe punched Simone in the lip, she swung at her again and punched her in the eye.

I jumped up yelling, "Help me, Emma!" Emma said, "Nope, I'm going to let this tacky bitch get her ass beat. She needs one good ass-whipping because she's always spreading rumors like wildfire and lives up to them. I want to see her get her ass beat. I would jump in, but it wouldn't be a fair fight. I want her ass next."

While Emma was talking, I was trying to get Chloe off of Simone. Chloe was on top of Simone going in left and right as she called her all kinds of names. With each hit she said some-thing. She hit Simone again and said, "This is for starting a rumor saying the football team ran a train on me." Chloe hit her again, "This is for lying about Bree last year, saying she takes steroids, knowing she has asthma, and she got kicked off the cheerlead-ing team because you wanted to be captain."

Last year was pure hell. I wanted to let Chloe beat her ass, but I couldn't let Chloe ruin her life over Simone. As I was rum-bling with both of them, tired and didn't have any strength left in me, I yelled, "Enough! Enough, Chloe!" I was being thrown here and there. A couple of teachers broke through the crowd and yelled, "What's going on?"

As I was being hit all over my body, I yelled, "You see what's going on! Y'all help me!" I yelled again, "Chloe, stop, you are going to beat her to death!" More and more people came to help me get Chloe off Simone. Someone yelled, "Simone finally got her ass beat!" People were laughing and yelling, "It's about time! I bet next time she's going to keep her dirty mouth shut!"

Everything from there just faded in the background. I never imagined today would turn out like this.

CHAPTER FOUR 4

OVER THE WEEKEND, I WALKED AROUND LOOKING LIKE A zombie. I didn't go to the game; I didn't feel like cheering. Plus, I didn't want to see Brian. I called off work because I didn't want to be bothered with anyone. I felt sick. I guess this is what "love-sick" feels like.

My mother knocked on my door as she slightly pushed it open. She had on her silk rose pink Soma's pajamas. Her pants slightly touched her cotton rose pink slippers. I was surprised she noticed something was wrong because she's always working and never pays attention.

"Breana, honey, are you okay? Are you sick?" she asked.

I had on my purple nightcap. My nightcap complimented my nightgown. I was comfortable under my comforter. I took the covers off my face and said, "No, I am not okay."

"Do you want to talk about it?" she asked.

59

Again, I was surprised. I said, "Really?"

She replied, "What you mean, really? You know I am always here if you need me!"

I said softly, "To be honest, Mom, no, I didn't know that. You are always so busy. When I want to talk, you are never around. If you are around, you are always too busy to talk. If you do ask about anything, you are more concerned about cheerleading and it seems like my popularity as well. As long as I am "well known" and "accepted" by everyone you are good to go—but I never thought you cared about my feelings."

My mother asked, "Breana, is that how you really feel?"

"Yes," I answered truthfully.

I added, "Mom, you hardly ask me how was my day. If you do it's only about my classes, grades, cheerleading, but it is never sincerely or heartfelt, Breana, how are you feeling today."

I rolled up in the fetal position, respectfully turned my back and said softly, "I am used to it—so it doesn't really matter. I make the best of what I am given when it comes to our relationship. That is why I talk to Dad, because he takes the time out to listen. Mommy, I feel like it is all about status to you. Like, when some mothers are stage moms when it comes to their children's acting career. You are a status mother when it comes to me and Summer because everything is all for show. I am not that type of person. I live life day by day without seeking the approval of others. I do not care what they think about me. My life is about making me happy. If I am not happy then, who will be happy for me? Who will make me happy? Nobody, because happiness starts within me first."

"I never knew you felt that way. Are you unhappy? Do you really think I am a quote "status" mother who seeks the approval of others?" she asked, as she sat on my bed and rubbed my back.

"Mommy, it seems like you only make time for Luke. You never make time for your girls. When I came on my cycle for the first time, I told Daddy before I told you because you weren't around. You were at work. When you came home that night, I was sleep, and you already left for work the next day. When you found out I was on my cycle that was like five months later. I decided not to tell you because you never had time." I said numbly.

I turned over, sat up and sat back on my pillow. I pulled my covers up to my stomach and said, "Mommy, I am not trying to hurt your feelings but you never make time for Summer or me. I make sure I give Summer attention because I want her to know she has me in her corner. I want her to know she can always come and talk to me and that I will always be there. There were times when Summer needed to talk to you, but either you weren't home because of work or you were too busy in your office writing up contracts. The only time we really have a conversation is at the dinner table when we all talk about our day but never talk about what is really going on in our lives. After dinner, you go back to your office and start where you left off. That is why I said Summer and I are used to it now."

She looked shocked as she rubbed my leg and said once again, "Breana, I never knew you and Summer felt this way. I didn't think you two needed me as much as you are saying."

I looked at my mom with tears in my eyes. They didn't fall, because they were tears of frustration, hurt and pain. They were tears of 'how could you not know?' I asked her, "Mom, why would you think Luke needed you more than your girls? Luke has you and Daddy in his corner. Summer and I only have Daddy. We, as your girls, will always need you." Tears started to roll down my cheek and my voice trembled as I said, "We needed you, Mom." My mom gave me a hug, "My sweet Breana, come here."

As she was hugging me, I said, "Mom, if you didn't understand or know, you do treat Summer and me as if we are status symbols. We know you want to be proud of us but when it comes to your girls it is all about numbers. Such as, what are our grades looking like; are we number one in the school? (Popularity-wise). That is why I ran for prom queen. To let you see I am well known, but Mommy, I do not care if people know me or not. As long as I am learning something about myself every day, what other people think of me doesn't matter. Just like I tell Summer, we should always be unapologetic for our flaws and all. I love myself, and I am happy with the way I am. Every day, I try to improve something about myself, but Mommy, I do not need anyone's approval. You make Summer and feel that we need the world's approval to make it in life. The world will lie to us and leave us where we stand. I teach Summer to be true and honest with herself. I never understood your motives."

My mother looked as if this was the first time she'd heard Summer's and my concerns. We had a family meeting about a year ago and expressed our thoughts—and nothing changed. Summer and I took it for what it was worth, made the best of it, and moved on.

"I apologize if you and Summer feel this way. I tried raising my girls different from how I was raised. I guess I fell into my mother's trap because I was always taught to make sure the world approved of me. If not, I wouldn't ever have anything in life. By being in a biracial family. I felt like I always had something to prove to someone of every color. My father's dark rich color wasn't good enough for the world. He worked for city hall until he died. He was a black educated smart man with multiple talents, but it wasn't good enough for the world. He never was accepted or acknowledged for his brain—only for what he could do for others to gain them profit. Just because my mother is white, her skin didn't hold any value because she married a black man. Back in our time, believe it or not, she was called a "nigger lover". You would have thought that those days have gone. No, baby, there are still people who use those terms freely."

I looked at my mother as she continued. "As for my siblings—my brother had it hard because he was always told by people he wasn't good enough because he was black. My brother Trip always told your Aunty Piper and me to never let anyone tell us otherwise. He preached to us on a daily basis that we are a human race and that our color doesn't define us."

My mother continued, "I made the choice to be a "people pleaser" because I wanted everyone to like me. I didn't want to fight every day. I made the decision to let what people thought of me define me. That is how I become the most popular girl in school, prom queen, captain of the cheerleading squad, etc. Because it mattered what people thought of me. Your grandmother told me to do what I had to do to be accepted."

As I continued to look at her, I was disgusted. I didn't feel any sympathy for her. I didn't know her struggles caused her pain, nor did I walk in her life on a daily basis, but I do not believe in lowering your human rights to get where you 'fit' to gain approval of others. I felt like my mother sold her soul to people who used her and they knew Vanessa would do anything to be liked and wanted by others.

I said, "So you wanted Summer and me to dislike ourselves for the approval of others?"

My mother replied, "No. That wasn't my intention. I wanted you to be liked and loved by other people."

I tried to maintain my composure when I asked her, "Mommy, how did all of that make you feel?" She replied, "It made me feel good and accepted." "Accepted. Wanted. Used. And afraid to speak up for who you were as a person because you didn't want to fight the battle of racism?" I asked. "Breana, I didn't know any better," my mom answered.

"What did Grandpa say about all of this?" I asked. "He didn't know," she answered. "I'm sure he would have been ashamed," I told her. "Why do you feel like you couldn't be a better mother to Summer and me than Grandma was to you?" I asked with a curious voice. "I tried, but I see I failed at it," she said, as her tears began to flow.

"Summer and I needed, and until this day, still need your attention, love, and support. We need your ears to listen, we need your arms to hold us, just like you did just now. We need your hands to rub our backs when we are down and out. Your touch will let us know things will be okay without words. Do you remember Summer and me voicing how we felt during our family meeting?" I asked. My mother sat there in a daze. I asked again, "Momma, you don't remember the family meeting last year? Summer and I talked about how we felt. The same topic of conversation as now." "No, Bree. I do not remember," she said, as if she was trying hard to remember. I didn't have any remorse and I was frustrated. "Don't worry about it, Mom. I am okay. Summer will be okay too. We will be okay." "Bree, talk to me. I am here. I want to be here," my mom said as she sincerely looked concerned.

I looked at my mom and told her, "Mommy, I want you to be here. But I do not want you to tell us to lower our standards to make other people happy. Honestly, Mommy, you shouldn't lower your standards either to make other people happy. I understand you have been that way all your life, but Mommy, it is time to change that. It is time to learn who you are as a person, love on yourself, and accept Vanessa for her flaws and all."

My mother smiled, "What have I done to deserve such a wonderful daughter?" I hugged her and said, "Children sometimes can teach adults and our parents a thing or two. We learn from each other regardless of how small or big we are. By the way, you have two wonderful daughters!"

She had tears rolling down her cheeks. I said, "Mommy, you are going to make me cry too." We were both wrapped in each other's arms and we rocked each other from side to side, crying. My mother said as she held me tighter, "It is time for a change. I am going to be a better mother. I am going to learn more about myself. I am going to love on me and work on being unapologetic for my flaws and all."

I hugged her as tightly as I could, "I believe for some things it is too late, but in a situation like this—it's never too late for change. It's never too late to become a better person." I looked at my mom, wiped her tears off her cheeks and said, "Mommy, I am glad we had this talk. Most importantly, I am proud of you!" My mom replied, "Thank you, Breana. That touched my heart. I am so proud of you too. After all these years, you've taught me a valuable lesson. Thank you again. I am here to listen and I want to hear what is going on with you."

I took it for what it was worth to give her a chance. Since she had time, I was going to take advantage and take her up on her offer. "Brian broke up with me," I told her. "Again," my mother said. She continued, "How many times is that boy going to break up with you?"

I noticed she didn't say, I told you so. "I don't know, too many times," I replied. "What happened?" my mom asked. "He got mad because I didn't have time for him last week and because I didn't answer my phone the other day," I replied. I continued, "What really made him mad was, I didn't buy him pizza."

She didn't say anything. She listened. But her facial expression told it all.

"Then he flirted with this girl named Angel in my face. He kissed her and was touching all over her. I had a panic attack in the locker room and the EMS was there..." My mother abruptly cut me off and said, "EMS was there for who? You?" "Yes, because I lost it," I said. "Breana, why didn't you tell me? When did all of this happen?" she asked. "A couple of days ago," I replied.

She called for my daddy, yelling his name, "Luke Senior!"

"Mom, please don't tell Daddy," I begged her.

"Senior!" she yelled.

I heard my daddy running up the stairs saying, "Is everything alright?"

"What is going on?" he gasped, as he was out of breath.

My mother looked at me and told him, "That damn boy, that is what's wrong. Have you noticed your baby walking around here, moping about?"

"Yep, but I figured it was boy problems. Bree knows she can talk to me anytime. I figured she would come talk to me when she felt like it," he replied.

"No, Bree had a panic attack because that damn fool broke up with her and was flirting with some little girl, and the EMS had to come out to the school because Breana lost her mind," my mother said, still looking at me. She continued, "Bree is going to let this damn boy make her lose her entire mind."

My daddy said, "Wait. Just wait a minute, Bree. EMS came out to the school for you? When? And why?"

"Yes, Daddy, but I am okay. I just was upset, because Brian broke up with me and started talking to another girl. My head started to hurt and I was dizzy, that's all. I am okay. It is over. I am fine," I replied.

"The thought didn't come to your mind to tell us anything?" he said angrily.

"Daddy, I had it under control," I answered.

"Where is your phone?" he asked.

"It's in my dresser drawer," I told him.

He looked in the top drawer and asked me to turn on my phone. I turned it on, and it was going off non-stop.

Sunday, 11:38 a.m.
"I got your man, bitch."

Sunday, 11: 40 a.m.
"Don't even think about asking him back. He is done with you."

Sunday, 11:41 a.m.
"I can give him what you can't."

Sunday, 11:43 a.m.
"If I see you with him I am going to beat your ass. He is mine now. Don't even think about looking his way, bitch!"

"Who is this? Is it that little tramp he's talking to now?" my mother asked.

"Babe, you can't be calling the little girl a tramp. She's just a child," my daddy said to my mom.

"She's a tacky tramp, calling my baby all kinds of damn names," replied Momma.

Daddy looked at her, "I am going to hush my mouth."

I answered my mom, "I guess Brian gave her my number or she got it out of his phone."

"If that girl puts her hands on you, you better beat her ass," my mom said.

"Wait a minute, Vanessa, she is not going to be fighting over a boy," Daddy protested.

She was mad as she retorted, "Luke Senior, she will not be fighting over that damn fool. If that girl comes for my baby, Breana's going to beat her ass. And I mean she's going to beat her ass good, too. This is some crazy mess. Breana, you better not show her any mercy."

"Get your butt out of bed. You been lying in bed all weekend over this no-good boy. You should never give anyone power over you," my mother said as she threw my covers on the floor.

I was looking at my daddy, thinking he was going to help me or something. "Well, I am going to head out and look at my movie," he said.

"Daddy," I pleaded.

"Bree, baby, I can't help you this time around. I am going to let your mother handle that," he replied.

My mother told me to put on my clothes and told me to come downstairs to help her make breakfast.

CHAPTER FIVE

SUMMER HAD A GAME LATER THAT AFTERNOON.

I was in a daze because I felt like Brian had gotten the better of me. My heart was crushed into a trillion pieces. I shouldn't care, but in reality, I am human. Sometimes I do not want to see what is in front of me, but I see clearly that if it's not one thing with Brian, it's something else that isn't good for me.

I heard the crowd yelling but I was in such a daze that they sounded like they were underwater or at a far distance, but I am front and center in the midst of it all.

I looked around. We all had on sky blue shirts with our yellow mini towels.

The other team colors were dark green and black. However, their supporters had on all kinds of colors. Maybe, our team is too serious when it comes to soccer. We come to represent.

As I continue to think... it amazes me how someone can turn your world upside down and not even care. Brian doesn't give a shit about my feelings. He doesn't give a damn about how badly he hurt me. He is carrying on with his life as if everything is just fine. Well, maybe everything is fine in his world. It's because he never cared. He didn't invest in as much time as I did. He wasn't there for me like I was there for him. He is the true definition of a selfish person.

The soccer ball was kicked my way. I had to think quickly because it was coming forwards my face. The referee had his hands up and said loudly, "Out!"

I quickly covered my face and I moved to the side.

"I'm out here, Bree-Bree," Summer yelled with her hands cupped around her mouth.

That was my key to snap out of it.

My mother laughed, "You know Summer likes all eyes on her during the game. You know she likes to have your attention." She continued, "Try to get that boy off your mind. Try your best to enjoy the game." I laid my head on her shoulder for a couple of seconds, "You are right. Thanks, Mommy."

I told myself as I smiled—*I can get used to this attention from my mommy. I love it!*

I waved at Summer and gave her the two fingers eyes signal to let her know I see her. I yelled as I continued to do the two fingers eyes signal and yelled, "I see you, Love Bug!"

The other team kicked the ball out of bounds. Summer ran over my way so she could throw the ball in to continue the game. Before she threw the ball to her teammates, she looked at me and said, "Love Bug? Really? I prefer Summer when I'm out in public." I smirked, "Okay, Love Bug."

I looked at the time, and goodness, time went by so fast. I didn't know the game was almost over. Daydreaming had taken up most of my time. I missed ninety percent of the game. No wonder Summer kicked the ball my way. I couldn't help but think—that's is what Brian does—he takes up most of my time.

He took up most of my time when we were together and he is taking up my time when we are not together. I have seriously got to get it together. ASAP.

Summer threw the ball and ran towards the goal since she was playing an offense position. I was like, goodness how did she get to the other side of the field that quick? Her teammates were yelling, "Summer, try to break free. Find an open spot!"

Summer ran left and then quickly ran to the right. The little girl on the other team was confused, and she fell. Maybe she was dizzy because Summer was moving around so fast! As if she was a tsunami. They passed the ball to Summer. Summer took control of the ball. Her footwork was so fast and perfect. A parent yelled, "Help Summer out!" Another parent yelled, "Defense!"

The game was intense. The other team gained on Summer and managed to take control of the ball. The little girl on the other team who had control of the ball was running really quickly down the field.

Rachel's mother on our team yelled, "No, do let them score on our field! Not today! Not today!"

Kristen's dad got out of his chair and yelled, "Knock their heads off! Do not let them score! Defense! Get on them!" As he flung his arms in the air he didn't notice his T-shirt was too small because his stomach was showing when he raised his arms. He ran down the field, out of breath, yelling, "Kristen, what are you doing? Keep your eyes focused on the ball."

For a minute, it sounded like crickets. Everyone looked at Kristen's dad.

Kirsten's mother said, "David, really? Knock their heads off! Come on babe. We can't promote that kind of behavior." Some of the parents started laughing because Mr. David was serious.

The other team tried to score, but Brenda, our goalie, caught the ball. Our team supporters got up yelling, "Yes! Good job, team! Great teamwork! Brenda, way to go, good catch!"

Rachel's mother yelled again, "Not on our field! Not today!" She took off her hair bow and put it back on and took it off again. She didn't know what she wanted to do. She wrapped it up in a bun.

Everyone yelling, "Summer, you got it!" I yelled as loud as I could, "Take it to the goal, you got it! Psych them out!"

My mother's hair was blowing in her face as she stood on her feet, clapping her hands and yelling, "Run it! Baby, run it! Take it to the goal, baby!" My daddy got out of his chair yelling, "That's right, baby girl, stay focused and keep control of the ball."

A girl on the other team was saying something to Summer. My daddy yelled, "Summer, baby girl, block her out. Don't listen to what she's saying. Stay focused. Keep your eyes on the ball and score or pass when you are ready."

The game was tied 4-4. It was so intense and everyone was on their tippy toes.

Summer did all kinds of tricks with her feet. She passed the ball to her teammate Penny. Penny did her thing and passed it back to Summer. Summer paused for a nanosecond as she positioned herself to prepare for a goal. She kicked the ball with all her might. It went slightly over the goalie's head. The little girl ducked and the ball went in.

Everybody got out of their chairs, yelling, "Great teamwork! Great job, Summer!

The final score was 4-5. Our team won once again!

After they paid their respects to the other team, Summer and her teammates came over and got their snacks. Everyone congratulated them on another win.

Mr. David said, "Summer, you were going to knock her head off." Summer winked her eye and smiled as she said, "No, sir that wasn't my intention—she just so happened to be in the wrong position. She was smart enough to duck."

Summer pretended like she was going to punch me in my stomach. I reacted to it quickly and I had a quick reflex. While she was opening her Gatorade, she said, "Breana Anderson, what was on your mind? Or maybe I should ask, who was on your mind?"

"My bad," I said as I smiled slightly and gave Summer a side hug.

I continued as we walked together, "You did your thing out there."

"Yeah, it was teamwork like always. But big sissy, you know I have to hear your voice to get in the groove. You were silent today." Summer said after she took a sip of her drink.

"I promise, no more distractions," I replied as I gave her a quick kiss on her cheek.

She wiped it off, "Ugh. What are you doing? That's nasty!"

I laughed.

Summer said, as she peeled her banana, "For real, Bree, today I missed you while I was on the field. I missed your voice, that is why I kicked the ball your way."

"I got you baby sis, next time. I pinky promise!" I agreed as I held out my finger.

Summer, gripped her pinky with mine and said, "Okay! I know you do. You always got my back, big sis! That's why your Love Bug loves you so much!

CHAPTER SIX 6

AS I WAS DRIVING TO SCHOOL I READ AN AFFIRMATION THAT I'd placed on my dashboard months ago. It said, "At the moment you cannot see it, but everything is going to be alright." I couldn't focus because I'd been crying for days; it feels like it's been months. I always swore I would never be the victim, but I feel like the victim. I cannot wrap my head around how Brian would treat me like this after all I have done for him. Forget about all of what I've done, but I was there for him mentally. I kept him afloat with his pathetic and frantic life. That's the problem, I carried him and he didn't appreciate anything I did.

I am so angry!

There were many days when I had to push myself to make it through another day because I was talking to him all night, listening to his problems and giving advice. When he didn't have anyone in his corner, I was there. I cannot understand why he would treat the one he's supposed to love this way. It is a fact — he doesn't love me—he just loved what I could do for him.

The pain is weighing on my heart. There are times when I want to be alone, and there are times when I want to talk to someone. I do not feel like being judged. I know if I talk to Chloe, she's going be like, "Girl, how dare he do that to you? He ain't shit, and blah blah blah." I want to talk to my parents, but my mother might be tired of listening to me talk about Brian, and my daddy just might break Brian's neck.

Okay, Google, call big brother.

(ring... ring......)

Luke answered. He sounded like he was busy. As he answered the phone he was talking to someone before he said, "Hey, little sis, to what do I owe the pleasure for this call?"

Hearing my brother's voice made me feel at home and comfortable. I busted out crying.

Luke quickly said, "Bree... Bree... what's wrong?"

I didn't answer because I was still crying.

He said again, "Bree... Breana... talk to me. What's wrong? Say something."

After I blew my nose I said, "Brian broke up with me."

Luke took a deep breath, "Again?"

Still crying, I blew my nose again. I couldn't stop crying but I managed to say, "Yes."

Luke sounded like he was tired of the same shit as he said, "Bree, why do you keep putting up with his no-good ass? I know this is hard to say, but you do this to yourself. Brian has broken up with you, shit, I don't know how many times and you keep taking his worthless ass back. Why? Why? Bree, why do you keep putting yourself through his bullshit? You know what you're going to get out of this—unnecessary hurt, pain, tears and stress."

Still crying, I agreed, "Yeah, I know."

Luke said, "Well, Bree, why do you keep putting up with it?"

"I don't know," I answered.

"Yes, you do know, Bree. Why? I told you he wasn't a good fit for you. You will get over him soon if you stop taking him back," Luke said angrily.

"Luke, I called you because I didn't want anyone to judge me," I said, as I felt worse than before I called him.

He tried saying something. I didn't let him finish. "I am so sorry I called you. Never mind. Carry on with your day. I didn't mean to bother you."

I hung up the phone.

Luke called me back but I didn't answer. He called me back again a couple times but I let it ring. I didn't feel like being criticized.

I parked my car and cut off the engine. I am not up for classes today, but I have an exam at eleven. I am not prepared for the test. I haven't studied because I cannot focus. My mind isn't in motion. I feel like my mind is paralyzed from the emotional, physical, mental, and traumatized shock. I really have to get myself together because I look and feel like a mess. I sit in my car and cry. I am tired of trying to cry my pain and hurt away. They say it takes time, but how long? I have about an hour before my class. I need to look over my notes, but I am so sleepy. I am going to lay my seat back and close my eyes for a quick second.

"Breana." (I heard tapping on the window, but I didn't want to open my eyes because this was the first time I'd really had some good sleep in days). "Breana." (I heard my name. Maybe if I kept my eyes closed they would go away). "Breana."

I kept my eyes closed and slurred my words. "Please go away."

The tapping continued. That person kept calling my name, but it was more of an out-of-body experience.

The tapping continued.

"Bree. Wake up." The voice said as the tapping on my window continued.

I opened my eyes. It was T'eo.

I let my seat up, rubbed my heavy eyes, and sat there for a minute to get my mind right.

He was speaking through the window, "Breana, are you okay?"

I rolled the window down, "Yes. I am okay. Thanks for asking."

I really didn't want to talk about what had been going on in my life. T'eo was looking at me like he knew I wasn't going to open the door. I rolled the window back up and unlocked the doors.

He got in the car and sat on the passenger side. He asked, "Breana, are you really okay? You face looks puffy and you look ill."

"I am okay," I replied as I looked in the mirror trying to do something with my hair.

"If you say so, because you don't look too good," he said in return.

"Yeah, I am okay. Thanks." I assured him as I turned my head, looking at the bright orange car parked beside me.

I came back to reality, and yelled as I gathered my books, "Wait! Oh, my gosh, what time is it? I have an exam at eleven o'clock!"

I was rushing, gathering papers, my phone, backpack, calculator. I picked up my book and lip gloss off the floor. As I opened the door with my index finger my book and paper fell out of my hand. My phone fell right after and the screen cracked. I fell back on the driver's seat and yelled, "Why? Why? Why?" I begin to beat my steering wheel and yelled, "Why? Why? Why?" over and over again until T'eo said, "Owwhh, Breana, what is going on? Talk to me." He gripped my hands and pulled me to him. I hesitated because I didn't want to be comforted.

"Breana, it's going to be okay," he whispered over and over again as he gently pulled me to him. I laid my head on his shoulder. I closed my eyes as I cried and cried.

"Bree, it is okay. Let it out. It is okay and it will be okay," T'eo said as he rocked me in his arms. I opened my eyes and laid my head on his shoulder. His skin was showing through his white t-shirt because of my tears. I lifted my head and said, "T'eo, I apologize for wetting your shirt." He looked at me with sympathy in his eyes, "No, Breana, it's okay."

I sat back in my seat, not paying attention to the signal warning making me aware that my keys were in the ignition and the door was open. "Oh shoot, my books and everything are on the ground." "Don't worry about it. I got it," T'eo said as he ran over to the driver' side.

I helped him as he picked up my belongings. He walked back to the driver's side and said, "I don't want to alarm you, but... it is past three." I yelled, "What? Past three a.m. or p.m.?

T'eo was looking confused because it was light outside and he slowly replied, "p.m."

"What? Are you kidding me? I got to go and see if I can talk to my professor to make up my exam." I gathered my things in a rush. "Breana," T'eo said.

"T'eo, thank you for waking me up and being here for me, but I have to run to class. My calculus class is in session now. I have to go." My voice shook as I slammed the door and started running.

"Bree. Wait!" He raised his voice to get my attention. "What is it, T'eo? I have to go!" I replied impatiently.

He smiled. I was looking like, "He's got to be kidding me. He wants to smile while I am telling him I have class." "Breana, all the classes were canceled today due to a gas leak on campus." I was looking confused, and a damn mess at the same time. Most definitely, not a good combination, "Wait. What?"

He laughed, "I was trying to tell you, but you were moving like a bat out of hell." I laughed, "Like a bat out of what? hell?" T'eo laughed back at me, "Yeah, like a bat out of hell. You never heard that saying before?" I turned up my lips, arched my eyebrows, smirked and said, "No. You are weird and funny at the same time."

He laughed. I softly punched him on his shoulder, "By the way, your joke wasn't funny." T'eo smiled, "I'd rather see you smile than cry any day." He then said very slowly, "Unless it is tears of joy and happiness." I smiled and started to cry. "T'eo you are a good person. Stay that way." "What's wrong?" he asked again. "I don't want to talk about it right now," I replied as I looked up at the sky, wiping my eyes.

I walked back to my car and T'eo walked back with me. We didn't say anything, but my heart was happy that he was in my presence. I couldn't find my keys. I put my books on the top of my car to look for them. T'eo said, "Bree." I was focused on finding my keys, "T'eo, give me a second. I am trying to find my keys They are in here somewhere."

T'eo said, "Bree, you are not going to like what I have to say, but your keys are in the ignition." I dropped everything and said loudly, "Shut up! No way!" I ran to my car looked in the window and tried opening the door. For sure, they were locked in the car. I slid down the driver's side door. "Ugh. What a day. I cannot believe this shit."

"Bree, don't worry about it. We can call the insurance company and they will send out a locksmith. If not, we can use mine," T'eo said calmly. I smiled, "Superman, you have a reasonable answer for everything. Thank you."

I used T'eo's phone to call my insurance company. They said it would take around three hours to come to the site. I also called my parents to let them know what happened. My daddy said he would come out and wait with me, but I told him I was in good hands. He insisted that he come. I asked him to trust me when I say I am in good hands.

It started to rain. T'eo and I ran across the street to the school's Treehouse. The Treehouse is a cabin. The inside is completely made of wood. It has a full kitchen, chairs, a table, and an open bar (for parties). Downstairs it's very cozy with a large pool table, air hockey table, sofas, table, chairs, and my favorite, a dart board.

Our Treehouse has a deck with rocking chairs on it, a pond to watch the ducks, and a water fountain. It's very relaxing. I was surprised to see nobody at the Treehouse, but I forgot the campus is closed because of a gas leak.

I picked up the darts and threw them at the dartboard. I hit the red target every time. "Damn, I wouldn't want to be the person you're thinking about," T'eo said. He looked serious as if he was feeling the pain from the darts. I looked at him and pretend to throw the dart at him. I smirked and told him, "Well, you better not act like these bust-ass little boys." He laughed, "I am a fully-grown man." "Good," I said as I turned around and hit the red target perfectly again.

After a while, I sat down on the couch as T'eo sat on the other couch. We watched the rain fall and listened to the rain play a melody on the roof. I closed my eyes, smiled and said, "This feels right." "What feels right?" T'eo asked. "Freedom," I replied as I smiled with my eyes closed. "Freedom?" He repeated.

"Yes. Freedom. Freedom is peace. Inner peace, outer peace and peace all around you in general. Freedom is joy and happiness on the inside as it faithfully shows on the outside without forcing a smile. Freedom is knowing you are alive on the inside and out. As opposed to faking being happy on the outside knowing you are completely dead on the inside. Freedom is truly knowing your self-worth. Freedom is loving yourself by putting yourself first. Freedom is always there, but we do not know it because we are trapped in someone else's shit. Freedom is truly always there, but we are stuck in sinking sand because someone else's drama is sinking us further and further in, to the point where the sand has reached our necks. The awful thing about it is, the person who pulled you under isn't willing to pull you up out of their mess. Instead, they pour water over your head as if the sand isn't enough. I learned today that I have to use the water they're throwing on me to my advantage. I have to start to wiggle myself out the sand as my ex pours the water. As the sand is being washed away, I have to keep moving to break up the sand. If not, I am going to drown in the water or the sand is going to suffocate me. Today, I used the water that was thrown at me to break free from the sinking sand."

T'eo was engaged as he shook his head, "Damn, that's deep, Bree. I like that!"

I smiled, "Yeah, I love it too, because I finally broke free. I am free. I am alive. I am restored and renewed. As I look at the rain, I feel like it is washing away the remains of the sand that once stuck to me. The rain has officially cleansed my sorrow, hurt, and pain, and restored my frame of thinking. It is a wonderful thing. It is going to be a work in progress, but T'eo, I am willing to put forth the effort and get through it. When I think about giving in, I am going to think about this day. I thought it was going to be the second-worst day of my life, but actually, it has been one of the best days of my life. Thanks to the Great Divines for the gas leak!" (I laughed), "You, T'eo, aka Superman, for being here for me, and to myself for being open-minded and taking note."

"I would ask you what happened but I want to keep you in the mood you're in," T'eo said. "I'd rather not talk about it. Let's talk about you," I replied. "What do you want to know?" T'eo asked. "What is your race?" I asked. "I am of the human race. I do not identify with one race, because I am one of many. Therefore, I tell myself and others that I am one race... human... the human race," he replied. "And another one," I said, smiling. He smiled back at me, "Another one? What do you mean?"

I looked at him and smiled, "When growing up, my grand-mother always told my siblings, cousins and I that we are a human race. My daddy's mother is white and Indian and my daddy's dad is very dark. He is black like the crayon."

"Really? So, you know about the human race," he replied. "I sure do. I am a human race, but I identify myself as African American. I am proud of the skin I'm in and I wouldn't have it any other way," I said. "I see. I understand. I wouldn't have it any other way either." T'eo replied.

He added, "If you must know. I am Columbian, black, Italian, Cuban, part Indian, and white. My mother is Cuban and Indian. Her parents are Italian and black. My father's mother is white and my father's father is Columbian and black. So, I am all in one! How about your family?"

"Well, my mother's mother is white. As you know, my dad-dy's mother is white and Indian. Everyone says my grandmother is mean, because she never smiles, and she always looks mean. But she isn't mean and she smiles, just not around people as much. Also, her high cheekbones make her look mean. My mother's daddy is no longer here. We were so close. I miss him so much. He was black and white. His papa was white and his mother was black. My granddaddy's mother died when giving birth to him. So his papa raised him. With that being said, I am all in one too. Therefore, I am a human race. Believe it or not, all of us are close. My father's family knows my mother's family. We are one for all and all for one," I replied.

"That's what's up!" T'eo said. He went on to say, "Well, I know where you get your high cheekbones from." I smiled, "Yeah, from my grandmother." "Are your parents together?" I asked. T'eo paused, "Well...When I was five years old my daddy left my mother to be with his mistress." "Oh...Woow..." I replied. "Yeah, but it's all good. My mother is a strong woman." T'eo said. He continued to say, "It's me and my mother. She gave up a lot for me to have a good education. When my father brought my mother to the States, she couldn't find work—so she cleaned houses for a living. She went back to Africo, Italy, to be with her family. She still struggles here and there. I want to make her proud, get a job and get my mother out of Africo. That is why I am focused and work so hard, because soon, and very soon, I will get her out of there."

I didn't know what to say. I broke the silence and asked, "Why doesn't she come back to the States?" T'eo said, "She tried, but she was deported. I was born here, but it's hard not being able to see her every day." "Are you the only child?" I asked. "Yes. I am my mother's only child—as for my father, I have no clue if he has other children."

The rain let up and we went outside. We rocked in the rocking chairs as we watched the ducks cross the pond. The sound of the raindrops falling from the trees was so peaceful, calm and relaxing. The fall colors of the trees made a huge impact on the scenery. The gentle breeze topped it all off.

"The weather is changing. It is finally feeling like Autumn," I said as I took a deep breath. "I agree, Fall has finally stood up to Summer," T'eo said. We both laughed.

I said, "That is a good way to put it. You are funny. I guess Autumn is a man and Summer is a woman. Therefore, Summer said, "It's a woman's world and Autumn will start when she feels good and ready to leave. I hear you loud and clear, Summer!"

"I like your way of thinking. I never met a lady like you who thinks of the oddest things. You draw out the meaning in life. Most people think on top of the surface. Not you, Bree, you think deep below the surface. That's pretty cool. You are not like a normal girl," T'eo said.

"I like thinking under the surface. Honestly, I give thanks to all the people who have fucked me over. They helped me to think deep under the surface because I've been cut, back-stabbed and done wrong so many times in so many different ways. So, I have to choose... either make me bitter or use it to make me a better person. Live, love, learn, grow, and keep it moving," I replied, smiling from ear to ear.

"That is a good way to put it. Why are you smiling?" T'eo asked as he smiled and giggled. "Ha! You are giggling! Too cute!" I replied in a high-pitched tone, laughing. "It seems like you bring out the best in me, Ms. Breana," T'eo said as he watched a rain-drop fall from a leaf.

"I think people bring out the best in one another when we all listen to each other. That is how we learn what the other person likes and dislikes. Also, when we listen to each other, the other one is communicating, then it goes back and forth. Therefore, listening and communicating is key. I also think the key is being honest. What I mean by honesty is telling the truth, meaning we don't always have to have an answer for everything. We should be comfortable saying, I do not have an answer for that at the moment, but if you give me time to think about it in a couple days, I will. You know?" I asked

"See what I mean? You are a thinker, but I wouldn't think of it too deeply. I truly know what you mean. It is okay to not know at the moment, but eventually have a concrete answer. I agree, communication, listening, and honesty are the keys to success in any kind of relationship in life," he answered, smiling from ear to ear.

"Now you are smiling, showing all of your teeth! I was smiling because life has a way of showing you what it has in store for you. Life has a way of putting you on the right path at the right place and time. Even if it means my keys are locked in the car," I said as I laughed.

We were quiet, but we both were smiling as we rocked in our chairs.

I broke the silence, "T'eo, thank you. I needed an ear to listen. I needed all the laughter we shared. Most definitely, I needed to smile. I haven't smiled in days. You just don't know how you made my soul smile again. Thank you. I truly appreciate it."

"You're more than welcome, Bree. You've made my day. Life has a funny way of making life better. I was having a challenging day. Life brought me to you; I didn't think about my situation. You made me realize that this too shall pass; and it *will* pass," T'eo said as he looked at the ducks crossing the other side of the pond.

I looked at T'eo and said, "This too shall pass. It is so, it is done, and it is completed."

My daddy called my phone. I couldn't answer it because the screen wouldn't allow me to swipe. Next thing I knew, T'eo's phone began to ring. It was my daddy.

T'eo put his phone on speaker. He answered, "Hello, Mr. Anderson. I am T'eo. How are you doing?" "Hello, T'eo. I am fine, thank you. How are you doing?" my daddy asked. "I am fine, sir, thank you for asking," T'eo said without fear or hesitation. "That's great to hear. Is Breana nearby?" Daddy asked.

Before T'eo could say anything, I jumped in, "Hey, Daddy! I'm here." "Hey baby, how are you doing? Are you okay?" Daddy asked. "Daddy, I told you I was in good hands. Yes, Daddy, I am okay. Thank you, Daddy, for asking," I replied, smiling from ear to ear. Blessed to know my daddy cares. "I had to ask, baby. The locksmith is at your car as we speak. Where are you?" Daddy asked. "We are at the Treehouse at the school. Daddy, call them and ask them to wait. We are going to walk over there. It should take us about three minutes," I replied.

"The Treehouse. Oh yeah, that's a nice place. I will call him and let him know to wait five minutes as you all walk over there," Daddy replied, sounding relieved. "Okay, thanks, Daddy," I replied. "You're welcome, baby. T'eo, thank you for staying with my baby girl. I truly appreciate it," Daddy said. "You're welcome, Mr. Anderson." T'eo looked at me and said, "I wouldn't rather be anywhere else. I just so happened to be at the right place at the right time."

T'eo and I walked to my car. Instead of crossing the street, we took the longer route. We walked across the bridge that would lead us directly to the parking lot.

I put my hand in my pocket.

"Are you cold?" T'eo asked as he put his coat around me. I took it off and said, "Thank you, but I am not cold." I was kind of cold, but I didn't want a repeat of what Brian did and fall for that slick move. Not this time. I'll rather freeze this time around. I was thinking to myself, *I know T'eo and Brian are different, but I'll rather take a chance at freezing before I wear his coat.* Besides the walk was only about two to three minutes.

After my car was unlocked, T'eo gave me a friendly hug and said, "I am glad you are feeling better." I smiled. "Thank you for making me feel better. It meant a lot to me. I truly appreciate it." "I wouldn't have it any other way, Breana Anderson," T'eo said as he walked to his car.

I got in my car to warm up and watched him walk to his car.

After he got in his car, he waited until I drove off before he pulled out of the parking lot. He was right behind me. However, I turned left and he turned right. We blew our horns and went our separate ways.

CHAPTER SEVEN

7

EVERY DAY DURING PRACTICE, PEOPLE WHO I KNOW AND WHO I don't care to know, come up to me left and right, asking me if am I okay. The showdown happened weeks and weeks ago. I know time heals all wounds, and I try not to be rude, but I say to myself, *what do you think?* After Simone's "It's not my story to tell" notion, I wonder if anyone even cares. I wonder, *do they ask me how I am doing so they can go back and tell another story?* It is funny how you tell someone one thing and they go back and tell a whole different story. It's really hard for me to trust anyone. With that being said, everyone who asks—I tell them I am okay. Okay, is all they need to hear. I am not going to vent and tell them anything. They are not going to spread my business and lies about me like wildfire.

I know Chloe was looking out for my best interests, but Chloe had anger built up inside of her; and my issues were the perfect time and place for her to get revenge. She could have taken advantage of the opportunity because Simone made Chloe look like a slutty ho after making up those rumors.

Speaking of Chloe, as I pulled up to Jackson-Miles, she walked to the car and said, "Hey, Superstar. I haven't heard from you. You must have been on a fast."

I looked at her and laughed, "What you mean? We talk every day."

Chloe looked at me with a 'you gotta to be kidding me' face and said, "Ugh. No. We haven't talked every single day."

I smiled slightly, "Well... No, not every single day, but we talk. I've had too much going on. I've just been laying low and thinking about life."

Chloe replied, "Well, don't be thinking too long or else you're going to start to think wrong."

"Yeah, you're right," I agreed. I tried to hold in my tears and keep myself together as I told her, "I look a hot mess. I do not feel like a Superstar."

She looked at me, opened her arms and said, "Aww, my Bree-Bree, come here. What's been going on?"

I fell into my best friend's arms, cried like a big baby. "I know I shouldn't care, but I am hurting and in pain. I am in so much pain, Chloe."

"Shhh... Shhh..." Chloe said as she rubbed my back.

She continued, "I know, Bree. Remember, we are Yin and Yang. You are the Yin. You are the light. You will grow from this, Bree. I know you gave so much to his sorry ass, but focus on your passion; and that's school, and becoming a better you."

I hugged Chloe tighter and said, "Thank you, Chloe."

"That's what sisters and best friends are for." She hugged me tighter too.

"I can't breathe," I said.

She laughed, "You can't breathe? See, that's how Brian's clueless ass is making you feel. Renew your soul. When was the last time you fasted or cleansed your chakras? You know, all that stuff you do to ground yourself."

I looked at her as I wiped my face. "It is not called stuff—and yes, I've been trying to cleanse my chakras. It helps a lot. I am trying to stay focused."

"Well, it is about that time to cleanse that negative energy completely away, Bree," Chloe said as she smiled and fixed my hair.

She continued, "Goodness. We need to do something with your hair. You look a damn mess."

I looked down, "I know."

"Don't worry, your bestie is here. I got your back," she said as she pulled out some black bobby pins from her purse.

Chloe parted my hair with her fingers and she braided it in two and put some pins in it for it to stay in place. She pulled out a mini mirror and said, "Girl, miracles do happen!"

I looked in the mirror. "You did that! Thank you."

I walked into Jackson-Miles for cheerleading practice.

Guess who was leaning on the lockers talking to Daryl? Ugh, Daryl, he is a boy-ho, he will fuck anything that has a vagina. Both him and Angel fit the bill. Angel was wearing a skank-ass short yellow skirt, with a dark turquoise shirt, and red Reebok's. I thought my hair looked a hot mess. Her hair looked a hot *damn* mess. I guess she tried to put it in a puffball, but her hair couldn't fit in the bow. The back of her hair was sticking straight up. My pinky was longer than her puffball length. Do I need to say more? Her ends were very dry and thirsty (in need of water). It looked like dandruff, but it was white flakes from her cheap-ass gel. She was tore up from the damn floor up. She looked at me as if she was saying to herself, *I got your man.*

Chloe said, "What the fuck are you looking at, sloppy ho?"

Angel replied, "At a girl who can't keep or satisfy her ex-man."

I was going to ignore her ass, but I wasn't going to let her talk shit and think I am a pushover. I laughed. "Angel, you can have his tired ass. I got rid of my headache. He is all yours now."

Angel turned her chapped lips up and as she put her hand on her hip said, "No baby. Correction, he got rid of your tired ass."

I couldn't help but look at her nails. She was badly in need of a manicure. Her nails had its own design on them as the polish was chipping off in the most horrible way ever.

I dusted my hands off and said, "You're right, he did, and that was the best thing that ever happened. Be happy, you got him now. There's no need for shitty talk. He's all yours now."

I kept it moving as she kept talking shit. I was saying to myself, *girl bye, you are a headache just like his dumb ass.*

Chloe said, "You know I had your back."

I replied, "I know. Thank you."

Chloe said, "No problem. I am glad you said something back, but you didn't have to."

I looked at Chloe as my eyes got big. "No, I had to. It wasn't like I was trying to prove a point, but I wasn't going to let her trashy ass talk shit and think I was going to walk away. Nah, not on my watch."

Chloe hugged onto my arm, laughed and said, "What the fuck she had on? And did you see her ends? They weren't laying on her scalp, they were sticking up waving, saying hello to us."

I laughed. "Girl, only you would think of that. Chloe, girl, you are crazy!

We had a good laugh as we walked downstairs.

* * *

After practice, Brian was waiting by my car.

I said to myself, *what the fuck he wants?*

I already had my keys out (my daddy always says, before you walk out the mall, school, a friend's house or wherever, make sure you have your keys in your hands. He preaches to us—never ever try to get your keys out as you look for them in your purse or pocket, make sure they are always ready in your hands to get in the car.

I ignored Brian. I am getting good at that.

"Bree, you see me right here. You know you see me," he said with his arms open with that, "What did I do?" expression on his face.

I'm looking back at him like, *bitch, please. I have no words for you.*

A security officer was sitting by the gate. He waved, "Hey, Breana, how are you doing today?"

I waved back, "Hey. I am fine, thank you for asking. How are you doing this evening?"

He said, "I am doing well, I appreciate you asking."

I smiled, "No problem."

I pressed the button to unlock my door.

"Bree, I need a ride," Brian said.

I said to myself, *no this busted-ass fool didn't just ask me that!*

I got in my car, locked my door and put my stuff on the passenger side and drove off.

I said out loud, "That dummy got to be an idiot. As if I would."

My phone started to ring. Google said, "Phone call from Asshole, do you want to answer or ignore?"

I said, "Ignore, Google."

My phone rang again. Google said, "Phone call from Asshole, do you want to answer or ignore?"

Once again, I said, "Ignore, Google."

Brian texted me I do not know how many times, over and over again. I didn't look at them when I had time, I deleted the Asshole thread.

* * *

I met T'eo for dinner at Juno's Pizza. I love this place. They have the best vegan pizza in the world! It is a cozy spot, with a 360-degree city view. The windows are beyond huge. After I put my car in park I looked up and saw him sitting in a booth. He was on his phone, talking to somebody. He had on a blue jean shirt, his curls falling in his face, and eww, he just dug his finger up his nose—I mean he's all the way up in it too!

I texted him. "I just pulled up. About to walk in. Also, go wash your nasty finger. I saw you digging up your nose, lol!"

He was looking at the door, waiting for me to walk in. As I walked in, I was smiling and looking cozy in my PINK light blue shirt, baggy pink sweat pants on with the word PINK spelled out in glitter on the side, and my flipflops. My fingers and toes were painted cotton candy (my favorite nail polish), and my hair was still braided in two, looking cute and fresh.

I continued to smile as I said, "Hey, Mr. Booger Man."

T'eo laughed. "Ha! Bree-Bree got jokes. What's a man supposed to do when he has a booger in his nose. Huh?"

I rolled my eyes. "Ugh, what a normal person would do... Go to the restroom, blow it and clean it out. Afterwards, wash your hands and dry them."

He smiled, "I'll remember that next time."

I said in a jokey way, "I'm glad I taught you something new today!"

T'eo pretended to put his finger in his nose, saying, "We learn something new every single day."

I laughed and said over and over again, "No... No... No... No... That is gross."

He laughed and asked, "How are you feeling?"

I smiled and replied, "Better. I have my days here and there. Every day is progress. Thanks for asking. How was your day?"

T'eo looked down at his phone, looked back up and said, "It was good, thanks. I am waiting on my grade to post."

"I know you did good," I said with confidence.

I continued, "Do you remember when we talked at the Treehouse and we walked back to our car you said I made your day too. I meant to ask you. What was going on? I wanted to give you space because you looked like it was getting to you. I thought if you wanted to talk about it you would have that day. Since some time has passed, I hope you are feeling better from whatever it was."

T'eo smiled. "You remember that after all you went through?"

"Yes, I do. I listen when people talk."

He said, "Thank you for asking. Well, I had a rough day that day because I found out my mother has breast cancer, but it is in its early stage. With that being said, weeks ago she had surgery and they said they got all of it. Now she's getting treatment. There's hope that it will not come back."

I felt bad and said, "Oh my, T'eo, and you decided to listen to my nonsense and here you had a real situation. I feel so bad right now. How are you holding up?"

He blushed. "Bree, no offense, but you had major problems that day too. If I wasn't there you would have slept in the parking lot all night and who knows what might have happened. You were in bad shape. Don't feel bad. I am glad I was there to help."

He paused and said, "To answer your question, I am doing well. Like always, I talk to my mom every day. She's holding up, and she's a warrior. I am amazed by how strong she is. We're supposed to be strong for her, but she is the one keeping us together."

I smiled and said, "That is what you call a strong woman who will not take no for an answer. She is going to execute this battle."

I looked at T'eo and said softly, "And she will win!"

T'eo smiled, "Thank you, Bree. I needed to hear that."

I smiled back and told him, "I am always here for you, T'eo. Do not hesitate to call me anytime"

I looked around. "Did you order? I know I didn't because I walked right in and sat down."

"I ordered you a small vegan pizza and I ordered me a real cheese pizza," he replied, as he looked down at the menu, knowing he was being funny with his words.

I laughed, "Ohhh, okay, I am going to let you have that one."

I looked over at our mini jukebox on the table and said, "What do you want to hear?"

He looked at the options and asked, "Do they have *In Due Time* by Outkast?"

"I see you T'eo! You are an Outkast fan. Me too!" I said nodding my head to the song that was playing (Molly Hate Kestner's *Compromise*).

I didn't see it on the table jukebox so I got in line to see if they had it on the big jukebox in the corner.

I walked back over and told him, "Yep! They had it!"

He smiled, "You are someone special, Breana."

I smiled back and started singing, "*I won't compromise. I don't care if you're satisfied. You're never going to change me. I won't compromise*"

T'eo said, "I see you love this song."

I replied, "Yep." as I got up and started dancing. I reached out for his hand.

He was blushing. "Nooo... I am good."

As I danced, I said, "Come on!"

He got up and began to move from side to side. I laughed. "T'eo you are off-beat and stiff as a pole."

I took his hands, put them in mine and made a fist as I took the lead. I danced around him as I held his hands. He loosened up, put his left hand on my back while our right hands were tightly gripped as he dipped me and spun me around.

I laughed and said, "Look at Mr. Tin Man loosening up."

He laughed too, "What can I say, you were the oil that loosened me up. I didn't have a choice."

I looked over at the jukebox because I wanted to pay for another song, but the line was long.

T'eo said, "We can dance to whatever song comes on."

I smiled, "Oh you're a pro at dancing now?"

The song changed... JP Cooper's *Passport Home*

It's kind of a slow song, with a nice upbeat. We had a little pep in our steps as T'eo started singing, *"Oh, don't you know you're my passport home. Keep the light on. Keep the light on..."*

I looked at him, surprised, and said, "I didn't know you could sing."

He smiled, "There are a lot of things you do not know about me as of yet."

As we continued to dance. Joss Stone's song came on, *Super Duper Love (Are You Diggin' on Me)*. It's more upbeat and everyone started to do the step. We didn't know what we were doing, but we were doing something. We had a ball and so much fun!

The songs kept coming back-to-back. I love me some Luther Vandross! *Can I Take You Out Tonight* came on and I said out loud, "Oh, this is my jam!"

T'eo and a couple next to us started laughing. T'eo began to sing, "Can I take you out tonight, to the movies to the park, or Juno's pizzas?"

I laughed, "Ugh, you cannot mess up Luther's lyrics."

T'eo kissed my hand and said, "You are too cute"

As we continued dancing the lights dimmed and we danced to another Luther Vandross song, *So Amazing*.

I laid my head on T'eo's chest and we slow danced the rest of the evening away.

It felt so good to not focus on the time. For sure time got away from us. We stayed on the dance floor for hours. When we walked back to the table our pizza was hard and cold.

The manager came by and said, "Don't worry about it—I have both of your pizzas in the oven as we speak. You two were showing out tonight!"

We laughed!

T'eo said, "She put me up to it!"

I laughed, "Well, after you were comfortable, you freely led the way!"

He looked at me and rubbed my pinky and said, "Bree, I had so much fun! Thank you so much!"

I looked at T'eo and replied, "You're more than welcome. I haven't had this much fun in a long time, and it felt great!"

The manager came by our table and asked, "To go or for here?"

We both looked at the time and said at the same time, "To Go."

I laughed, "Stop copying me."

He smirked. "Get out of my head, Bree."

I said, "Ha! Ha! You are too funny!"

The manager brought our food to the table. He packed them separately and told us, "It's on the house"

My mouth was slightly open and I said, "Oh wow, thank a bunch! That is so kind of you."

T'eo agreed, "That is kind of you, but I do not mind paying for our food."

I said, "T'eo, look at it this way—you're always giving, now it is your turn to receive and accept."

The manager told T'eo, "You have a smart young lady here. I will not accept any money from you. It is on the house. It's always wonderful to see people enjoying themselves and full of light and peace. I was happy seeing you all enjoying yourselves this evening."

T'eo said, "Thank you. We truly appreciate it. We will most definitely be back."

I texted my parents to let them know that I would be home within thirty minutes.

T'eo walked me to my car and said, "Bree, I had such a wonderful time tonight. We have to do this more often."

I replied, "T'eo, I had a blast and I haven't had this much fun since I don't remember when. Thank you for tonight. Thank you for willing to pay for my food too. I want you to know, your mother will be in my thoughts."

T'eo smiled, "Thank you, Bree."

I gave him a hug and got in my car. He closed the door and said, "Text me to let me know you made it home."

I smiled, "I will, and you make sure you do the same."

I waited until he got into his car and once again, we went our separate ways.

I thought to myself... *until next time.*

CHAPTER EIGHT 8

I WAS GOING TO CHEERLEADING PRACTICE TODAY, BUT I SAW Brian and Angel outside on the steps, kissing. It was so disgusting—it was one of those nasty kisses, at that. I felt confused because I never understood how someone could move on so fast without healing or giving a care in the world. I shouldn't care, but in reality, I do. I invested so much time and energy into that boy. I can't believe it's been a little over a month and things are still intense. Everyone is talking about the fight. As I walk in to debate club, I hear people whispering as they look at me. I don't know what they are saying; it shouldn't matter, but it does.

I can't stop thinking about them outside. I have to be honest, it hurts. My wounds are still open but they will heal in time. As I continue to think about them out there slobbering each other down—I remember, just a week or two ago, he asked me for a ride.

I looked at everyone in the debate club and walked out. I am not going to sit there while I am the topic for today. I decided to pass on cheerleading practice too.

My heart is broken into many pieces. I got in my car and cried and cried until I felt like I didn't have any fluid left. I looked over and read an affirmation that I'd placed on my dashboard months ago. It says, "Tears cleanse the soul. Cry if you want too. Scream if you have too. Afterwards, everything will be A.O.K!" When I thought I was done—I cried over and over again. When a girl's heart is broken sometimes there isn't any coming back from that. Sometimes we lose hope because dudes ain't shit. They are so selfish in so many ways.

As I was driving home, I pulled up at my favorite nearby park and sat there in silence for a couple of hours. I cut my phone off and just begin to think about life. I said to myself,

Love is so hard.

Love is so complicated.

Love hurts.

I feel like love doesn't give a fuck about anybody. Love is so selfish and steals your joy. Love is cut-throat.

Love isn't fair, because the person who needs you, you don't want them; you want someone else. Most of the time the person you want is taken or don't want you in return. Love sucks. Love doesn't give you who you want, more so, it sends you who you need. Then... That one person who needs you doesn't give up... but you pull away. As you pull away, that one person keeps walking toward you. That one person never gives up, because he said he needs you. What do you do?

The thought crossed my mind, *would I want to try again?* My heart and mind said, *hell no!* This time I asked myself out loud, "Would I want to work it out?" But when reality hits me, I told myself, *Nope, because I will be smothered. I am who and what he needs to get by. How is that fair to me? He always burns me; as a matter of fact, he burns me all the time but I always turn around and walk straight into his arms.*

When my heart is broken, I always ignore it and go back to the same person who broke my heart.

As I always welcome him back into my life, I am cautious. Broken promises are never put back together—they are shattered. It is impossible to put the same broken pieces of glass together. If it was possible, the glue would represent my scars. Superglue may keep it together, but the pain is stronger.

He dries the tears from my eyes, but he does not know he is the reason why I am crying. My emotions are weak. My mind is tired. My body is traumatized. Understanding isn't an option anymore.

Love. If you know what I need—why don't you feel my heart's desire/ My heart is in tremendous pain. This isn't love. I am so tired of carrying his memories of pain. They do not belong to me. They are not mine to bear. I am lingering on because I do not have anything left of me to give. This unhealthy relationship is too demanding.

Love, you hurt me more than him. I need help finding the courage to let go. I cannot make his life better. I am so young and have so much life ahead of me. This is draining, but I keep coming back. Help me. I know you see my suffering. I know you hear my cry. I know you feel my unbearable pain. This is too much to handle. I am going to walk away with or without your approval.

I am tired of hearing him say, "I need you, Bree."

Or, "Bree, I need you in my life."

This is a good one. He always says this to make me come back: "You complete me. I am so sorry for what I've done. How do I go on living without your love and support? I need you. Please. Bree."

When I stand my ground, he would say, "What am I supposed to do?"

Then he will add another, "I am so sorry Bree."

To top it off he would say, "We can fix this. Right, Bree?"

The icing on the cake—as he blows out the candles and his wishes come true. He knows how to get me back. He would say, "What do you want? What do you need? Tell me, Bree, how can I change? I will do it. I'll do anything. I need you, Bree. Please."

As I sit in the car in silence I am thinking to myself, *what do I do? I tell myself, it is time for me to put my best foot forward. Mean what I say, and say what I mean without sacrificing my worth. It is time for me to be unapologetic for my flaws and all. No ifs ands or buts about it.*

* * *

I had to get a new phone since the damage was beyond repair. T'eo and I have formed a friendship, which is pretty cool. I am loving it! Meanwhile, I have my moments. I stay up at night crying because it isn't easy getting over someone you invested time in and deeply care about. With that being said, I protect myself, because ever since Brian's "ho" moment I purposely keep my distance from him. I haven't talked to him in a while and I am trying to keep it that way. When someone talks to me about him, I cut them off quickly.

Since I only take classes at BSU, I am good because I do not have to see Brian. I haven't been to cheerleading practice for a while. Which means I cannot participate and cheer at two games. Basically, I am on probation. I am so fine with that. No hard feelings. I must say, since I haven't been up at

Jackson-Miles High, my load is lighter and I have more free time to do what I want to do.

Sooner or later we are going to cross paths. I just hope it's not anytime soon. I am enjoying my peace.

Come to think about it, I am not cheering in homecoming after all, because I am in the running to be Queen!

* * *

I really do not want to get up and go to work. I have no choice because I made a promise to Sage that I will fill in for her. I need the detraction. I got up, got dressed and called it a day.

Brian is blowing up my phone. I am not going to answer his calls or text messages. He is the reason why my head hurts. I have to block him out. Before I pulled out of the driveway, I blocked his number. As I was driving to work, I popped in one of my favorite artists, Jhene Aiko. I love Jhene Aiko; her music opens up the vibration of the soul and takes it to a higher state in the mind. As I turned to one of my favorite tracks, *Frequency*, it soothed my mind right then and there. I put it on repeat; that way, I can play it over and over in my head while I work.

I walked into the café. I took a deep breath with hopes that the smell of coffee would soothe my headache. Unfortunately, it isn't working today. Normally, the smell of coffee takes away my worries for the moment. Well, I have no choice but to get through today the best way I know how.

For some reason, the walls in the café are so bright. As I walked into the open area, I noticed the pictures in the gallery are different. Just last week there were dark and mysterious colors. Today, there are bright sunshine yellow and orange pictures on the walls. The brightness is so vibrant because of the mirrors on the other side of the room. Gosh, I do not see how anyone can focus in here. Maybe it is just me, because my head hurts so badly to the point my eyes are really sensitive to the brightness. One thing I do know for sure, my chakras are not balanced.

My back pocket was vibrating. I looked at my phone and it was Brian the Asshole calling me from his friend Leon's number. I know it's Brian because Leon never calls me.

"Hey, Breana, are you okay?" my supervisor asked. "I am okay. I have a bad headache, but I'm sure it will go away soon. Thanks for asking," I replied. "Are you sure you are okay?" she asked. "Yes, I am sure," I answered in return. "Okay." She looked concerned.

I smiled. She rubbed my back and said, "I asked because the Breana I know always greets everyone with a smile. The Breana I know is always filled with so much joy. I know something is wrong. If you want to talk or need today off, I am here."

"I am okay, thanks. It's a minor problem that I can handle. A little stressed here and there, but I will be okay," I said. I tried to smile but the brightness and the music felt like a ton of bricks hit my head all at one time. With a serious but concerned look on her face, my supervisor said, "Okay, let me know if you need a break or if you need to leave early." Once again, my phone is vibrating. I wasn't going to look at it, but I was curious and it was nobody, just Asshole. I cracked a smile and said, "Okay, thanks."

I walked over to get an apron off the rack and said hello to everyone. I couldn't deal with Brian's ass today. I walked to the back to put my belonging and phone in my locker.

As I tied my apron, a guy with blonde hair, green eyes, and a fresh, even tan smiled with pearly white straight teeth and said, "Hey." I was saying to myself, *damn, he is adorable and gorgeous.* I replied, "Hello, how may I help you?" He smiled and said, "I know you from somewhere? I looked around and asked, "Who? And I pointed to myself. "Me?"

He laughed.

I said to myself, *oh, my goodness, when he giggles its adorable.* He replied, "Yes, you. You are in my Anatomy Physiology class and AP lab at BSU." I played it cool and said, "I have no clue. Maybe I am. There are so many people in the class. I just keep to myself and do what I have to do to pass."

He laughed again. "You are always so serious. I see you sitting on the far left up near the rear door, focusing. After the professor dismisses us you are a ghost. It's like you snap your fingers and disappear, Ms. Breana Anderson."

He looked down for a second and looked back at me as he bit his bottom lip and said, "Yes, I know your name. I've been trying to keep up with you for the longest, but you never give me an opportunity to introduce myself."

I said to myself, *damn. Okay, that was cute. Goodness gracious, when he bites his lip, he is so damn sexy. Okay, Bree. Get it together. Keep your composure. Act like you don't give a shit. And you better not let him see you looking at his lips. And his eyes. His perfect tan skin. Damn, Bree, just look the other way.*

Ding, the bell rang. I turned around and smiled as I got the lemon blueberry crumble cake out of the oven and said, "I have places to be." He bit his lips again and asked, "Like?" "Come again?" I said. He smirked. "Like. Like where? Where do you have to be?"

Good gosh almighty, his smirk is so sexy. I said to myself, *Bree, do not look at him.* I walked over to get a knife to cut the cake and told him, "I have business to take care of. Like. Making sure I am all set for graduation." I looked at him with a serious face and said, "And the list goes on."

He nodded his head, "Yeah, I heard you were a senior in high school." I arched my eyebrows and said, "Okay. And?" He replied, "I didn't mean anything by it. I wish I would have taken that route. I think that is smart of you. That's all I am saying, no pun intended."

As I put the lemon crumble bread in the bakery case I said, "No offense taken." I was focused on putting the bread in the case as I asked, "What is your name? And why are you asking people about me? No pun intended, but you sound like a stalker?"

He stepped back with his hands in the air said, "Whoa!" I cut him off, laughed and asked, "Why are you surrendering?" He laughed as he stepped back two more steps, "No, I am not a stalker. I value my life. I think you are very attractive and smart. I love your style and your personality." He had on white Converse with mismatched no-show socks (light blue and white), a black v-neck shirt and low-cut black jogger pants. I noticed he had a tiger eye bracelet on his left wrist.

I walked over to the tables to collect the dishes that were left for pickup and said, "I have two more questions." He smiled as followed me and helped with the dishes and said, "Go for it." I wiped off the table, "Thank you for helping, but you know you are not on the clock, right?"

He laughed, "I knew you had a funny side to you. It is my pleasure to help you, Ms. Breana. If it gives me more time with you as you work, I am willing to sweep the floor too. If I have to, I will mop it as well."

I smiled.

I walked to the next table. I wiped it down after I put the dishes in the black bin and said, "Well, let me go get you the spray to clean the restrooms. While I am at it, let me get the black bags and toiletries." He laughed and said, "Okay. I'll be waiting. Just like I am waiting on your two questions."

I stopped in my tracks. "Are you real or am I imagining you?" He laughed out loud and said, "Breanna, no, you are not crazy!" I laughed so hard and remarked, "I was just checking to be on the safe side." We walked to the next table and I said, "Okay. Why do you have on different colored socks? Don't you have better things to do than be here?" Again, he laughed. He was about to say something, but I cut him off, as I was flattered, saying, "So you are going to laugh at everything I say?"

As he walked towards the corner, he reached out for the broom and said, "First, I have to assure you that I am not a stalker. I have good instincts and I know a good woman when I see one. Second, I asked your lab partner about you, since you vanish into thin air after lab and lecture. Just to let you know, I tried to get your number, but she said no. I asked her for your email address too."

I stopped washing off the table and looked at him as if he was crazy. He laughed so hard as he slapped his leg and said, "I was just playing around. Girl, I didn't ask for your email address." I turned my lips to the side, saying, "Yeah, right." He still was going to town laughing and said, "No, seriously, Bree, I didn't ask for your email address. All jokes aside, you have my word on that one." I replied, "Okay."

He continued to sweep the floor. "I never wear matching socks. I'm surprised they are not bleached, as I do the best I can when it comes to washing clothes and matching up socks. Just like you, I am focused on my studies. On the other hand, unlike you, I know how to have fun too."

I walked over to get the dustpan and said, "All you have to do is wash the colored clothes together and use cold water, and the white clothes together and use hot water. It's that simple." I had more to say, but he cut me off. He asked, "Why do we always have to live in a divided world?" I was looking lost, "What?"

As he took over the dustpan and swept the trash into it, he continued, "You said all I have to do is separate the colored and white clothes and use cold and hot water. I choose to wash all my clothes together because I feel like we have more than enough separation in the world."

I said, "Okay. I understand what you are saying, but I am talking about your clothes. If you wash them together, all of your clothes are going to look like tie-dye." He said, "That's fine with me." I didn't know what to say after that.

He said, "I didn't answer the most important question." I told him, "Okay, answer it." He sat down and said, "We did a good job! Are they closing early or something?"

"No," I replied. "They are having a 'Speak in the Mic' session tonight. People show off their talent. It's pretty cool. You can stay if you like." He smiled. "Are you asking me out on a date?" I hit his leg (which I didn't mean too), laughed and said, "Ugh, I do not even know your name."

He put his hand on his heart and said, "Well, let me answer the most important question. Do I have other things to do? Yes, I do... but I took advantage of this opportunity to speak to you. Since you were working, I knew you weren't going to clock in, clock out and vanish into thin air. With that being said, I wanted to take a chance and speak. I didn't know you would capture my heart and have me working for free. I mean, really, I washed down tables, put dirty dishes in the bin, and swept the floor. That means you are something special, Ms. Breana Anderson."

I smiled as I turned my eyes to the side and said, "So that was the most important question? I would have thought it would have been your name. But, thank you. Also, thank you for your services today." He looked me in the eyes and said, "Yes. That is the most important question that I had to answer."

"Why so serious?" I asked.

"So, serious because I want you to see how sincere I am," he replied.

I looked down at his mismatched socks, busted out laughing and said, "I apologize, but I can't. Your socks. I just can't." I laughed so hard and put my hand over my mouth, trying not to cause a scene.

"I'm glad I am making you laugh. I am going to wear mismatched socks all the time if it puts that huge gigantic smile on your face," he said as he smiled from ear to ear. I continued laughing, "Nooo... Nooo... Nooo..."

I looked up and saw my supervisor. She waved her hand and asked me to come here.

I nodded my head.

"Hey, I have to get back to work," I said. I continued, "I enjoyed your company. Thank you. Humm."

"Humm what?" he said.

"Humm... I don't know what to call you," I replied.

He looked at me and said, "Breana, my name is Eli. Eli McNair"

I smiled, "It was a pleasure, Mr. Eli McNair. Thank you for your help."

"The pleasure was all mine," Eli said as he watched me walk away.

Two hours passed. Speak in the Mic started. I was looking for Eli. I was thinking to myself, *if he was so interested, why didn't he ask me for my number or my email address? What am I saying, email address? I am totally tripping. Well, I've come to the conclusion that Hi, makes things harder. Maybe he was here just for the moment. I will admit, I really enjoyed his company. It's funny, my headache went away and I didn't even notice it.* I laughed at myself and said, *maybe he was a figment of my imagination. Its official, I am totally losing it.*

I clocked out and took a seat and stayed awhile for Speak in the Mic night. There was a guy who walked up with a daisy shirt on and a daisy in his hand. He had on blue jeans with yellow clogs on. I guess his favorite color is yellow. He cleared his throat and tapped the mic. He spoke in the mic and said, "Check. Check."

He cleared his throat again and said, "Hi, everyone. My name is Mike. Mike Miller. I am going to read a poem I wrote called, *Rose*."

He cleared his throat once more and said, "Rose, close the door and let's talk. Rose, I cannot see you. Rose, close the door so we can talk. Rose, are you there? Rose, the door is open, let yourself in. Rose, where are you. Rose. Rose. Rose, you know you hear me."

Everyone was looking around looking like, what the hell?

He went on to say, "Rose, you are such a selfish bitch. You are all about me. Me. Me. Me. But what about me, Rose? I cannot take this shit anymore. I want to love you, but loving you is too much. Rose, I gave you all of me." He raised his voice. He turned his head and looked at a lady in a purple shirt and said, "Sabrina, I love you." Sabrina blew and kiss and replied, "I love you too"

Mike yelled, "No, the fuck you don't! If you loved me you wouldn't be fucking Rosemary. I saw you! I saw the both of you!"

An officer ran up to the stage because the speaker jumped off the stage as he walked quickly past Sabrina. The officer showed Mike to the door and asked him to exit the property. The officer came back and asked Sabrina to leave as well.

The owner of the shop canceled the 'Speak in the Mic' night in fear that Mike would come back to do something tragic.

After everyone left the café, I helped the owner clean for business tomorrow. Later on, I gathered my things, checked my phone and noticed I had twenty-six missed calls from Brian. As I scrolled down, I had so many messages from him, there wasn't any point in counting them. Chloe had called a couple times. I'll call her back later tonight.

The owner and my supervisor said, "Lights out." They both thanked me for staying over to help.

Just when I was about to call Chloe, Eli walked up and said, "That's what I forgot to give you. My number! Speak in the Mic night is over already?" "What makes you think I want your number?" I asked. "Because you said you enjoyed my company today," Eli replied. I smirked and said, "Ummm, okay."

I continued, "Yeah, it is over. This one dude confronted his girlfriend because he was cheating on him with somebody named Rosemary. So the owner shut it down because she didn't want him to come back and do something crazy."

Eli put his hands in his pockets, looking shocked and asked, "Damn, are you serious?" "I am dead-ass serious. You look shocked. What? You knew him or something?" I said, trying to be funny. "Aww, so you are going to go there," he said, smiling. I didn't say anything. I just smiled back at him.

He got out his phone and asked, "May I have your number, please? If so, Ms. Breana, will you put it in my phone?" I put my hand on my hip and tapped my foot and said, "I'll think about it."

Eli put his phone back in his pocket and said, "Okay, I'll respect that." I laughed. "Look at you! I was kidding. But I liked how you respect my decision."

"I try not to overstep my boundaries," he replied. I didn't say anything. He broke a couple seconds' silence. "If you don't mind me asking, where are you going?" he asked. "I don't mind you asking. I am going home so I can rest," I answered. "Are you hungry?" Eli asked. "I ate here," I replied. "Okay, well. Can I call you tonight?" he asked. "Sure, if you like. That is fine with me." I answered.

Eli walked me to my car and said, "Breana, I had a rough day, and you just don't know you made my day. Thank you." I smiled and told him, "Eli, you're more than welcome."

As I drove home, I was feeling good. Eli just doesn't know he made my day too.

CHAPTER NINE

BRIAN BEEN TEXTING ME EVERY DAY FROM SOME UNKNOWN number. Every time I blocked each number he managed to call from another unknown number. I am so proud of myself! I normally would have given in and called Brian or answered his calls. Maybe this is a sign that I am getting over him. Who am I kidding? I've had a distraction. Eli and I talked every single day. He asked me out a couple times but I am not ready because I am still in the healing process.

I am enjoying my peace and getting a lot done without being distracted with all of Brian's many problems that he dumped on me and left me to figure out.

Summer yelled loudly, "Breana, you have company! Do you want me to send her up?"

I yelled, "Who is it?"

"Confident Chloe!" Summer yelled.

"Yes, she can come up. Thank you!" I yelled.

Knock. Knock. (on the door)

"Anyone home?" Chloe asked, smiling as she waited for me to say come in.

"You silly, girl. Come in," I said as I was cleaning off my bed.

"Bree, I've never seen your bed clean. You are either cleaning it off or stuff is still on it. We just sit on stacks of paper and at times books, pens, thumbtacks stick us on the ass, or we get attacked by all the papers on your bed and get a paper cut," Chloe said as she sat on a stack of papers.

"Well, since you are used to it and making yourself comfortable there's no need for me to clean off the bed," I said as I sat across the bed with it being half cleared off.

"What's been up your ass?" Chloe asked as she looked at her sky-blue nails.

"What you mean? I've been chilling, taking it easy and getting a lot of work done. I am loving it. No pressure. I am not responsible for anyone but me," I said as I picked up a sheet of paper I'd been looking for, for the longest time.

"Umm, okay," Chloe said as she rolled her eyes and put a piece of gum in her mouth.

She started to chew her gum, "I don't appreciate you putting me on pause. I've called you a couple of times and you never called back. Needless to say, I've texted you too."

I was looking confused and told her, "Girl, stop. I talked to you the other day. You filled me in on Darius and how he played the victim because you told him you are not going to have sex with him."

Chloe popped her gum, put it back in her mouth and said, "Okay. Go on."

"You told me over and over again Brian was asking you about me. You caught me up on ol' girl Shay's baby daddy drama and come to find out Marcus is the daddy. Must I go on?" I asked.

"Yes," Chloe said as she took off her shoes.

"What? Girl, bye. I am not going to tell you what you already told me. You must not remember," I said as I looked at my phone.

"I remember. I just wanted to make sure you were listening since you've been in your own little world. Lately, you been all about Bree and you haven't checked on me once. I know you and Brian are going through stuff, but dang, you can call and check on your girl. Or have you been too busy to even think of anyone but yourself?" She asked with an attitude.

I paused and said to myself, *oh no she didn't. This is the shit I've been trying to stay away from.*

"Chloe, you are right. I've made my life all about me. At the beginning and end of the day, nobody but me knows what I am going through inside and out. I am trying to stay positive and focus on all the stuff I need to do and give myself some me time. I deserve that. When we texted each other, I asked you how you were doing. You never answered. I asked you again and you read it but didn't say anything. I assumed you were fine or upset with me. If you are upset with me, I don't know why because I didn't say or do anything for you to be upset about."

She tried to talk, but I talked over her and said, "No, let me finish. I feel like when I need a little time to myself everyone thinks it's a crime or some shit. I wish people would for once under-stand where I am coming from or at least give a shit about how I feel. I am going through a lot of shit with Brian, I haven't gotten a letter from the school I want to attend. I am working my ass off with school, working, homecoming stuff, and trying to make everyone happy. With that being said, who asks Bree how she's doing? Nobody. Instead, everybody wants to complain and say, Bree, you haven't done this or that. You haven't answered my calls or text messages. Bree, you didn't ask me how I am doing. Well, excuse the fuck out of me. I wish someone, shit, just anybody, would ask Bree how the fuck I am doing? I guess that's too much to ask. I am tired of being everybody's keeper." I paused and yelled, "I am not Perfect Breana! I am human and I have feelings too!"

I paused, pursed my lips, blinked my eyes, walked to the door and said, "You know what? I do not have time for this shit today. Chloe, with all due respect, please leave. You can be pissed off or whatever. Right about now, I really don't give a shit."

Chloe jumped off the bed and said, "I think it's fucked up that you are taking your shit out on me. It's all good though."

She put up the peace sign and she walked down the steps.

I sat on my bed and laid my head on my pillow. I felt a touch on my back. "Bree, are you okay?" Summer asked softly.

"Summer, I am okay. Thanks for asking. Everybody wants too much from me. I am only one person. If everybody could have their way; they would clone me. I wish they would and the real me would be able to breathe for once," I said as my pillow was wet because of my tears.

"I wasn't trying to be nosy, but I was standing outside the door. I heard everything. What happened with you and Brian?" Summer asked, as if she was innocent.

I smiled and said, "You weren't trying to be nosy, but you were standing outside the door. That was your choice to stand outside the door. Girl, it is sealed, stamped and approved that you are the Secretary of State. You know everyone's business."

Summer continued to rub my back as she said, "I'm glad you are smiling."

"You're trying to be slick and trying to get off the subject. I am smiling, you're acting like you are so innocent. One day, you

116

are going to hear something you're not supposed to hear," I said as I hugged my pillow.

"If I didn't know anything else, I know you let Chloe have it," Summer remarked.

"I don't think I was wrong. I am tired of always being everyone's hero. People think I should stop everything I am doing to console them. I am tired of it. I just want a break from everything and everybody. Summer, you are the only one who asks me how I am doing. I appreciate it." I told her as I hugged her with one hand.

Summer took off her shoes and said, "Bree, you are more than my big sister, you are my best friend. I love you so much. I know you have a lot on your plate. I think you should take a break too."

I got up and hugged Summer as I squeezed her tightly with my eyes closed, I said, "I love you too, baby sister."

A familiar voice asked, "Can I get in on the hug too?"

I opened my eyes and it was Chloe.

"I want some sisterly love too," Chloe said as she hugged Summer and me.

"I apologize, Bree. I was too hard on you. I know you are going through a lot. Will you accept my apology?" she asked as she almost squeezed the life out of me.

"You know, my girl, and yes, I accept your apology," I said as I hugged her back with one arm as I continued to hug Summer with the other.

"I am going to let you two be," Summer said.

I smirked. "Yeah, right."

"I am for real, my favorite shows come on back-to-back so you all are lucky!" Summer said as she walked backwards out of the room.

"Bree, Really. I am so sorry." Chloe said as she reached to hug me again.

"Chloe, I apologize if you felt like I wasn't there for you when you needed me. I just needed some time to myself," I said.

"Girl, I wasn't going through anything. You were right, we talked. I guess just not as long as I wanted too, but you did make time for me. I should have been calling you asking you how you were doing, but I understand we all need our space," Chloe said as she chewed the hell out of her gum.

"I appreciate it," I said as I moved a box into a corner. "How are you doing?" Chloe asked as she watched me move boxes around.

"I am good. You know Brian been blowing up my phone? I miss him though, but I am tired of his shit," I said as I stacked the boxes on top of each other.

"Yeah, I hear you. He asked me about you. I told him he gotta talk to you because you are my girl. He told me to tell you he misses you and to answer his calls," Chloe said as she took off her shoes and lay on the bed as if my bed was her bed.

I turned around before I stacked the last box, and replied, "Chloe, girl, he broke up with me three times in one day. You know he's good for breaking up with me when he doesn't get his way. Girl, I am just tired of his ass. As if I got to put up with that shit. I am too good for that. I know my worth, and honestly, when it comes to Brian, I settle for less. The sad part is I knew I was settling for less when I got involved with his ass. I don't know why we girls know we're settling for less, and accept it."

Chloe was shaking her head as she focused on filing her nails and said, "Hell yeah, we know better. We either think we can change a dude or we settle because there aren't any good boys out here. Either way, it is our fault because we know what we are getting ourselves into and do it any damn way."

"Yeah, so true. After listening to Brian's story about his mom and dad I really thought I could make him a better man, but girl, the only thing I've done is made him depend on me and treat me like shit. I feel like I was his mother, not his girlfriend."

I paused and said, "Well, an ex-girlfriend once again. I don't know how many times he's broken up with me as long as we've been together. And my dumb ass takes his ass right back. This time, I am like, fuck it, because he knows that he can do what he wants and I will take him back. I'm drained and I am so sick of it."

I walked over to look at myself in the mirror and said, "I love me too much to let a boy talk to me to any kind of way. We as women teach a man how to treat us by what we're willing to accept. I love him, but I am so tired of all the straight-up bullshit."

Chloe looked at me and said, "Bree, I hear you. Darius broke up with me today because I told him I am not ready to have sex for, I don't know how many times, too. He flat out said...

Chloe's eyes watered as she repeated herself, "He flat out said he didn't want to have sex with my fat ass anyway."

I turned around so fast my head was about to fall off my shoulders. "His ugly ass said what?"

Chloe was crying a river of tears. I walked over to give her a hug. I rocked Chloe in my arms as I said over and over again, "Let it all out. It's going to be okay."

Chloe continued crying as she asked me, "Bree, do you think it's going to be okay?"

I reassured her as I rocked her in my arms, "I know it's going to be okay."

Summer opened the door, walking in the room with her arms wide open and said, "I apology for eavesdropping again, but Chloe, it's going to be okay."

Summer hugged Chloe and put her arm over me and said, "Remember, you are confident, Chloe, and you are tough as nails. Screw Darius, and I agree with Bree, he was ugly anyway. You should have told his ugly butt if you had sex with him you would have had to put a pillow over his face so you wouldn't have to look at him."

Chloe and I start laughing and said, "What?" at the same time.

Summer started laughing and answered, "Well, I'm sure you wouldn't want to look at that ugly face while having sex. Ugh. I'm just saying."

We all laughed because Summer is something else.

I looked at Summer with a curious face and said, "Hold up. Wait a minute. What do you know about sex?"

Summer looked at me as she put her hands on her hips and said with her sassy mouth, "Bree, you talked to me about it in elementary school, don't you remember? Mommy and Daddy talked to me about the birds and the bees right before I started middle school. They said they wanted me to hear it from them first because they did not want me to hear it from anyone else. Mommy and Daddy talked to you and Luke about it too around my age. So, Bree, do not act surprised."

I was thinking about when I talked to Summer. "Summer, I don't remember," I said.

"Sure, you do, Bree. Remember we had a picnic at the park? You brought a blanket with some snacks. Remember?" she asked.

"Ohhh, yeah, I remember! That was about two years ago," I said.

Summer looked at me with her mouth open. "Duh, Bree. I tell ya, sometimes you are not the brightest—but I will give you another pass."

As Summer settled herself comfortably in my room she said, "I told Mommy and Daddy I do not understand why people call it the birds and the bees. Clearly, that is not how sex happens. My take on the birds and the bees is—the bees are the boys because they are drones. They mate with the female bees and leave them alone to take care of the mess they made together. Drones are good for nothing—they do not produce pollen. They cannot do anything but make a mess. They are powerless because they do not have a stinger. They are just for nothing. The drones stay in the hive during the summer and the female workers and queen bee kick them out during the cold seasons. They kick them out because they do not participate in gathering food or making honey. We as girls need to have the mentality of a female bee. We have to know our worth. We must keep in mind we are soon to be young ladies and women and that we hold the power. We hold the key because we are powerful. What we say goes."

Chloe said, "Summer, girl, you better preach!"

Summer looked at Chloe and said, "Wait. You interrupted me. I am not finished. Girls are birds too We all know birds lay eggs, but I'm speaking hypothetically because the guy has gotten her pregnant, that is when the girl bird has to provide for their child or children. Such as nesting, finding them a home, providing food for their child. As the saying goes, the early bird catches the worm. From what I see all the time, birds are always protecting their young as well and taking on all the responsibility in caring for their babies. We as girls need to take note from the worker bees and the queen bee. We have to believe and know that we are in charge and it's our call."

Summer paused for a minute and continued, "The other day, I played chess at recess with this boy name Kale. He looked at me with a straight face and said, "The king piece can move anywhere he likes on the board. He's the man." I told him, "That is true, but like always "the man" is powerless because the queen protects the king. Shouldn't the king protect the queen?" I told him to keep in mind guys are good for moving around here and there and always bragging, but the queen is the most powerful piece on the board—and the most powerful in the world. Man cannot dare do what a woman can do. He then said I wasn't any fun to play chess with. I told him, "See, a typical man. Leaves with he wants to and cannot handle the truth."

I looked at Summer and gave her a high five, saying, "Girl, knowledge, wisdom, and power!" As Summer took her hands off her hips she said with a confident voice, "As Breana always says, (Summer looked directly me) we as girls do not need to apologize for our flaws. Instead, we are unapologetic for our flaws and all!"

Summer winked her eye, took a bow and said, "Ladies, that's all I have to say."

I looked at Chloe and bumped up against her. "Girl, you dodged a bullet."

I smiled at my sister and said, "So, Ms. Know-It-All."

As I was sitting on the bed Summer jumped on me, kissed me on the cheek, hugged all over me and said, "I am proud and honored to have you as my big sister. You are not the smartest at all times, but Bree, I never ever forgot when you talked to me about sex for the first time. I will never forget when you told me I should know my worth. I will never ever forget when you said that I should always be unapologetic for my flaws and all. I listen to you, Bree. I thank you for always taking time to listen and be here for me."

I hugged Summer so tight and told her, "You're welcome, Love Bug!"

Love Bug has always been my nickname for Summer. When she was little, she always loved and hugged up on me; and she still does it until this day. That is why I call her Love Bug.

Summer rolled over on the bed as she was out of breath. "By the way, I am Ms. Know-It-All because you taught me eighty percent of everything I know."

I tickled her and said, "Well, that's good to know."

I got up and opened the door and said, "Summer, the realist and the comedian, and an added bonus, Secretary of State, who knows everyone's business; and to top it off, Ms. Love Bug. We thank you for the laughter and the knowledge. I must say, Ms. Know-It-All, it was very delightful; however, you have to exit my room because Chloe and I gotta have a well-needed girl talk."

"No problem. You all are more than welcome for my services," Summer said after she gave Chloe another hug.

I walked over to my dresser and put on some music so Summer couldn't hear our conversation.

I received five text messages in a row. Chloe was about to pick up my phone as she said, "Damn, who is that? Brian?"

I rushed to pick up my phone before she picked it up.

"Umm... are we keeping secrets?" Chloe asked as she tried to reach for my phone.

I moved back quickly as I read the message from Eli.

Thursday, 7:39 p.m.
"Hey, Breana!"
"WYD"
"Can you talk?"
"I hope you had a great day?"
"Hit me up when you can."

"Secrets? I met this guy named Eli, but he's just an associate," I replied.

"Damn, that is why it's been so easy for you to not respond to Brian," Chloe said.

"Nooo... I am tired of Brian's shit. Like I said, Eli and I are just associates," I repeated.

"Eli," Chloe said as she forgot all about her breakup."

"Is he cute?" she added.

"We are not going to talk about him right now, but he's alright. Are you okay?" I asked.

"What is our motto?" Chloe asked.

We said at the same time, "We are the Yin Yang sisters. We can get through anything and problems are temporary."

"No, I am not okay. I helped Darius when he didn't have shit," Chloe said.

I nodded my head and agreed. "Yep."

"I made that fool who he is today. If it wasn't for me, he would be nothing," Chloe said as she got up, pacing around the room.

"Exactly, that is how I feel about Brian. I was the one who made him better," I said as I punched a teddy bear that Brian gave me in the face.

"What the hell are you doing?" Chloe asked as she just about died laughing.

"That was the teddy bear Brian dumbass gave me," I laughed.

Chloe walked to her purse and took out a picture of Darius. She walked over to my desk and got a pair of scissors and tape. She got the teddy bear Brian gave me and taped Darius' picture on it. Chloe punched the hell out of the teddy bear as she said, "You ain't shit. I made you who you are. You are a user, a punk, and fake as hell."

Chloe punched the bear one more time and said, "Screw you! I love the skin I am in and I am beautiful! I am the shit whether you see it or not!"

She ripped off the picture, got the scissors and cut it into as many pieces as she could.

She fell on the bed, out of breath. "Damn, I am tired. That was a workout. I am going to miss his dumb ass, but time heals all wounds. Bree, I am going to pull your move and keep my distance. What the hell am I talking about? Damn, I cannot do that, because we are in the same classes."

We both laughed.

I said as we both laughed, "Block his ass. You won't have to wonder if he called or texted you. Trust me when I say it helps. That way, you will be on the fast track of getting over his no-good ass."

I lay on the bed beside her and said, "Chloe, we have to be strong. I miss Brian. I want him to see he cannot treat me the way he does. He doesn't see it, because the messages he's been sending me are so disrespectful."

I reached for my phone and read the messages to Chloe that I'd saved to help me not to give in.

Saturday, 9:19 a.m.

"Bree, you can be such a spoiled bitch at times. You think I should be kissing your ass."

Saturday, 9: 22 a.m.

"Fuck you, Bree."

Saturday, 10:37 a.m.

"You think you're better than me."

Saturday, 10:43 a.m.

"I should come up to your job to make you talk to me."

Saturday, 10:46 a.m.

"Bree, I am on my way up there."

As Chloe was reading the messages with me, she said, "Oh my gosh, Bree, I didn't think it was that bad. I didn't know he was this disrespectful. Did he come up to your job?"

"No," I answered.

I continued, "He's always been disrespectful. I never told anyone."

"Bree, has he ever hit you before?" Chloe asked.

Slowly I said, "Well, he pushed me a couple of times. He shoved me on my car a couple of times. He also grabbed my arm a couple of times, but he never punched or slapped me."

"Before, you say anything," I continued, "I know that's abuse and unacceptable but I knew he needed me. I figured if he didn't put hands on me then..."

Chloe cut me off, "Oh my God, Bree. Why didn't you tell me? Why?"

"Because I didn't want people to judge Brian's and my relationship," I said as I started across the room.

I asked, "Chloe has Darius ever put hands on you?"

"No. He hasn't. We got into a couple of arguments, but we never put hands on each other."

Chloe hugged me and said, "Bree, I am so, so, so, so, so sorry you had to go through this alone. You know I am always here. Always."

Chloe and I gave each other the longest hug. I told her, "I know you are here for me and I am always here for you too."

CHAPTER TEN

10

I HAVE A BUSY WEEK THIS WEEK. I HAVE EXAMS BACK-TO-BACK and Homecoming is this week! I hope Faith wins Ms. Tenth grade! Speaking of Faith, I totally forgot to call her. I've had so much going on. I have to call her before the week is out. As I walk to the library, I waved at T'eo as he was rushing to class.

He yelled, "Bree, are you going to the library?"

I yelled back, "Yep, I have to study. My professors canceled our classes this week so we can study."

"I will be there when my class is over," he yelled.

"Okay. See you then," I yelled back.

I walked into study room one—it's not too big, but it is big enough for three or four people. I took my books out of my book-bag. I laid them out on the table, closed the door and started to study.

A knock on the door... I looked up. It was Dr. Wright. I said to myself, *what does he want and why is he in the library?*

"Ms. Anderson, it is good to see at least one of my students taking advantage of the time I gave you all to study," Dr. Wright remarked.

I wanted to say, I am not studying for your class.

I looked up for a split second. "Hello, Dr. Wright."

"That was a dry hello," Dr. Wright said as he welcomed himself into the study room.

I kept my head in my book.

He sat down and asked, "Will it be okay if I take a seat? Do you mind?"

My phone was in the seat beside me. I picked it up without him noticing, put in the password and pressed the record button. I said, "Dr. Wright, I do mind because I am trying to study." He touched my hand. "My apologies. I was trying to reach for your pen. May I use it?" I pulled my hand back and said, "Sure." I looked up and noticed he'd closed the door. I asked, "Dr. Wright, will you please open the door?"

"The door was closed before I walked in. I figured you wanted me to close it," he replied. "Dr. Wright, I prefer that you open the door, please. I am not comfortable being in the room with you alone," I told him. "Ms. Anderson, I am not going to bite. You're acting like I am going to hurt you," he remarked, as he looked at me and smiled. I said in a firm voice, "Dr. Wright, please open the door. As you open the door, I would appreciate it if you would please leave."

Dr. Wright didn't open the door. I got up to open the door. He touched my hip and asked, "Ms. Anderson, where are you going?"

"Please take your hands off me, Dr. Wright!" I said loudly. "What's the matter, Ms. Anderson? It's a friendly touch," he answered with a creepy smile on his face. He reached to touch my breast. I yelled, "Stop! Please leave!" Nobody heard me because study room number one is the last room and further back in the library.

He opened the door and asked, "What has gotten into you? What's your problem?" I yelled, "You are my problem! You talked and touched me in an inappropriate way."

"Nobody is going to believe you if you say something. It's going to be your word over mine," he commented as he wrote his number on a sheet of paper. As he walked out of the room he said, "Ms. Anderson, I told you, you need an older man. I wrote my number down just in case you need help with your assignments." He winked.

After he left, I closed the door. I picked up my phone to make sure it had recorded everything. It had. I called my daddy in a panic. "Daddy," I said, scared and afraid as I packed my books and crammed my papers in my book bag. "What is it Breana, are you okay? He asked. "No, Daddy. No. My professor came in my study room and touched me inappropriately."

I walked out of the room as I was talking to my daddy. He yelled through the phone and said, "What! Where are you?" "I am walking out of the library now. I am about to walk to the police office to report him," I answered. "No, stay right there. You do not need to walk alone. I am on my way," he said in a hurry.

* * *

It started to rain. I was nervous and watching my back. I felt pressure on my back. I jumped up to prepare to defend myself.

"Bree, Whoa, My bad. I didn't mean to scare you." T'eo said and he jumped too.

"Don't creep up on me like that!" I yelled. I started to pace back and forth.

"Whoa, Bree are you okay? What happened?" T'eo asked as he tried to calm me down.

"I am waiting on my daddy," I replied.

"Why? Do you need a ride?" T'eo asked out of concern.

"No. My car is fine." I answered.

I looked out the window and I saw my daddy running. I grabbed my book bag and ran outside in the rain and into his arms. I cried and cried with relief because I knew I was protected.

"Where is your professor?" Daddy yelled. "Where is he, Bree! Show me now!" T'eo came outside and said, "What is going on?"

"Is this him?" Daddy asked as he ran up on T'eo. I yelled, "No! Daddy! That is not Dr. Wright!" T'eo's heart was about to jump out of his chest when Daddy asked him, "Who are you?" T'eo was thinking quickly and on his toes as he said, "No, sir, I am not Dr. Wright. I am T'eo."

Someone had called the police, as they were running down the stairs yelling at my daddy, saying, "Put your hands up, sir! They yelled again, "Let us see your hands, sir!" I yelled, "Daddy! show them your hands, Daddy! Show them your hands!" My daddy showed them his hands. They patted my daddy down as they asked, "What is the problem?"

I showed them my college ID to let them see that I was a student. Officer Smith said, "Breana Anderson, what is going on?" Officer Smith is always at the front gate checking for cars without a student tag, as he put tickets on them. I always say hello and goodbye when coming and leaving. I was so happy he was there today because he is the only officer I knew here.

I was speaking fast and told them what happened. "I was sexually harassed by my professor, Dr. Wright. This man, right beside me, is my daddy. He didn't want me to leave campus because he didn't want me to walk alone."

Officer Smith said, "Let's get out the rain."

We walked inside the library building. We were soaking wet.

Officer Smith said, "Ms. Anderson, do you know what you are saying? You are accusing a professor of something serious." I replied, "Yes. I know exactly what I am saying and I know precisely that what he did is not acceptable."

As I tried to talk, Daddy asked in a harsh tone, "What are you saying? My daughter is lying?"

Officer Smith said, "Sir, I understand your concern, but I need for you to calm down."

I tried to talk, but apparently, my daddy's voice overpowered mine as he said, "Don't tell me to calm down. My daughter is telling you all that she was sexually harassed. I believe my daughter! Do you have a daughter? If so, would you think she's lying?"

Officer Smith said, "That's beside the point."

Daddy replied, "What the hell do you mean, it's beside the point?"

I yelled because I knew they weren't going to let me say anything, "Everybody, listen to this!"

I played the recorder back, and as I played it, I sent it to my mother, sister, brother, and my daddy to make sure they all had a copy. I also sent a copy to all of my personal email addresses and our lawyer.

I put the recorder up so everyone could hear it loud and clear. After it was completed, I asked the officers, "Now do you think I am lying?" I continued, "If I didn't record the situation you wouldn't have believed me." My daddy said, "I didn't raise a fool."

Officer Smith said, "Ms. Anderson, we are going to need your phone as evidence."

Daddy said, "We have rights, we are not handing anything over until our lawyer gets here. Baby, I am going to keep my eyes on them while you call Attorney Davis.

As I called our lawyer, my mother called. I asked Daddy to call Momma as I talked to Attorney Davis. After speaking with Attorney Davis, he told us not to hand over anything until he got there.

I called my mother back and she said she was five minutes away from the school, she stayed on the phone as she listened to what I told her had happened.

T'eo was still standing in his spot in the corner. I walked over and asked him was he okay. He said, "I am fine. Are you okay?"

"No, I am not. Thanks for asking," I answered.

"It seems like you all are going to be here for a while. I am going to go home and bring you back some dry clothes. Will that be okay?" he asked.

"Yes, thank you, because I am freezing," I replied.

* * *

Just about fourth-five minutes passed and my lawyer finally made it. T'eo made it back before Attorney Davis showed up. He went to the store and bought my daddy and me gray sweat suits and socks. That was very thoughtful of T'eo. Attorney Davis apologized because he was stuck in traffic because of the rain.

He said he listened to the recording over and over again. He made us aware that he'd called the news station about what happened. They were all over campus. Our lawyer had paperwork for the officers to sign before I turned over my phone. After they signed the paperwork I looked up and saw Dr. Wright walking out the science building in handcuffs.

My daddy ran outside in the rain again as he said, "That's him!" Five officers had to hold him down because he was running full force to jump on Dr. Wright.

It was a long night. I wasn't allowed talk to the news anchor until my lawyer and I had a chance to sit down and talk about the entire story. Attorney Davis had on a black suit with a white shirt and baby blue tie. As he looked in the cameras he said, "We will not release the victim's name at the moment. All I have to say is we will keep you all posted after the facts have been given. Until then, we will be in touch soon."

This is going to be a long journey, but I will not keep quiet that I was violated, disrespected, and sexually assaulted on so many levels that are not, and will not, be acceptable.

* * *

Slowly but surely the week is picking up. BSU has been on the news on every station. Attorney Davis said it is not time for me to talk. He wanted me to stay behind the scenes for a couple more days. Until then, I am going to carry on and prepare for Homecoming which is in two days. Last week my daddy bought me a new phone since the police still have the other phone for evidence.

I picked up the phone to call Faith. "Hey, Faith. This is Breana," I said after she answered the phone. She replied excitedly, "Hey, Breana! How are you doing?" I appreciated Faith asking me how I was doing. I said, "I'm holding up, thank you for asking." I continued, "I know it took me a long time to call you. I apologize. I have a lot going on."

It took Faith a second or two to say something. She said, "Breana, I understand. You do not have to explain anything. I thank you for calling. I know you have a lot going on and a lot on your mind." She paused again, "I am glad you are holding on. I cannot imagine what you are going through." I said, "Yeah, but life goes on slowly but surely."

"You can say that again," Faith said after she took a deep breath. She took another deep breath and said, "I've been catching hell left and right from these jealous girls."

"I heard all of the things are you going through. You have to have thick skin because these girls are like vultures, but what they fail to realize is that they are making you stronger. Stay focused on what's important to you and do not let them side-track you from your goals. With that being said, how are you holding up?" I asked.

"I am feeling better after you said that," Faith told me. I heard her voice trembling as she said, "It is hard." She repeated herself as she cleared her throat, "It is hard. You're right, those vultures are trying to rip me to shreds." I felt bad for Faith as I said, "When you are alone at home, cry your eyes out if you have to, but not around them. You have to act like you don't give a shit. When you act like you don't give a shit, believe me when I say, it gets under their skin. Carry on as if everything is fine. I am here if you need to talk."

"Thank you, Bree. Oh, by the way, I am moving out of state next year so there's no need to talk to anyone about me joining the varsity squad. Thank you anyway," she said. "Why are you transferring? I asked. "Because I want to start fresh. I am going to stay with my grandmother next year," she answered. "You are not letting them run you away, are you?" I asked. "No, I just want to start fresh" I laughed and said, "Well, there isn't any better way to leave a bitter and sour taste in their mouth as you leave as Ms. Tenth Grade." Faith laughed, "You're right about that! You made me feel so much better. Thank you, Bree."

"You're more than welcome, Faith. Anytime," I said. I heard someone calling her name in the background. "Well, I have to go," Faith said. "Okay, I'll see you soon at Jackson-Miles High, Ms. Tenth Grade!" I said. She laughed, "Okay, Queen of Jackson-Miles High!" I smiled and said, "Thank you! See you soon!" She replied, "See you soon."

As I hung up the phone with Faith, Chloe called. I answered, "Hello," She asked, "My, Yin, are you okay?" It is something when someone you care about asks if you are you okay. You become emotional. I started to cry and said, "Yang, no, I am not." Chloe said in a soft voice, "Guess what, Yin?" I asked, "What?" She replied, "It is okay to say you're not okay. It is okay not to be okay, as long as you talk to someone about it. Right now, that someone is me, your Yang." I thanked Chloe and we talked and fell asleep on the phone.

CHAPTER ELEVEN

11

I LOOKED IN THE MIRROR AS MY MOTHER PINNED UP MY HAIR and put on the finishing touch of my make-up. I asked myself, *"Brenna, are you happy?"*

I asked myself again, *why are you asking yourself this question on Homecoming night? You just might be the queen.* Being queen hasn't crossed my mind. I ran for Ms. Jackson-Miles High because I knew it would make my mother happy. Indeed, it has made her happy and I am happy to see her happy.

A month ago, we went shopping for my dress, and I must say it is beyond beautiful! I look like a princess; well more so, I look like I am a bride in a sweetheart royal blue backless ball gown. I can't help put to think I am going to freeze out there tonight, but I love the dress. It has tiny crystal beads here and there that sparkle.

As my mother looked at me, she was looking serious. She asked me to turn around to make sure everything was in tiptop shape. I am happy and blessed I am sharing this moment with her and my sister.

My mother looked at me in the mirror and asked, "Breana, what's on your mind?"

I looked at the black bobby pins that I was holding in my hand and said, "Mommy, there's been a lot going on. I am overwhelmed because I have a lot on my plate."

She pulled up my purple footstool and asked me to sit down. She gently put her hand under my chin and she slightly pulled my head up. She looked me in the eyes and said, "Breana, you are not in this alone. I know what your professor did was horrifying, but sweetie, you are safe, and justice will be served. You have a courageous team on your side and we are putting up a good fight." Tears formed in my eyes as I said, "Yes. I know, Mommy."

She continued, "I know you are having unsettled emotions about that boy Brian, but things will get better. I know it is easier said than done, but time heals and sooner than later he will be your past. I also know you get tired of hearing this—but everything happens for a reason. Breana, you have a lot going for yourself. You've worked hard to get where you are today. You have sacrificed a lot of your freedom to enjoy your high school career to get ahead because you want more, and you know exactly what you want. I am so proud of you!

I smiled and said, "I knew I wasn't going to miss out on too much in high school. It's a lot of drama and senseless issues that I carelessly became involved with. Early College, helped me to realize that life is what you make it, and why waste time knowing I can make it happen now? My goal is to graduate with an Associate degree before I graduate from high school. That way,

I will have two years left in college and I will use the two years to attend and graduate with my Masters."

My mother gave me a hug and said, "I wish I was like you growing up. You have your head on your shoulders right at an early age."

I was crying and laughing.

She gave a slight laugh and said, "Breana, I am serious. If I'd had a mind like yours when I was young, shoot, I would be just like you —unstoppable."

I put my hands together as my eyes filled with tears. As I looked down at my hands, two teardrops fell on my thumb as I said, "Mommy, it hasn't been easy. People do not understand how hard I've worked. They think I am a goody-two-shoes. I know where I want to be and I know how to get there. I know the road will not be easy, but I am trying to take the right route and bypass the unnecessary heartache and pain, yet it seems that regardless of what route I take I cannot manage to get past the pain that has built up along the way. As for my professor, I know for a fact my voice will be heard. As for Brian, I am dealing with his betrayal the best way I can. You're right, Mommy, sooner or later I am going to get over it. It is taking longer than expected. I managed to cleanse my chakras and meditate to keep myself grounded, but my energy is being pulled in opposite directions because of my feelings for him. I feel myself shifting gears for the better. I'm healing, slowly but surely."

The tears kept falling as I said, "Mommy, I gave him so much of me. I gave him more of me than I gave myself. I felt like I loved him more than I loved myself. I helped him any way possible with every fiber of my being, and nothing was ever good enough." I could hardly talk when I said, "Mommy, what did I do wrong? I was there for him. Why would he do me like this? Mommy, what did I do wrong?"

She wiped my tears and said, "Breana, you didn't do anything wrong. Just as you told me once before, we cannot change a person, nor can we let a person change us."

She held the side of my face in her hand. My cheek lay in the palm of her hand as she softly smiled. Her eyes filled with tears as she said, "You know, a smart young lady taught me a valuable lesson. She told me, what people think shouldn't matter when you know who you are as a person. For the people who think you are a goody-two-shoes, they are jealous and wish they could walk in your shoes. As for that boy Brian, Breana, I knew when I met him for the first time he was going to lean on you. I knew you were going to be his crutch because that boy came with many problems that weren't solved and never will be solved unless he seeks professional help. He will always be a young boy who depends on others to do stuff for him. I know you did a lot for him. There were days you and I got in many arguments because I told you to leave that boy alone. However, Breana, sometimes we have to learn the hard way and see for ourselves. It isn't your fault. We all get caught up and it is up to us to see for ourselves if we are willing to carry the load of others, give it back to them or leave it on the wayside. Breana, look at this situation as a lesson learned. One thing I know is that you know your worth. I think this situation has taught you that you cannot help everyone who doesn't want to be helped—and most definitely you cannot be everyone's hero."

I couldn't hold in my emotions. I cried. Cried and cried.

My mother said, "Crying is good for you. Let it all out. You know when I was younger than you, before I met your daddy, I dated this guy named Bobby who I knew was going to get me in a lot of mess. I knew he was trouble, but I thought I could save him by always being there when he needed me. I knew he wouldn't change for the better, but he was the best mistake

I ever made. One day, I was at the store with his sister, Clarity. Most definitely she didn't live up to her name. She asked me to put two cans of baby milk in my pocketbook. I told her no, I wasn't going to do that. She told me I was a goody-two-shoes and a sellout. I told her to call it as she may because I wasn't going to jail so that her baby could eat. When Bobby found out I didn't steal the baby milk he told me I was worthless and no damn good. He told me he couldn't be with someone like me who is too scared to take a chance on life. Breana, he really thought taking a chance on life was stealing and doing whatever possible to get what he needed by any means. I was so hurt when he said that because I did so much for him and his sister. After I went home I realized they used me for what I had. I had a car, they didn't. I had a family who was stable. They didn't. I was going to school. They weren't. Unlike them, I had plans for myself and I knew I was going places. They were content and I knew that wasn't the road I wasn't going to take. Just like Brian, Bobby broke up with me so many times, and I took him back. But that time, I didn't take him back, because he had shown me one too many times what he thought of me. I really thought I could change his world. When he told me I was basically good for nothing, a light switch turned on the bright lights in my head and I said, I love myself too much to get caught up in this life. I loved me too much to sacrifice my life for someone who didn't give a damn about my life. A couple of mornings after he broke up with me, I found myself having bad cramps. Blood was all over my sheets and there were thick blood clots all over my bed. I ran to the bathroom and so much blood ran down my legs. I didn't know what to do. I couldn't tell my mother. I had to figure it out. Later that evening I went to the ER because I was in so much pain. The doctor gave me an ultrasound and I was told I'd had a miscarriage."

She paused, took a breath and said, "Yes, Breana, I lost my virginity when I was in ninth grade because I didn't have a mind-set like you. I wanted to be "liked" but I wasn't ready to have sex. I let peer pressure get the best of me every single time. I am so happy you didn't have sex with that boy, or anyone for that matter, because it isn't worth it."

I looked at her, and I didn't know what to say. She had never opened up this deeply with me. I was speechless. After I collected my thoughts I said, "Mommy, I'm sorry you had to go through that. How do you know that I am still a virgin?"

She said, "Trust me when I say a mother will know whether their son or daughter tells them or not. There are so many signs. Number one sign, your attitude would have changed."

I hugged her and said, "Mommy, I'm so sorry you went through that alone. I never would have known if you hadn't told me. Wow. Did you ever tell the guy?"

"No. I never told him. I tried, but when I called him, he blocked my number," My mom answered.

She added, "That is why I didn't like Brian when I met him. He didn't have to say a word. I knew what he was about. I didn't tell you because I didn't want you to think I was trying to tell you what to do. Some kids have the tendency to do what they are told not to do, and I didn't want you to try to prove a point to me or your father. I didn't want my story to backfire on me."

I looked at my mother because, in a way, she was right. The more my parents didn't like Brian, it pushed me closer and closer to him. Now I see why she fell back and let me make my own decisions. As I looked at her, she said, "Don't feel sorry for me, Breana. It was all my doing. I saw the signs but I ignored them big time. I should have believed him the first time he showed me he didn't care about my wellbeing. I learned the hard way, and that boy put me through so much pain. I hurt badly every day because he cheated on me all the time and I always took him back. Unlike you, I didn't know my worth. After I kept getting burned by those no-good guys I slowly realized my worth. When I met your daddy, I gave him a hard time because I didn't trust men. My bad decisions had my mind made up that I was going to be single for the rest of my life. Your daddy knew how a woman should be treated. He changed my life so much for the better. I know God will send you the right man too later on in life. Right now, you have your journey cut out for you; and you will succeed because Grace is guiding your steps."

My mother smiled and said, "Breana, you are going to be okay. I know you are because you are strong. It's hard, but the way you feel is making you stronger every single day."

She looked up and read an affirmation on my wall. She smiled and said, "A wise young lady once wrote, *Life is beautiful. We will have our ups and downs. However, we must take one step at a time; and as we take one step at a time, we must make each step count, and count each step as pure joy.* The affirmation you wrote is beautiful, Breana."

Her voice trembled as she said, "Breana, your mindset is very strong and powerful. I wish I could take some credit for how powerful your mindset is. You are a remarkably wise young lady who is going places."

I hugged her and said, "Well, Mommy, as they say, the apple doesn't fall too far from the tree. Believe it or not, you and Daddy are my inspiration. I haven't come this far on my own. We all need help along the way, and I thank you and Daddy for your love and support."

She said sadly, "I knew I could have been there more; and I apologize a trillion times for my neglect of communication."

As I continued to hug her I said, "Mommy, that is the past. What counts now is the present. You are here now and this is what matters." I added, "I will never forget this conversation or this day."

We hugged and wiped each other's tears. She said, "Let's get you ready to be Ms. Jackson-Miles High." A couple of minutes later Summer came in the room and said, "Oh wow, Bree! Look at you! You are gorgeous!" Summer helped me with my dress as I prepared to walk down the stairs.

As I stood at the top of the stairs, my daddy was smiling from ear to ear as he said, "I hope you are not wearing a glass slipper. I do not need any dudes coming to the house trying to claim my princess." I laughed and said, "No, Daddy."

As I walked down the stairs, he teared up as he said, "Wow, one day, I will be walking you down the aisle." I smiled and told him, "Daddy, don't cry. And the only aisles I will be walking down is to get my Associate degree, high school diploma, and getting my college degree shortly after."

My mother said, "Bree, turn around and let me get a good look at you one more time." I turned around as I looked towards the kitchen. I closed my eyes as I turned around towards the family room. When I opened my eyes, my brother Luke was standing there!

I put my hands over my mouth, screamed, jumped up and down and said, "Oh my goodness! Oh, my gosh! What in the world are you doing here?" I ran over and hugged my brother because it was so good to see him. I said excitedly, "This made my day!" After I hugged my brother he said, "Bree, you know I wouldn't miss you becoming Ms. Jackson-Miles for the world!" I was smiling from ear to ear.

Luke said as he smiled, "I wanted to be here to do the honors to put Mother's necklace around your neck as you carry on the tradition of running for prom queen." My brother put my mother's necklace on me and said, "Bree, you are so beautiful!

143

You, Mother and Summer look like triplets." I smiled as I looked at my mother and Summer and said, "Yeah, we do look like triplets."

My daddy said, "Well, I want to be the one who puts the fresh baby's breath flowers in your hair." He gently tucked the flowers in my beehive.

I looked in the mirror and the flowers were beautiful! They brought out my bangs, skin and the color of my dress. Everyone was so excited and wished me many blessings as we prepared to walk out the door.

* * *

I stayed in my own lane as everyone was preparing for the potential queen and king to get in their car to drive out of the tunnel. As I looked around I saw that Angel ran for Ms. Jackson-Miles High as well. I kept my eyes on the prize—and that was me! I made sure my blue glovettes were on correctly. I saw she had on a red short strapless dress with silver high heels. The other girl that was running was called Autumn. She had on a green dress with yellow flats. I wondered what she was thinking, but to each his own. I wore blue because our school colors are blue and yellow.

The potential kings were drunk and off the chain. Needless to say, all of them were athletes. Jodee is such an ass. He's in 12th grade, but he plays on JV. I call him Jodee the Jerk. He thinks he is better than everyone. He always has the latest phones, clothes, and cars too. What he does best is look down on people. He's wearing Prada from head to toe. I'm not hating, but I wish he would understand materials things sooner or later will become dated.

Winter, yes you heard me right, Winter is a guy, he tells everyone his mother named him Winter because she was always freezing when she was carrying him—and when she gave birth to him the temperature was an all-time record low of 11 degrees. I agree with his mother, she gave him the right name because he is colder than an iceberg. He is very blunt and cold, but sometimes that's how a person has to be. I'm learning that when you are too nice people take advantage in the worse way. Winter looks very handsome—he has on a black tux with a royal blue tie. I'm trying to understand why in the world he has a football in his hand. I do know he knows he's going to win, too.

Ronald, he plays basketball. We call him 'ocean eyes' because his eyes are so beautiful. The girls are breaking their necks to go out with him just to look in his eyes. Needless to say, he's a player. He's cool, though. He has on blue jeans with a blue Jackson-Miles hoodie and white sneakers. Again, to each his own.

As I come out of the tunnel I wave my hand from side to side as my name is announced. Oh, my gosh, it is freezing, but I smile and I find myself in a daze. I cannot believe I am in 12th grade, my life has flashed before my eyes. I am going to be stepping out in the real world. I can't help but think am I ready. I am already going with the flow and I am always prepared. But will that be enough?

There are so many people out here. As I look up at the stands, I see Brian. I see him looking at me, but he isn't smiling. I can't help but look at him. I looked at him until the car turned the curve. I didn't turn around.

I hear so many people calling my name. I thought to myself, *this just might be the same crowd that will be at graduation.* I continued to wave and smile. I hear someone yell, "Breana, I love your dress!" I heard a group of people say, "Bree is Ms. Jackson-Miles High!"

As I smile and wave, I start to tear up, because I see my daddy blowing kisses. I looked at him and caught a kiss. I continued to look at him as I put it on my heart. Summer is jumping up and down, waving out of control. My mother has her hands on her heart. My brother has his hand around his mouth yelling, "Bree! Bree!" Chloe was right beside Luke yelling my name too.

As we line up on the field. The former Ms. Jackson-Miles walked up with the crown on her head. Wow, it's all so beautiful!

My heart is beating a million miles per hour. The crowd is going wild as the announcer steps up with the mic and says, "And the runner up is—Autumn."

The crowd is going crazy as everyone says at the same time, "Bree is queen! Bree is queen! Bree is queen! Bree is queen!" I was so emotional I started to cry because it felt so amazing to see so many people have so much love for me.

The announcer said, "Please everyone, quiet down." The stands were slightly calmer. Someone in the stands yelled, "Come on, man! Hurry up! Damn."

The announcer said, "The Queen of Ms. Jackson-Miles is--- Breana Anderson!"

The crowd yelled my name. "Bree! Breana! Bree! Queen of Jackson-Miles! Bree!

I had been freezing my tail off, but now the blood rushing through my body with excitement as Ms. Former Jackson-Miles crowned me queen. I slightly bent down as she put on the yellow sash that read, Queen of Jackson-Miles High 2019!

I waved, and as I waved, I turned around and blew kisses at everyone. I put my hand on my heart as I said thank you to everyone.

Dr. Chapman, my principal, walked up to give me a dozen red roses.

I said, "Thank you!"

He replied, "Breana, you deserve it."

* * *

Jackson-Miles High won our homecoming game. After the game one of the players on the basketball team threw a party. I wasn't going to go, but I decided to go. I went home to change and asked my brother if he could be my date to the party.

Chloe met me at my house as she got out of her car, she said, "Hey, Queen!"

I laughed and said, "Hey, Queen!"

Chloe laughed, "Girl, you know word's going around that you got eighty-five percent of the votes; Autumn got fourteen percent and Angel got one percent of the votes."

I laughed!

Chloe held on to my arm as we walked to Luke's car. We laughed so hard and said, "I guess Brian was the only one who voted for her!"

We both had a good laugh!

* * *

When we pulled up at the party there were so many people there.

Chloe said, "Damn!"

Luke said, "He invited all the schools in the county."

I walked up to the door. Word travels fast because Brian walked up and said, "I heard you just pulled up."

I looked at him. "Well, you heard right."

Brian looked at me and touched my hand. I pulled back and said, "Brian, excuse me."

Brian looked me up and down and asked, "What?" with an ugly-ass expression on his face.

"I said, excuse me. As matter of fact, excuse you," I said as I tried to walk away.

Brian blocked me in. "So you're too good to talk to me."

I turned around and walked the other way.

Brian ran in front of me and said, "Bree. I apologize. Let's talk."

"I'm good Brian," I told him as I looked past him and made eye contact with Chloe.

"I'll hit you up later," he said as he licked his lips.

Angel came out of nowhere and asked, "Who are you going to hit up later?"

Brian said, "Angel, chill out."

Angel replied, "Don't tell me what the fuck to do."

She looked at me as she said to Brian, "Baby, come dance with me."

Chloe and I laughed as we walked in the house and started to dance with each other.

We weren't in the house for long before we heard someone scream and the crowd ran to the commotion.

"Leave me alone!" someone yelled loudly.

Halfway across the room, I saw it was Faith, screaming and crying.

I kept my eyes on her as I fought through the crowd. Out of nowhere people started to throw rotten eggs at her. The smell was horrible.

A girl came out of the blue and ripped the side of Faith's shirt.

I pushed the girl and said, "Get the fuck off her!"

I reached for Faith. "Come on, Faith. I got you."

Faith's shirt was ripped apart to the point her bra was showing. Some dummy yelled, "Faith showed a tit!"

I yelled, "Shut up, asshole!"

As I helped Faith get through the crowd, I covered her up with my jacket.

Luke yelled, "Bree, I am over here! Are you okay?"

"I am fine, "I told him as I held Faith in my arms as we continued to walk.

"Where is Chloe?" I asked Luke.

Luke looked up and said, "I don't know."

He yelled Chloe's name.

Chloe was yelling my name and Luke said, "Chloe, we're over here!" as he waved her down.

We got in the car, locked the doors and tried cleaning Faith off.

In a hurry, and cleaning her off as best I could, I asked her, "Faith, did you see who did this to you?"

"I don't know," she said as she cried.

Chloe took off her sweater, gave it to Faith. "Let's try to warm you up."

Faith was shivering as she said, "Chloe, you don't have to do that. You're going to be cold."

As Chloe tried to warm Faith up she told her, "Don't worry about me. I have on a t-shirt."

"Where do you live?" Luke asked Faith.

We drove Faith home.

Chloe and I stayed with Faith for a while to keep her company. We didn't say much as we held each other and listened to music.

* * *

After I prepared for the next day and for bed. I walked past my mother's office with my chamomile, lemon and honey tea in my hand. She was working on an assignment, humming, she had a white and pink candle lit and the aromatherapy diffuser on as it smelled like lavender oil, and she was listening to *The Holiday* soundtrack.

I didn't disturb her because she was focused. I mentality blew her a kiss and said I love you, Mommy!

I smiled as I walked up the stairs. I opened Summer's door. It was dark in her room, but the aromatherapy was on, changing colors, and Summer was knocked out asleep.

After I finished drinking my tea. I said to myself, *this is so far the best day of my life!* I turned my light off and went to sleep.

CHAPTER TWELVE

I RAN DOWN THE STAIRS TO MAKE SOME PINK ROSE TEA. I love the aroma as I put half a teaspoon of honey in my cup. I held the warm mug in my hand as I closed my eyes to smell the sweet fragrance. I walked outside and sat in the swing on the porch. The weather is cooling off, but it still doesn't feel like fall.

As the swing moves back and forth, I begin to think about how precious life is. Lately, I've been happy. My life has been so peaceful. Although I've been busy working, preparing for my exams—life has been so good to me. I've been doing everything I wanted and needed to do. I did not feel rushed and I had time to spare.

Life is good, weeks ago, there was no way I would be sitting here on my porch enjoying the fresh air. I am loving it! Today, I have a day off of work. I am all caught up on everything that I had on my agenda.

Eli and I have been talking and texting more than often lately, but not too much—he understood I had to go on a phone fast so I could prepare for my mid-terms. Which I passed! I might call him today to see what he's up to.

My phone vibrates. I didn't know I put my phone in my housecoat. I looked at it and saw it was Brian. I remembered I forgot to block him since I got a new phone.

> **Saturday, 10:02 a.m.**
> "Bree. Can you talk? Please?"
> "Breana, I miss you."
> "Please talk to me. Please."

Maybe I should text him back. I miss him too, but I do not miss the drama. I am in doubt. If I respond I am more than sure he is going to interrupt my peace.

I thought about it for a couple of minutes. I guess I can hear him out. I hope I do not regret it.

> **Saturday, 10:13 a.m.**
> "Hi, Brian."

> **Saturday, 10:13 a.m.**
> "Bree!"
> "Hey!"
> "How are you doing?"

> **Saturday, 10:15 a.m.**
> "I am fine. Thanks for asking."

> **Saturday, 10:15 a.m.**
> "I miss you, Bree"
> "Can I come by and see you?"
> I do not know if I want him to come by. I don't want to meet him anywhere either.

> **Saturday, 10:17 a.m.**
> "Brian, we can text or talk on the phone."

> **Saturday, 10:17 a.m.**
> "Bree, may I come see you, please. I need to talk to you. Please."

I am not ready to see him.

Saturday, 10:18 a.m.
"Brian, maybe another day. Today is not a good day."

Saturday, 10:18 a.m.
"Why"
"What are you doing today?"

Saturday, 10:19 a.m.
"Brian, I am not ready to see you."

Saturday, 10:20 a.m.
"Bree, give me a chance to apologize face-to-face."

Saturday, 10:21 a.m.
"That's the problem, Brian, I've given you too many chances."

Saturday, 10:21 a.m.
"Bree, please give me one last chance. I just want to see you."
"I just want to talk, Bree."
"I want to make it right."

Saturday, 10:23 a.m.
I thought about it—or maybe I didn't.
"Brian, be here no later than 11:30 a.m."

Saturday, 10:23 a.m.
"Really?"
"I am on my way now!"

Saturday, 10:25 a.m.
"Okay."

I walked into the kitchen and I noticed the garaged door open. I peeked my head in the doorway, and said, "Good morning, Daddy!"

"How is my baby girl this morning?" he asked.

"I am fine, thank you. I was enjoying my tea and Brian is on his way over," I said.

"I saw you on the porch. You looked like you were in deep thought. Are you sure you are okay?" he asked.

"I am fine, Daddy." I said as I ran upstairs to get ready.

Summer met me halfway as she ran downstairs with her luggage. I stopped as I turned around and asked her, "Love Bug, where are you going in a hurry?"

"My soccer game was canceled. I am going to spend the night over Robin's house," Summer said as she jumped off the last two steps.

Summer had on some skinny blue jeans with a cute designer pink shirt, with her pink and white Converse, pink watch, and her hair was in two pom-poms with pink ribbons.

"Well, you look cute this morning," I said.

Thank you. You know when I go out, I have to look my best. The first impression is always the best!" she replied.

As I walked into my room, Daddy said, "Knock. Knock." I sat on my bed and said, "Hey, Daddy, what's going on? My daddy asked, "Did I hear you right just a few minutes ago? That boy Brian is coming over here?" I put my tea down and told him, "Yes, Daddy, is that okay?" Daddy looked at me for a minute. "Breana, no, it is not okay. Why is he coming over here?" I didn't know what to say. My daddy yelled my mother's name, "Vanessa!" She walked up the stairs and said, "Good God, with all that yelling, you are going to wake up Jesus!" My daddy ignored my mother's remark, saying, "You know Bree just said that boy Brian is coming over here." My mother put her hand on her chest and said, "What! Why? I thought we got rid..." Daddy cut her off. "No, Vanessa. Most definitely not the right time." I knew why my daddy said it's not the right time because my mother was going to say, I thought we got rid of him, and my daddy doesn't want words like that to make me fall for Brian again. I looked at both of my parents and told them, "He wants to apologize in person. I am not going to get back with him." My daddy snorted, "Ha! Yeah, that's how they try to reel you in." My mother said, "Sweetheart, this is your life. We can only show you and tell you what is best for you. You are older now, so you make the decisions for your own life. Pick them wisely."

I opened my closet and pulled out a long orange sundress. I moisturized my hair and shook it out so it would have volume. I head the doorbell ring. I grabbed my blue jean jacket out of my closet, put on my flip-flops and walked downstairs.

I heard Brian and my daddy talking. I sat on the steps for a little while as I tried to listen to the conversation.

Daddy's voice is deep. I heard him say, "Brian, how are you treating my baby girl?"

I heard Brian say, "As well as I can."

"I heard something different. You better not put your hands on her or disrespect her if you know what's good for you," my daddy said.

My momma scared me when she whispered, "What are you doing? "

I jumped, put my hand on my chest and cried out, "Momma, you can't be creeping up on people like that."

Momma had a good laugh and said, "Well, you shouldn't be eavesdropping on your father's conversation. That boy Brian must be here?"

"Yes," I replied.

We both walked down the stairs.

Brian said, "Hello, Mrs. Anderson."

My mother said, "Hello Brian."

Daddy said, "Well, baby girl, I will leave you and Brian be. I am about to head out and cut the lawn."

"Okay, Daddy."

Brian and I walked outside and sat on the porch.

"Bree, you look nice. Like always," Brian said as he stared at me.

"Thank you. You do too," I replied.

Brian started to talk but I didn't hear a word he said. I had butterflies in my stomach. He is so handsome. He had on some dark-rinse pants, with a black, gold and white Nike shirt that read, *Just Do It,* and to top it off he was wearing black and gold Jordan's.

He put his hands in his pockets. His arms were muscular and toned. He had a fresh hair cut like always. I feel like I am falling in love all over again.

I sat on the swing.

"So, I can't get a hug," Brian said as he had his arms wide open.

I wanted to fall into his arms, lay my head on his chest and hear his heartbeat.

"I'm good," I said as I looked at the chimes hanging on the porch.

"Ha!" Brian laughed.

He looked at me and asked, "It's like that now? You going to leave me standing here with my arms wide open, waiting for you to give me a welcome and a friendly hug."

I sat there and watched him standing there. I placed my hand on my chin and arched my eyebrows saying to myself, *he doesn't deserve a hug.*

I looked at him and said, "Feel free to sit down when you feel like it."

"Damn, Bree. You are cold," he complained as he sat beside me on the swing.

He sat there for a minute and said, "I want to apologize for yelling at you a couple of months ago. My bad for breaking up with you again too. I was emotional and very frustrated because you always bring it out of me. I don't ask for much. I need and want you to be here for me when I need you. I miss you around. I miss talking to you, and Bree, I miss you in my life. I know I apologize all the time and my apologies are getting old. For what it's worth, I mean all of it this time. I won't ever yell at you again."

I didn't say anything. My facial expression spoke louder than any words that could have come out of my mouth. I sat there, not believing a word he said.

"Bree. I know you do not believe me. The only thing I can do is show you," he said, trying to sound sincere. He looked at me as he put his hands on my legs, "You looked so beautiful at Homecoming." "Thank you," I replied. He said as he rubbed my leg, "I never got a chance to say congratulations."

I looked at him and said, "Brian, it's been three weeks and counting. You had plenty of chances to say congratulations—you just choose not to." He slightly laughed, "Maybe I didn't feel like saying congratulations at the time."

I didn't say anything.

He looked at me, popped his knuckles and said, "Bree, today is a special day. Or did you forget?" I took a sip of my tea and told him, "Brian, I know what day it is." I took another sip and said, "That's why you should be with your girl and not me." He put one of his hands in his back pockets and said, "We are doing something later."

I smiled. "That's cool."

"Well, aren't you going to at least say Happy Birthday," he asked. He was getting frustrated.

"Happy Birthday, Brian. May God bless you with many more," I said, then took another sip of my tea.

I received a text message from Eli:

Saturday, 12:13 p.m.

"Breana, what do you have going on today? Do you want to catch a movie?"

Saturday, 12:14 p.m.

"Catch a movie??? Who's going to throw it to us? LOL!"

Saturday, 12:14 p.m.

"Ha! Ha! Ha! You are too funny? Do you want to see a movie?"

Saturday, 12:15 p.m.

"I would love it, but my ex is over here at the moment."

Saturday, 12:16 p.m.

"Bree, do not sell yourself short. Why are you talking to that loser? You know you deserve better than him. Right?"

I had talked to Eli about what happened with me and Brian. I told him about how he always broke up with me and my dumb ass always took him back. Eli was shocked. He told me I do not seem like the type of girl to let a dude disrespect her in that manner. Honestly, I'm not that girl, but when it came to Brian, I had a weak spot for him.

Saturday, 12:16 p.m.

"I know."

Brian started to grind his teeth together as he said, "I came over here to apologize and your ass is on the phone, not giving a shit. See what I mean? You're always making me look like a damn fool."

I wanted to say, *Brian, you don't need any help in that department.*

I started to shake my head and remarked, "Brian you didn't mean a word you said, because your temper proves it all."

I paused, "What do you want Brian? I am here listening. You've been over here about twenty minutes now and you have yet to..." Brian cut me off.

"Put your phone up, Bree!" he yelled

"I don't have to put up my phone," I told him.

I can hear the lawnmower going in the backyard.

He yelled again, "Put up your goddamn phone, Bree!"

I got off the swing and said, "Brian, leave."

He raised his hand.

I yelled, "Leave now! You are not going to disrespect me, my parents, or my home!"

He snatched my phone out of my hand and threw it so far it landed in the street. I took a couple of steps down off the porch. He grabbed my hand and said, "Where do you think you're going? I hope a car runs over that bitchy-ass phone."

He pushed me as he let my hand go.

As I was walking to get my phone, two cars and a moving truck ran over my phone.

Brian looked at me, "Well, I guess I am going to have your undivided attention now."

I clenched my lips together and said, "Brian, leave my house now. If I tell my daddy what you did, you will not leave here alive. I am giving you a chance to leave. Now."

He looked at me coldly. "I don't have to go no damn where."

Right before I opened my mouth to say something, my daddy came out of nowhere with his gun. He quickly ran up the steps and forcefully pushed Brian on the glass door (the door shattered) as he had his hand around his throat.

I screamed very loudly out of fear as I shouted, "Daddy, no! You are going to kill him!" I yelled as loud as I could, "Mommy, help!" I didn't know what to do. I was scared as I saw him hold Brian against the shattered door. Holding the gun under Brian's chin, Daddy said, "You punk bitch, better get the fuck off my property before I shoot to kill your ass."

My mother yelled, "Luke Senior! What are you doing? Put the gun down before you do something you will regret!" Daddy's expression was very scary as he looked directly into Brian's eyes. He said, "I will do anything for my children, even kill if I feel like they are in harm's way."

My mother said, "Please, Senior, please let him go. He isn't worth it." My face was wet with tears. I walked over to Daddy, my hands shaking. I put my hand on the gun and said, "Daddy, I am okay. I am not hurt—I am fine. Please let him go. Please."

I had a tight grip the gun. As I slowly, pushed the gun down kept saying over and over again, "Daddy, I am okay. I am not hurt. I am fine."

Daddy kept his eyes on Brian as he said, "My baby girl saved your life. Get your ass off my porch and I don't ever want to see you around here again."

Daddy let him go, and Brian ran as fast as he could without looking back.

My heart was pounding so hard it felt as if it was about to fall out of my chest. I sat on the swing and put my left hand on my chest, trying to catch my breath. I said to myself, *I am so happy Summer wasn't here to see this.* My mother looked Daddy and asked, "Senior, have you lost your damn mind? What happened for you to...?"

Daddy cut my mother off as he looked at her and said, "Vanessa, I apologize for that, but that little boy is not going to come to my damn house and disrespect my daughter, you, me or my goddamn house."

My mother was looking confused as she said, "You didn't answer my question. What happened for you to react this way?"

Daddy's tone changed as he looked at me. He was calm and patient. He saw that I was a nervous wreck and said, "Breana, I heard Brian yelling at you. That is when I walked over to my truck to get my gun. It pissed me off I saw him push and pull on you."

He looked at my mother and said, "That is why I ran up on that fool because I was going to kill him for putting his hands on my baby."

Mother looked at Daddy without saying anything as she started to shake her head. She looked at the glass on the door and said, "Let me call someone to fix the glass."

I know my mother had more to say, but she knows Daddy doesn't play around when it comes to his children. She knew that was a battle she wasn't going to win. I am more than sure that he knows he is never going to hear the end of what happened today. My mother will have the last word without me being in their presence.

Daddy sat beside me on the swing and said, "Breana, tell me what is going on. Don't you lie to me, either." I knew I couldn't lie to him, but I didn't want to tell him what's been going on because I was afraid he would load up his gun and head to Brian's house.

I looked at him then looked down at my fingers. The tips of my fingers were cold. I was nervous. My heart once again was pounding out of my chest.

He looked at me as he put his hand on my hands and said, "Breana."

I looked at him with tears in my eyes and said, "Daddy, I am so sorry. If I didn't invite him over none of this wouldn't have happened."

Tears started to run down my face as I tried to talk. I couldn't catch my breath, because my crying had gotten the best of me. I didn't want to disappoint Daddy, nor did I want him to put his life in danger for me.

Daddy looked at me, wiped the tears off my face. "Breana, baby, stop crying and talk to me." I laid my head on his chest and said, "Daddy, I don't want you to be disappointed in me." He rubbed my head. "Bree, baby, there isn't anything you can do to make me disappointed in you."

As I laid on his chest, I said, "Daddy, Brian and I have been broken up for some months now. Remember, I told you that he broke up with me a couple times in one day because I was tired of being his crutch? So, I started to say no because he wanted and needed too much of my time."

Daddy didn't say anything. I know what he was waiting to hear. He wanted to know if Brian ever hit me before. I went on to say, "I wasn't happy when I was with Brian. I know I should have listened to you, Momma and Luke."

He said, "Baby girl, we all have to learn on our own time. I always knew you deserved better than that boy, but kids nowadays want to do what they want to do. As parents, we have to step back, yet stay close." Daddy continued, and he got straight to the point. He said, "Breana, I want you to be honest with me when I ask you this."

I sat up and waited on his question.

He looked at me in the eyes and said, "Bree, has Brian ever hit you before?"

I looked at him and replied, "No, he never hit me before, but he has grabbed and pushed on me before. Months ago, he did say at least he doesn't hit me like his boys do to their girls."

His face was livid.

I put my hand on his hand and said, "Daddy, I am okay. We need you here, and Mommy is right, Brian isn't worth it. I know you want to protect me. You do a great job at doing so."

Daddy didn't say anything. He hugged me and rocked me in his arms.

For about five or so minutes there was complete silence until he said, "Brenna, I know you know your worth." I looked at him and nodded yes, and told him, "Yes, I do."

He looked at me with tears forming in his eyes and said, "My sweet baby girl, if a boy or man ever hits you, pushes you, pulls you, disrespects you, yells at you, please don't be afraid to let me know."

I cried because this was the first time ever that I'd seen him so emotional. "Daddy, I promise I will tell you." His lips trembled as he said, "Bree, you, Summer, Luke and your mother are my life. You all are my world and I wouldn't want anything to happen to you all. I will protect all of you with every being in my body."

He went on to say, "I never put hands on your mother and I never will. Your mother is my queen, she and I are one, and I wouldn't ever want to harm or hurt her in any way because I love your mother dearly."

I smiled because he spoke with so much passion when he talked about my mother.

He continued, "Bree, don't ever lower your standards to where you feel it is okay for a boy or a man to put hands on you to physically, mentally, verbally, or spiritually abuse you. If a boy or man pushes and pulls on you, that is a form of physical abuse. If a man yells at you, that is a form of verbal abuse. If he put you down in any kind of way, that is mental abuse. If he tries to break you down in any way possible that is spiritual abuse—meaning he is trying to break your soul and who you are as a person. That is when a person starts to think they are not worth happiness or start to believe in what they are being told."

He looked at me with great concern in his eyes as he said, "Breana, I never raised you to be abused in any kind of why.

I've led by example and will accept nothing less in our household. Breana, you know you are a queen and you deserve to be treated like one."

I looked at him and said, "Yes, Daddy, I know that I am a queen, and I know I should be treated like a queen and nothing less."

I hugged him and laid on his chest as I said, "Daddy, don't worry—I know my worth. You raised an intelligent young lady."

I smiled. "Daddy, I am blessed to have you in my life. Thank you for being the best daddy in the world!"

My mother opened the door and said, "I finally found someone who will be willing to come and fix the door tomorrow. I made dinner while you two had your 'daddy and daughter' talk."

My mother walked over to him. "Senior, I knew I was your queen from the day you said hello."

He put his arms around my mother's hips, kissed her a couple times and told her, "When I laid eyes on you for the first time, I knew you were my queen and I was going to be your king."

My mother and daddy were hugged up on each other as they talked and kissed. I let them be as I left them alone to have some lovers time.

When I walked into the house, I smiled because I want a relationship and marriage like my mother and daddy.

I do know there are some good men out here because my daddy is a prime example of one. The Universe sent him to my mother, and I know one day the Universe will send me a good man too. Until then, I am going to let the Universe lead the way as I focus on the now.

CHAPTER THIRTEEN

13

I LOVE FAMILY GATHERINGS!

Summer, my mother and I were up all night cooking Thanksgiving dinner. We had so much fun! Throughout the morning hours, Daddy came in to taste some of the food we'd prepared. More so the desserts! After we made the chocolate cake batter, he would sneak in and scoop up the chocolate batter that was left. My mother, her sister Piper and I laughed because he always knows when we are making desserts. He says he smells the aroma in the air. My mother said, "Luke Senior, you need to sneak some collard greens and mixed vegetables instead of the leftover cake batter." He put his finger in the leftover sweet potato pie bowl, put some of the sweet potato mix on my mother's lips and kissed her.

Summer's face told it all when she said, "Yuk, get a room!"

As I was putting the icing on the red velvet cake I smiled and said to myself, *I adore the relationship my mother and*

daddy have. I know one day I am going to be in a healthy mar-
riage and relationship just like my parents.

* * *

Later that evening, the family arrived for dinner. My Aunt
Rita bought her famous apple pie. I took it to the family room
and sat it on the table. The aroma of her apple pie was a cinna-
mon spicy sweet smell—I closed my eyes as imagined the taste
on the tip of my tongue and washing it down with some warm
homemade almond milk. My Aunt Rita is a hot mess; she doesn't
have a mouth filter. She speaks her mind and keeps it moving
without thinking twice. She's my daddy's sister—to let daddy tell
it, her mouth always got her in trouble.

As she walked into the family room, she called my name. I
turned around and smiled. Aunt Rita said, "What are you doing in
here all alone, my little precious sweet bug?" She always called
me her little precious sweet bug. I always wondered how she
came up with that. In my opinion, it is a long nickname. I smiled
and said, "I personally wanted to bring your yummy apple pie
in the room, that way, I know that nobody will sneak a piece."
As she walked closer with her tight red jumpsuit on, I must say,
it fit every curve of her body. Her butt looked like two juicy mel-
ons. She had on a green scarf and black shiny high-heel boots
that resembled a mirror—you really could see your reflection in
them. Her gold earrings were oval, and it seemed like they were
the size of her cheeks. I seriously do not know where she got her
style from. Her lips were glowing like always. She normally wears
cranberry lipstick but today she is rocking red cherry lipstick and
the finishing touch has to be a bright glowing clear gloss. Her
skin was so smooth—I always loved her brown blaze glow. She
looked as though she was going to a disco party because her

hair was in an afro. With every move she made, her curly hair bounced freely from side to side.

As she walked closer, she had her arms out to give me a hug. As she rocked me from side to side, she kissed me on my cheek and said, "How are you doing? How is school going? And how is that no-good raggedy-ass boyfriend of yours?"

I burst out laughing, "Dang, Aunt Rita, you get straight to the point and come in for the kill without hesitation." I added, "I am fine. School is going well—better than I expected. I am working hard to receive an Associate degree and high school diploma at the same time. I am going to make it happen, too. As for raggedy Brian, he is dismissed. I am surprised Momma or Daddy didn't tell you what happened."

Aunt Rita sat on the couch, patted the cushion beside her and said, "My precious little bug, they didn't tell me anything. What did that little shit do to you?"

I burst out laughing again, "It doesn't matter. I could care less to talk about it. I'm over it now."

Aunt Rita said, "Okay, as long as you are fine, we will not talk about it. I never cared for his ass anyway. He just wasn't any good for you. He really was a waste of your time."

I heard my mother call my name. As I got up, I agreed, "Aunt Rita, you are so right about that. He was a waste of time and drained a lot of my energy."

I put my hand out and said, "Come on, Aunt Rita.

The doorbell rang. Before seeing what my mother wanted, I answered it—and there was a boatload of people. My mother's brother, Trip, my daddy's siblings, and many family and friends. We had a houseful!

My mother and I made eye contact. I knew what that meant. I had to hide my mother's, Summer's and my belongings that were valuable, as Aunt Teresa would take them. Sad but true, my daddy's sister, Aunt Teresa, was always taking stuff. She calls it "borrowing." However, if you do not ask and take what's not yours, that is called stealing.

The house was packed. I peeped in Summer's room to see how all the little kids were doing. Summer was playing with my little cousins. Like always, she was telling them what to do. Believe it out not, they were following Summer's every move and word without hesitation.

The doorbell rang again, so I ran downstairs to open the door. It was Chloe and her mother. I gave them a hug and thanked them for coming. Chloe had on an ugly Christmas sweater. I told Chloe, "You know this isn't an ugly Christmas sweater party. Right?" Chloe smiled and said, "Momma, you owe me a movie day, with homemade popcorn in bed!" I was looking lost... Chloe's mother smiled. "Chloe and I made a bet that you would say that." I said, "Oh, okay, I see. Chloe thinks she knows me." Chloe said, "I know you very well!" She pulled out the Yin pendant we gave each other when we were younger, saying, "I am the Yin to your Yang and you are the Yang to my Yin." My eyes teared up because I had on my necklace too and pulled out the Yang pendant. Chloe said, "Stop it, cry baby," as she teared up too."

Chloe's mother said, "Breana, you look pretty. I am going to call you 'Ms. Lady Dressed in Red' tonight." I smiled and said, "Thank you." Chloe's mother continued as she touched my hair, "I see you blow-dried your hair out. You have beautiful hair. I didn't know your hair nearly touches your behind." I laughed and said, "Thank you, the shrinkage is real!" I added, "You two, come on in."

Chloe whispered in my ear, "Ms. Lady in The Red Dress, who are you trying to look good for?" I laughed and said, "What? Just because I straightened my hair?" Chloe pulled my arm and said, "Yep, because the Bree I know does not like heat on her hair." I said, "Hello, we are having a gathering. I want to look my best for *me*." Chloe looked me up and down. "Well, maybe it's the lady in the red dress personality trying to come out and do her thing instead of Breana." Chloe's mother said, "What are you girls chatting about?" We both laughed. She then added, "Breana, where is your mother?" "In the kitchen," I replied.

Chloe's mother had on her baby blue uniform because she just got off from work. She's a nurse practitioner and she's attending medical school. I admire Chloe's mother because she started from the bottom and worked her way up. She's always been a single mother, and she started off as a certified nursing assistant (CNA). She worked the midnight shift at an assisted living facility for the elderly and went to nursing school during the day to become an LPN. After she got a higher position, she continued to work the midnight shift as she went to school to become a Registered Nurse.

When she became an RN, she found another job and continued working the midnight shift as she went to school during the day to become a nurse practitioner. Once she became a nurse practitioner, she then worked the day shift because Chloe was older. Sometimes I envy Chloe and her mother's relationship because her mother made many sacrifices for her. The reason why her mother worked the midnight shift was because she did not want "the streets" to raise Chloe. She wanted to make sure after Chloe got out of school she was able to help her with her homework, feed her dinner, spend quality time with her, participate in her life by going to her activities, parent-teacher conferences, PTCA meetings, etc. She wanted to make sure she was there for every moment of Chloe's life.

After Chloe was old enough, she made the decision to work during the day and go to school as well. Chloe knows she's highly favored because she has a mother that always puts her first. Not to mention, Chloe and her mother have an amazing relationship. I asked her mother a while back, why she was going to medical school because she's doing very well for herself. She said because she's come this far, she might as well aim for the top, reach for stars and complete her journey. Chloe and her mother will be celebrating their graduation together. Her mother will be graduating from medical school, and Chloe from high school.

Just as I was going to close the door, I heard someone say, "Hold the train! Hold the train!" I knew that voice sound familiar—it was T'eo. He looked very handsome and very different. He had on a dark blue suit with a lilac dress shirt, dark brown dress shoes, and his hair was combed to the back. He was smelling so good. He kissed me on the cheek and said, "Bree, do you know you have a bright red lipstick tattoo on the side of your cheek?"

I laughed and said, "Oh my gosh, I forgot to wipe it off. My Aunt Rita put that there." I continued, "I am glad you came. How is your family doing?" He smiled and said, "I wasn't going to pass up on homemade food. I am tired of eating pizza. My family is fine, they were bummed that I couldn't make it. The price of the ticket was too high and I would have had to come right back to take my finals. I reassured them that I will be there for Christmas." I then asked, "How is your mother?" He said, "Better than expected. She is doing very well, thanks for asking. She's moving around and staying busy." I smiled and said, "That's always a good thing."

He put his hands behind his back, playing around as he said, "Well, am I going to stand on your porch or are you going to invite me in?"

I laughed and said, "You are silly. Come on in."

Summer and my cousins were running down the stairs, my mother smiled at me and said, "Breana, take your friend's coat and put it in the room." My daddy walked over and said, "You must be T'eo?" T'eo replied, "Yes, sir. I am T'eo. T'eo Jones." He shook my daddy's hand. Daddy said, "It's nice to finally meet you, T'eo—the right way. Please accept my apology for running up on you at the school. I shouldn't have assumed so quickly." T'eo said, "Sir, I accept your apology. If I had a daughter or son, I would have done the same thing." Daddy smiled and said, "Thank you for understanding. Please, T'eo, make yourself at home." Summer said, "So you are T'eo? Are you my big sister's boyfriend? She just got over a loser—I hope you will not break my sister's heart. If so, you will have to pay the price." My eyes were huge as I said, "Summer…" Summer said, "Bree, I'm just saying."

T'eo replied, "Summer, I won't ever hurt your sister's feelings." Summer walked off with her index finger swinging from side to side, with a mean, serious face saying, "You better not."

My brother Luke introduce himself and said, "Do you like football? If so, please feel free to join us in the family room."

Before T'eo could answer my brother's questions, my aunts and uncles, sipping on their drinks, prepared to drill T'eo with a million and one questions. My Aunt Rita said, "Mr. Redbone, looking GQ smooth over there." She looked him up and down as she sucked her teeth and said, "You're handsome. You are dressed very nicely, and smell so good. Are you my precious little bug's boyfriend?"

He looked at me and said, "With respect, Breana and I are just friends. Thank you kindly for your compliments."

My Aunt Rita sipped a little of her drink again and said, "Breana, you better make this one here yours, because he is a respectful good man."

My Uncle Sebastian is my daddy's older brother. He's chubby and he always talks about school. I feel bad for his children because they cannot bring less than an "A" home. They are always on lockdown and what he does not know is that they sneak out of the house to have a life. Yet he thinks they are better than us. If only he knew what was really going on I believe he would have a heart attack; however, Luke and I keep it to ourselves because my cousins don't have room to breathe. We feel bad for them. As of right now, they are in my mother's office reading a book. To me that is crazy. My uncle Sebastian said, "Well, young man, what are your goals and present plans? Where are your family? Where are you from? Do you go to school? What's your major?"

T'eo looked overwhelmed and very uncomfortable, but he kept a smile on his face. I can only imagine what he was saying to himself right now. All I could think about was, *I hope he doesn't return the favor when I meet his family.*

My mother cut him off and said, "Sebastian, why are you interrogating this young man? You are not Breana's father. Let this young man breathe." She introduced herself and said, "T'eo, it is such a pleasure to meet you. Thank you so much for helping and staying with Breana when she locked her keys in the car. My family and I truly appreciate it. Please make yourself at home and enjoy yourself."

T'eo smiled at my mother as he prepared to shake her hand, but my mother gave him a hug instead. He said, "Mrs. Anderson, you're more than welcome. It wasn't any trouble at all." He paused and looked at me and said, "Breana is someone special. She's such a loving young lady who's very independent and is going places in life. I hope I am a forever friend in the present and future. I will always be here for Breana if she allows me too."

I couldn't help but blush.

My mother agreed and said, "Yes, my daughter is someone special, with a loving heart, and I must say she is going places in life." She continued, "T'eo, I hope you will be a forever friend. You seem to be a nice loving young man."

T'eo smiled and said, "Thank you, Mrs. Anderson."

I was so happy when my mother cut the tension. While my mother and T'eo were talking, my family went on about their business. The men were in the family room screaming at the TV as they watched football. There is something about men and football. I never understood the sport. As they continued watching the game, the ladies were having fun chatting as we put the finishing touches on the food, desserts, and drinks.

* * *

As Chloe and I were helping prepare dinner. Chloe whispered in my ear, "Damn, Bree, T'eo is fine and handsome, I might add." I laughed and said, "He's just a friend." Chloe said, "Yeah, right, friend my ass. You like him." I blushed and said, "No, I do not." Chloe rolled her eyes and said, "You can lie to yourself, but you cannot lie to me, honey." I looked at Chloe and said, "Whatever." Chloe washed her hands before she cut and separated the cornbread and said, "I'm just saying he's a good guy. Cute is a plus, Handsome is a quadruple plus, and respectful! Now T'eo is on a whole other level, which is a good thing because sobbing over Brian's dumb ass isn't going to cut it."

Chloe couldn't stop talking about T'eo. She cut the cornbread in reasonable squares and started on making the sweet tea as she said, "Girl, your parents like him too! That is a blessing within itself." I said, "Yeah, but my parents like everybody." Chloe quickly retorted, her eyes looking like they were about to pop out of her head, "No they don't! They put up with Brian because you liked him. They like T'eo. Accepting and liking someone has a totally different meaning." I nodded my head and said, "Yeah, that is true." Chloe was going to town pouring the sugar in the tea dispenser as she stirred and mixed the sweet tea. I said, "God dang, Chloe, you are going to have us all in a coma." Chloe said, "This is called that Southern Hospitality Sweet Tea." She looked at me as she poured in more sugar and added, "You do not know anything about that, Ms. Drinking Pink Rose and Chamomile Lavender Tea." I looked at her, smirked, and said, "Exactly, the teas I drink are healthy and they are good for you. With all that sugar, good God Almighty! I will make sure I have my phone all set to call 911." Chloe eyed me as she continued to stir the tea and said, "I bet nobody will be complaining but you."

T'eo came into the kitchen and asked, "Do you all need help?" My Aunt Rita said, "Damn, look at him, he's a good man. How old are you baby?" T'eo looked at me as if he didn't know whether he should answer the question or not. I said, "Thank you, T'eo, but we are fine." My mother laughed and said, "Rita, I know you are not about to rob the cradle." My Aunt Rita laughed and said, "Vanessa, I am trying to rock the cradle." She laughed so hard and said, "T'eo, baby, I am just playing." We all laughed. Chloe raised her eyebrows, walked towards me and said, "Your aunt isn't playing, she is trying to take your man." She then softly bumped into me and said, "Seriously, Bree, at least get to know him a little better. He seems like a good guy."

After the ladies put the finishing touch on our dinner, my mother called the fellas into the dining room to help put the food on the table. We all gathered at the table and we talked about what we were thankful for. It was wonderful to hear everyone was thankful for good health and family. After I made my plate, I sat there for a minute as I watched everyone pass plates here and there, talking to each other, and stuffing their face with a healthy hearty meal (minus Chloe's killer coma tea). It was so beautiful.

* * *

Afterward, everyone made themselves a to-go box and helped clean up. Our family and friends were leaving one by one and soon after that everyone had left. As I dried and put up the last silverware, I took off my apron and put it in the laundry room. I was going to walk up the stairs, but I heard a couple of people talking. I walked into the family room and saw T'eo talking to my parents and my brother. I smiled and said, "What are you still doing here?" He smiled back and said, "Do you think I would leave without saying goodbye?" I said, "Right, how silly of me. I see that you are fitting right in." I walked over and sat on the sofa near my father. I kissed him on the cheek, laid my head on his shoulder and said, "Daddy, you're the best, and I love you." He squeezed my shoulder, kissed my hair and said, "I love you too, baby."

He said, "T'eo, thank you for spending Thanksgiving with us. Know that you are always welcome."

T'eo said, "You're welcome. Thank you for having me over. I truly appreciate." Like always, my family had a ton of questions. My brother asked, "I heard you are in school at Brubaker State University?"

T'eo replied, "I am. A sophomore, majoring in Economics. After undergraduate, my plans to go straight to graduate school to get my Masters. I have $200k in scholarships— might as well make the most of it!"

My mother smiled and said, "Really, that's amazing! Congratulations on your accomplishments. I see you are a hard worker and have business about yourself."

T'eo said, "I try. I'm not perfect, but I try to put my best foot forward and take advantage of the time that is given to me."

My mother said, "I agree. You know, I have my Masters in Economics."

T'eo said, "Yes, ma'am. Breana told me. That is very impressive."

My mother smiled and said, "Thank you."

My brother said, "Funny... I declared my major. It is Economics too."

My mother and daddy looked at Luke Junior and said at the same time, "So you finally made up your mind?"

My brother said, "Yes, I figured since I am good at business and math, why not stick to what I am good at and make myself better at what I know. I can say this much—it isn't easy. But I know I can do it. I am up for the challenge."

T'eo laughed and said, "Breana sees me in the library all the time struggling too. It is a challenge, but look at it this way—we are polishing up what we already know—as you put it, Luke, we are making ourselves better and more resourceful."

My daddy said, "Nice metaphor!"

Needless to say, we weren't watching the time, and the conversation lasted a little past midnight. My mother said, "Goodness, T'eo, we apologize for keeping you here for so long." She added, "Today was a beautiful and blessed day. I couldn't ask for more."

T'eo smiled and said, "Mr. and Mrs. Anderson, thank you for your hospitality and welcoming me into your home."

My daddy stood up, shook T'eo hand and said, "You're more than welcome. Again, thank you for coming. You are always welcome."

My mother gave T'eo a hug and said, "Any time. It was our pleasure."

My brother gave T'eo a dab and said, "T'eo, it was good to meet you. I will be in touch."

I smiled because I knew my parents liked T'eo, and to be honest, I liked him too. Today, I saw a different T'eo. I said,

"Daddy, I am going to walk T'eo to the door." He smiled and said, "Okay. See you soon, T'eo."

My daddy looked at my mother, walked over to the old record player, pulled out a Luther Vandross album, blew off the dust, put the needle on the record and said, "We had a wonderful, blessed, yet busy day. Mrs. Anderson, do you have time for one dance?"

If This World Were Mine begin to play.

My daddy put his hand out as he reached for my mother's hand. She said, "There isn't any place I would rather be but in your arms."

My brother said, "Well, that's my cue to head upstairs."

As I walked T'eo to the door, I looked at my parents and smiled. They were talking and smiling. Then my mother laid her head on my daddy's chest and he took the lead.

T'eo said, "Breana, that is true love. Pure love does exist." I smiled and said, "Yes it does. I know it does because I am looking at it." We walked on the porch. It was a little nippy, so I said, "I'll be right back. I have to run upstairs to get a jacket."

As I was about to open the door, T'eo said as he took off his jacket, "No you don't, you can wear mine." I smiled and said, "Thank you." T'eo helped me put it on and said, "Breana, may I have this dance?"

He held out his hand, I walked up to him and put my hand in his. He softly pulled me close and we dance as the music played.

My daddy put on Luther's Greatest Hits. *Endless Love* started to play. T'eo and I danced without saying a word. I laid my head on his chest and let him take the lead. I never experienced such gentleness. I was so used to the rough touch. I wondered why was that when my parents show me what true love is. My mind was racing with so many thoughts on why I settled for less with

Brian. My heart was about to fall out of my chest because I realized I really liked T'eo. I settled my mind and enjoyed the dance.

Can I Take You Out Tonight? came on. I looked at T'eo and said with excitement, "This is my song! You know I love me some Luther!" T'eo laughed and said, "I remember." We danced and danced for hours.

As T'eo and I prepared to say goodbye to each other, he reached for my hand, kissed me on my cheek and said, "Breana, I really enjoyed your family. I had a good time with you tonight. Thank you for inviting me." I kissed T'eo on the cheek as well and said, "I had a good time too, thank you so much for coming." As he let go of my hand—I was saying to myself *no, do not let go.* He smiled and told me, "I will text you when I get home." I smiled and said, "You better." I watched him get in his car and I waved as he pulled away.

I walked in the house, looked over at my parents and they were still in each other arms, dancing to Luther's, *So Amazing.* I smiled and watched them for about a minute and headed upstairs.

CHAPTER FOURTEEN

WHEN I WALKED INTO PSYCHOLOGY CLASS IT WAS STRANGE because all eyes were on me. I held onto my books tightly as I made my way to sit beside T'eo. There were some of my classmates rolling their eyes. Some of them nodded their head as they cracked a smile, and there were some students who just stared without any emotion on their faces. T'eo whispered in my ear and said, "Bree, do not pay them any attention. They are going to think and say what they want. One thing's for sure, they can't say much because they weren't in your position." I looked at T'eo and said, "I am not paying them any attention." I looked around at everyone and said, "They have a voice and know how to use their mouths. If they have something to say I am right here, front and center." I opened my notes and waited to see who replaced Dr. Wright.

Fifteen minutes passed. The dean opened the door as he walked down the stairs. He was wearing a dark purple suit and black dress shoes. He tucked his white shirt into his pants, cleared his throat, pushed his glasses up and said, "As you all might know, Dr. Wright is under investigation. With that being said, since we are a couple of weeks from finals, I am going to abide by the syllabus and take over his lectures for the time being. Today, we will discuss Chapter Fifteen. What we do not cover, please note that you will have to read on your own because it will be on your final exam."

He cleared his throat again, and said, "Does anyone have any questions?

A dude name Torrey raised his hand and said, "You didn't introduce yourself."

The dean looked very frustrated as he said, "I am the Dean of the Psychology Department. Do you have any other questions?"

Torrey said, "There's no need to get upset. I think it is only fair if you introduce yourself that way, we would know what to call you. You still didn't give us a name. Do you want us to call you Dean of the Psychology Department?"

The Dean answered, "Dean will be fine."

As the dean looked up, he noticed my face and said, "We all must be very careful what we say and how we say it."

I squinted my eyes and said, "With all due respect, are you referring your comment to me?" I stood up and said, "If Dr. Wright would have kept his hands to himself and his mouth shut, then..." T'eo cut me off and said, "Breana, it's not worth it."

Before I sat back in my chair I said, "Dean, I do not care if you believe me or not. I do not need or seek your approval. The cameras in the library tell the entire story. Also, your comment was..." The dean interrupted me and said, "Ms. Anderson, you need to apologize for your behavior. You are very disrespectful."

My lips were trembling, I balled my hands into fists because I was angry and said, "I am not apologizing for anything I've said. Your comment was unprofessional and most definitely uncalled for."

The dean looked at me and said with a firm voice, "Calm yourself. I am not going to force you to apologize. However, it would be the right thing to do."

I popped my knuckles and said, "I am unapologetic. That includes my flaws and all. You should be apologizing to me. I am not going to apologize for what Dr. Wright did to me. I am not going to apologize because I want my voice to be heard. Wrong is wrong, whether you see it or not, but I am not going to let Dr. Wright get away with verbally and sexually assaulting and harassing me. As a matter of fact, I have a class full of witnesses that heard your disrespectful comment towards me."

The Dean asked, "How's my comment disrespectful, Ms. Anderson?"

I opened my mouth to speak, but another young lady spoke up and said, "If you didn't know, you looked directly at her when you made your disrespectful, and I might add, biased comment." She paused and said, "Well, in my opinion, your (she put her two fingers up as if they were quotations and said) "comment" was discrimination." She stood up as she put on her brown jacket and said, "My name is Precious, and I too am a victim of Dr. Wright. He sexually harassed me this semester as well. I was scared to say anything because he told me it would be his word against mine and I would fail his class. I am standing with Breana."

Another girl stood up and said, "My name is Marshall, and I too am a victim of Dr. Wright's verbal and sexual harassment behavior. He started to sexually harass me when I took his History of Psychology class. From there, his harassment never ended. I too am standing with Brenna."

There was an older woman who kept looking at me. I looked at her without hesitation. She kept flipping her pen, then she would write something on a piece of paper. She looked nervous, but I centered my attention on a dark-skinned young lady who looked as young as me. She had on a light green sweatshirt that had the word *Brave* on it. Her blue jeans were ripped near the knees (that's the style nowadays) and she had on pink Converse. As she stood up, she put her hair in a ponytail and said, "Breana, I want to say thank you for speaking up. Most of us are not as strong, bold or brave as you. However, it takes only one person to make a difference. It takes one person to form an impact for change. Although you thought you were alone, you decided to stand alone and make it known that your voice was going to be heard." Tears formed in her eyes as she said, "Brenna, like you said, we should be unapologetic for our flaws and all. Who is Dr. Wright to take our voice? He had silenced my voice for way too long. I am a homeschooled junior in high school. I just turned seventeen years old. My name is Asia, and I too was touched in an inappropriate way by Dr. Wright. He threatened me and told me if I said anything, he would make sure I failed his classes. That was last semester when I was taking two classes with him. This semester he sexually harassed me too. I never said anything because I was scared. I am standing with Brenna as well."

The dean put his hands up and said, "Wait a minute. Wait a second."

The older lady who was flipping her pen yelled, "You shouldn't be saying wait a minute or wait a second. You must be on Dr. Wright's team and have verbally and sexually harassed students too because you are not taken aback by what is being said here. You should be investigated as well, you are swallowing down these victim's stories like smooth warm milk. I too was harassed by Dr. Wright. I had him for Educational Psychology class and he put his hand on my breast. He always pushed my hair out of my face, saying he wanted to see my blue eyes. This term he said I was too old to flirt with because he has younger girls in his class that he can catch. I too am standing with Breana."

The class was getting out of control. Word went around campus and the Vice President of the University came to our classroom and said, "Ladies and gentlemen, class is dismissed."

As I was walking down the hallway my phone went off and I received an email. It was a video from an anonymous person regarding what happened in class today. It said, "Breana, show this to your lawyer. Do not let anyone know of the video." I emailed that person back and said, "Thank you so much. I just sent it over to my lawyers and my parents." The person emailed me back and said, "Okay, great. I am going to send the video viral. It needs to be seen and heard. Brenna the brave, you are everyone's hero. Job well done!"

I knew it wasn't T'eo because he was walking beside me. I wondered if it was the girl who had the word *Brave* on her shirt. I had no clue, but I thanked them again for the video.

As I walked out the door, there were people saying, "I stand with Breana! I stand with Breana! I stand with Breana!" I didn't know whether to smile or cry. I pumped my fist and joined in, saying, "I stand with Breana!" There were so many people recording with their phones and the next thing I knew all of the news channels were setting up.

My lawyer called me and said, "If they asked you to speak, let them know you cannot talk unless your lawyer is there. I'm listening to the radio and I am less than three minutes away."

My daddy called and he asked, "Breana, are you okay?" "I am fine, Daddy," I answered. I heard a familiar voice yelling my name. I looked up, and it was my mother! She was pushing through the crowd, saying over and over again, "Excuse me. Excuse me." She hugged me in her arms so tightly that her breast embraced the left side of my face. She put her hands on my cheeks and asked, "Baby, are you okay?" She looked me up and down; she looked worried, as if I was injured and said once again, "Are you okay?" I looked at her and said, "Mommy, I am fine. All of this came about in class today. People decided to speak up and stand up."

My lawyer called me. I answered the phone. He asked, "Breana, where are you?" I answered, "I am standing right in front of the library with my mother." He said, "I see you on the steps."

Attorney Davis looked at me and said, "My, my what do you know? It is true, what is done in the dark will come to the light. I saw the video and all of this came from the dean asking you to apologize to him for making a disrespectful comment. I bet he never thought this would happen. Look at all these people!"

A news reporter was walking towards me as he asked, "Breana, what do you think about all of this?" I looked up at Attorney Davis. He nodded his head yes. I spoke into the microphone and said, "I do not know if I should cry or be happy." The reporter asked, "Why do you want to cry? I said, "I want to cry because it is beautiful that women are standing up and being unapologetic for what happened to them. They didn't welcome what was done to them with open arms. I was focused upon them and the unlimited and countless threats they faced. I want to smile because I am happy to see so many women unafraid. It makes me happy to see that fear doesn't have power over them anymore. Their voices are being heard—and that's as it should be."

Another reporter asked, "Breana, you said it is beautiful that women are standing up and unapologetic. What do you mean by 'unapologetic'?" I looked at him and said, "As I stated before, women are not letting fear take over their lives. Fear no longer has power. Women are loving more on themselves and they are being unapologetic for their flaws and all. Meaning, we as women do not need to seek the approval of others. As long as we approve of ourselves, that is what matters." The reporter said, "Wow, I love that! As a woman myself, I am going to carry that with me. I should be unapologetic for my flaws and all! What a bold statement!"

There was a journalist who came in on the end of the conversation and she said, "What do you mean, unapologetic for their flaws and all?" I didn't mind repeating myself again. I looked at the journalist and said, "You are a woman, how many times have you apologized for your flaws to people in general, whether you had to apologize to a male or female for your flaws, just for being you? Something that is a part of you—meaning you do not need approval from anyone. As long as you accept your flaws, you should be happy with who you are. Nowadays women have to apologize for some things we didn't do; or worse, because of who we are as a person. Not to mention, just like in this situation, the dean wanted me to apologize for what happened to me. I didn't ask Dr. Wright to verbally and sexually harass me, however, the Dean of the Psychology Department looked directly at me and said, "We all must be very careful what we say and how we say it." As if he was blaming me for what Dr. Wright has done to me and so many other females on the campus. What makes matters worse, he asked me to apologize because he felt as if I was being disrespectful because I spoke my truth. That is what I mean when I say women shouldn't ever have to apologize for what is right. We should always be unapologetic for our flaws and all, because who else will accept our flaws?"

The reporter looked at me without an answer. I look directly at her and said, "Nobody, only we as women will accept our flaws. With that being said, why not be unapologetic, we shouldn't ever seek approvals of others, because we are perfect just the way we are."

"Well said," the reporter said as she smiled at me.

All I could hear in the background was, "I stand with Brenna! I stand with Breana!

As I walked down the stairs, I gave a hug to many of the women I walked past. I smiled at the other women who I couldn't get to. Never did I think in my wildest dreams that today would have served a purpose for justice. I am so happy women decided to stand up and speak loudly for their voices to be heard.

* * *

During the evening after dinner, Summer turned on the news and said, "Breana is a superstar! You are famous."

As my family and I sat down on the couch the headline was: *Unapologetic for My Flaws and All*. Summer turned to another station and the headline once again was highlighted as *Unapologetic for My Flaws and All*. We flipped to all the stations and all of them had the same headline. I smiled.

After we looked at the news for a while, we all had a family discussion about safety. My daddy said, "Breana, I know you are a big girl, but I am going to come with you to school because I do not want any harm to come to you." I looked at him and said, "Daddy, you do not have to do that." He replied in a firm voice, "Oh, yes I do."

My mother looked nervous and worried. I hugged her and said, "Mommy, have faith and know everything will be okay. If it helps, we can meditate and clear our chakras." She smiled and said, "I think that's a good idea."

My phone rang and it was T'eo. I answered and he asked me was I okay. I said, "I am fine, thank you for asking." I added, "T'eo, thank you for being with me every step of the way today. I truly appreciate it." He said, "Breana, anytime. If you need me, I am a phone call away." I smiled and said, "Thank you." I then asked, "T'eo, are you okay?" He said, "Yes. I am. I wanted to make sure you were fine because you are on every news station. I must say, you most definitely made a statement, like you always do!" I smiled and said, "There's no other way to do it. I wanted to make a statement and I wanted it to be known and heard." I paused and said, "The biggest thank you should go to the person who recorded it in class. I wonder who that was. Do you know?" T'eo said, "Nope. I do not have a clue." "Strange," I said.

* * *

Before I settled down for bed my mother, Summer and I meditated and cleared our chakras for about an hour. I was surprised that Daddy joined us too. As I lay in my bed, I thanked the Great Divines like always, but today was totally different. I looked at today as a miracle, because one thing was for sure, today was teamwork and I didn't go at it alone.

* * *

A week has passed and the newscasters have been at the school for days. Chloe has called me every day to check on me. There were a couple of nights she came by to spend the night. We talked and like always, enjoyed each other's presence. I am happy I have a friend like her because she's been here with me through thick and thin.

As I walked on campus with my daddy to go to math class, I ran into the President of the school. "Hello, Breana," Dr. Wallace said. I looked concerned and said, "Hello, Dr. Wallace. Is everything okay?" He looked me up and down and said, "Yes, everything is fine. I wanted to catch you before you arrived in class." He cleared his throat and said, "I got approval from your professors to let you take your final exams early." I looked at him and asked, "Why?" He said, "I thought maybe that is what you would have wanted." I paused for a short moment and said, "Dr. Wallace, how could you have thought that if you didn't ask me? If you had asked me, then you would have known for a fact what I wanted. I do not want to take my finals early. I need more time to prepare, and I need to be in my lectures to know what is going to be on the finals."

Dr. Wallace looked at me as if I was making things complicated. I said, "Dr. Wallace, I believe you want me to take my finals early to end what is going on—on campus. Whether I am here or not, it is what it is because Dr. Wright caused this problem, not me. I am tired of the men on this campus blaming me and the females here who have been verbally and sexually harassed. The problem is not going to go away until we have justice. Truth be told, this is something we will have to deal with for the rest of our lives. With that being said, excuse me, Dr. Wallace, I have to get to class and prepare for my finals."

I looked at my watch and said, "Come on, Daddy, before we are late." He looked at me for a moment, smiled and said, "Look at you! I raised a fighter. You do not need me here, you talked to him as if I wasn't here." I smiled and said, "Well, Daddy, for a moment I did forget you were here. Thank you for letting me speak for myself. Believe it or not, Daddy, I got this, but I thank you for being here." He laughed and said, "I know you got this.

I know one thing, I wouldn't want to double-cross you. My baby girl is a wildfire!"

I walked into math class and once again all eyes were on me. This time around I received a standing ovation. Everyone was clapping their hands and yelling my name as they yelled, "Breana the Brave." I didn't pay attention to what they were wearing until my daddy said, "Breana, look at their shirts." I cried when I read their shirts. They read: *Standing with Breana The Brave: Unapologetic for My Flaws and All.* I put my hands over my mouth and said, "No way! This is unbelievable." One of my classmates said, "No, Breana, believe it. You opened the door for all of us. We are not afraid anymore, thanks to you." I have her a hug and said, "Thank you too. We all have to stick together and stand for something." Another classmate said, "Indeed. And here we are—standing with Breana."

My calculus professor, Dr. Gilbert, is a woman. She walked up to me and gave me a hug. She looked at my daddy and said, "I know you are a proud father." He smiled and said, "Yes, I am."

After the lecture was over. I was surprised to see how many people were wearing a black shirt with pink letters saying: *Standing with Breana The Brave: Unapologetic for My Flaws and All.* I looked over at some of the news reporters and they were wearing the shirt too. Today I learned it takes one person to stand up to make a difference. Once one person takes a stand, everyone else will freely come forward with confidence, hope, faith and have peace of mind, knowing this day has finally come.

* * *

The past weeks have been overwhelming with school and the court case. Final exams are around the corner and I am ready for the semester to be over. I deserve a well-needed break. I went up to Jackson-Miles High today to let the cheer-leading team know that I am resigning as captain. Not only as captain, but I will no longer be on the team. I have too much on my plate and I do not need any more responsibilities which I know I can't afford to take on.

Later that evening, I went to my job to study for my finals. My supervisor said, "Bree, I am so proud of you. You are a fear-less woman." I smiled and said, "Thank you, but this fearless woman is tired." After studying for a while, I helped the staff clean up, restock the tables and break down the chairs. There was a couple finishing up their conversation, as I looked over, one of the customers had on a *Standing with Breana The Brave: Unapologetic for My Flaws and All* shirt. I smiled, walked over to get the broom to sweep the floor. About thirty minutes later, my daddy pulled up. I took off my apron, gathered my things and said, "I will see you all next weekend!" My supervisor said, "Okay. See you soon!" As I walked towards the door my supervisor said, "Breana, I noticed you didn't clock in." I waved, smiled and said, "I did it out of love!" My supervisor said, "How nice of you, but I am going to pay you for a full shift because you didn't have to help. Like always, you come in, study, manage to find your way to put on an apron and start working." I laughed and said, "Well, you know me! Good night! Be safe, love you guys!"

CHAPTER FIFTEEN 15

I AWAKEN TO SO MANY TEXT MESSAGES BECAUSE TODAY IS my birthday. I am not doing anything exciting. My goal is to study for my finals. As I walked downstairs my mother, daddy, and Summer were singing Happy Birthday to me. I smiled, laughed, giggled and was filled with happiness. I said with excitement, "Wow, I am 18 years old today!" Summer said, "Don't get too happy, you are not fully legal until you are 21 years old." I started to shake my head and said, "Thank you, Attorney Summer." She smiled, jumped down from the stool and said, "Oh, no problem. I was just doing my job." My mother walked over and gave me a hug as she said, "Happy birthday, my sweet baby." I smiled in her arms and said, "Thanks, Mommy!" My daddy hugged me too and said, "Happy birthday, baby girl. May God bless you with many more!" I thanked him as well! Since it was a weekday, we all gathered our things and went on our merry way.

Later that evening, when I arrived home, I opened the door and all I heard was, "Surprise!" Chloe ran up to me and said, "Happy Birthday, bestie!" I said, "Thank you!" I didn't have a clue that everyone would be here. T'eo walked up to me and said, "Finally, 18 years old!" Summer said, "Well you two are not old enough to drink." T'eo said, "Leave it up to Summer to school us." I laughed and said, "Right!" My aunts, Rita and Piper, walked up to me and said, Happy Birthday as well. My mother asked were we hungry. She made me a birthday dinner, no meat, just veggies (organic kale, broccoli, kidney beans, and sweet and sour tofu). I am the only one in my family that doesn't eat meat. They like tofu but they do not eat it often. I was happy because the food was catered for me, and everyone that I love was there. Luke had to stay at college to take his finals, which I completely understood. After dinner, they sang Happy Birthday and I cut the cake. We talked a little and I opened my presents. Daddy got me a gift card to my favorite restaurant, The Farmer's Market. Mother and my aunties gave me what I asked for (BP gift cards), Summer wrote me a card which was so cute! Chloe got me an affirmation and astrology calendar for 2019. She knows I love my calendars! T'eo wrote me a letter and gave me a Visa gift card. I hugged and thanked everyone for my special day! I really enjoyed myself.

* * *

My final exams were a breeze. I am so happy I am done. As I logged in to see my grades, I was anxious and excited. I received an A in Psychology, Anatomy I, Anatomy lab and in Speech. I was disappointed because I received a B in Calculus. I worked my butt off in Dr. Gilbert's class. Overall, I am proud of myself because Dr. Gilbert is a tough professor. On RateMyProfessor. com she has a 1.8 overall. However, at the moment she was the only professor at the University that taught Calculus. My GPA for the term is a 3.8—my overall GPA is a 3.9. I have to get all A's next semester because I want to have at least a 4.0!

I had to make sure I passed all my classes before I registered for the Spring term. Since I am good to go—I immediately registered for my classes which are: Anatomy II, Anatomy II lab, Calculus II and Economics. I will have more than enough credits to graduate with an Associate's degree! I am excited. I went on the RateMyProfessor website to check out my Economics professor, which said, "Dr. Samuel is a joke. He doesn't teach. He tells us to read the chapters on the syllabus and dismisses class." I thought to myself, *well, that doesn't sound that bad*. There was another comment that said, "How did I flunk Dr. Samuel's class and he never taught us anything? I got an F for what? Showing up to class?" I said to myself, *damn that's messed up*. Another comment said, "Dr. Samuel is a jerk! He talks about himself and his problems all day. I think he is insane. I got a C in his class. Until this day, I am in awe because I always showed up to class just to hear about his problems. He should have given the entire class an A for being his psychiatrists." I had a good laugh at that student's comment! Overall, Dr. Samuel got a 1.0 score. That sucks. The other professor's name is Dr. King; overall score is a 2.5. His comments were better, but he is a hard teacher like Dr. Gilbert. Ugh, if I get two B's next term, I will not have a 4.0. A student said, "Dr. King is so boring and his exams don't cover anything we lecture in class." Another student said, "Dr. King take his classes too seriously. Hello! Economic is an elective, yet a requirement to graduate. Why? I do not know. Eighty percent of the university take this class just because it's a requirement. It is not our major. Needless to say, I got a C in his class. Glad I have to take him only one time." Their other comments were similar to hers. I do not have any good options to choose from. Gosh, why do some professors have to be so difficult? Looks like I will be registering for Dr. King's class. I submitted my schedule and I'm good to go for Spring semester.

* * *

Since I'm on break, I am going to take advantage of my time and with hopes to move into the attic. I do not know if I really want to move up there since I am going to be staying up there for about seven months or so. Moving seems like it would be a bit too much. I think I might unpack everything and stay in my room.

I heard my parents yelling my name. I ran down the stairs and walked into the family room. My daddy was standing up and my mother was sitting down, holding the remote control. Their eyes were glued to the television. My daddy pointed to the TV and said, "Look, Bree. Look!" Summer ran downstairs saying, "Goodness gracious, what is all the commotion?" My mouth was open and my eyes were getting wider and wider. The news reporter said, "We are here at the Correctional Center. Dr. Rodney Wright has been arrested at his home. As of right now, they just pulled up. They haven't got out of the car yet." My eyes didn't blink. The reporter said, "Wait. Wait. They are now escorting him from the police car. He is keeping his head down as the police officers walk him into the Correctional Center." There were people protesting, saying, "We are standing with Breana! We are standing with Breana! We want our voices to be heard! We are not apologizing for what he did to us. We are unapologetic for our flaws and all. We are human beings and we matter!" I looked at my parents with concern in my eyes and said, "I need to be down there!" My daddy said, "No, baby girl, not tonight." I yelled, as tears formed in my eyes, and said, "Daddy, yes I do! I need to be there down there fighting with them! I need to be protesting with them!" My mother said, "No, sweetheart, not tonight."

It started to rain and the reporter said, "I just got the word that so far Dr. Rodney Wright has been charged with twelve counts of verbal harassment and sexual assault. With two additional counts of sexual conduct with a minor. He also is charged for a sexual assault on a minor as well. In all, he has been charged with fifteen counts."

I dropped to the floor. I was shaking because I couldn't believe what was being said. Dr. Wright's secret verbal and sexual assaults all of those women, including me. I balled up my fist and I screamed at the top of my lungs. I cried because how dare he think he had the right to take from us? He really thought he was going to get away with it.

The reporter said loudly, "It looks like there are people still coming forward. However, so far it is fifteen and counting."

My daddy hugged me as I was curled up into a ball, crying and saying, "We got him, Daddy. We got him. He isn't going to get away with touching or talking to women any kind of way ever again. We got him, Daddy. We got him." He rocked me back and forth and said, "Yes, we got him. It took a brave little girl to stand up to burst the door wide open. There's no turning back, everything is out in the open now and justice will be served."

* * *

For a couple of days, I had a hard time sleeping because my mind was roaming a million miles per hour. My mother gave me some tea to relax. It wasn't disrupting to the point I had nightmares. My sleep was disrupted because I could not understand why Dr. Wright thought he could get away with hurting people.

I cleared my chakras on a daily basis to stay balanced. Got myself together and prepared for work. As I arrived at work it was busier than usual. Like always, I put on my apron and got to work. It was strange because I felt awkward. I ignored the feeling and kept working. My coworker Leeann said, "Breana, I heard what you did, and you are an amazingly strong woman." She lifted up her apron and she had on a Standing with Breana shirt." I smiled and said, "Thanks, but it wasn't all me. I give credit to all of the women who stood up as well." Leeann flipped her long bone-straight blond hair back, smiled, and said, "Well it took one person to speak up for them to stand up." I smiled and asked her, "Did you make the blueberry crumble cake?" She said, "I didn't." I said, 'Okay, cool, I'll stay back here and make it." Leeann said in a joking manner, "Breana, wants to stay in the back, that is a first." I smiled slightly and said, "Yeah, only for today. I need time to clear my mind. Plus, baking is therapeutic for me."

After I baked three pans of our famous blueberry crumble cakes I stayed in the back to wash dishes. My supervisor came to the back and asked, "Breana, are you okay?" I smiled and said, "Yes. I just wanted to be in the back for a while. I'm ready to go to the front now to get some fresh air. Has the crowd died down?" My supervisor rubbed my back and said, "It's okay if you want to stay in the back for the rest of the day. I understand. As of right now, there isn't a line. There are only a few people out and about, sitting down eating." I said, "Thank you for under-standing, but I am tired of being isolated." My supervisor looked at me with great concern and asked, "Are you sure?" I smiled and said, "I am positive."

I took off the kitchen apron and put on a dining apron to help serve the customers. My coworker Tony asked me would it be okay if I took orders out to the numbered tables. I didn't mind and said, "Sure." He said, "Thanks, Bree. This order here goes to table 21." I said, "No problem." As I gather the silverware I said, "Tony, by the way, I love your new do! ...Did you get a tan?" He said, "Really? I got tired of the bronze color and straight hairstyle so I decided to perm it to make it curly. Since my boyfriend and I've been on fire lately with so much passion, I dyed it red to show my affection." I laughed and said, "Well, damn, you did that!" Tony laughed and replied, "Yeah, my man loves it, so that's all that matters." He added, "Yes, girl, I got a tan because I was too pale." I looked at Tony and he said, "Bree, oh gosh, what is that face for?" I said, "It's good to know your boyfriend loves it, but what matters the most is that you love it too." Tony said, "Of course, I love it!" I smiled and said, "I love it too!" As I walked off, I said, "Do not change your eye color, your blue eyes are perfect!" He waved his hand and said, "Child, I won't. Thanks!'

I begin looking for the number 21 table in the dine-in area but it wasn't there. I walked over to the mini-library, as we call the cozy couch area, however, nobody was sitting there. I walked outside, and I'll be damned! It was Brian and Angel sitting at a table with the number stand 21. I had to be polite because I was at work. I said, "Good evening, I hope you all are doing well today. If you all need anything let me know. Enjoy your meal." Brian said, "Well…Well… Well… Breana the Brave. Or should I say, Breana the celebrity?" I didn't respond to his comment. I said, "Enjoy your meal and have a good evening."

As I looked straight ahead and walked away, I heard Angel laughing and I felt her looking at me. She had on a skanky out-fit—a fishnet shirt with only her bra under it. Eww, how disgusting. It's chilly outside and she had on some cut-up booty shorts. Hello, it is December. Who wears shorts in the winter time? Her hair looked like she just got into a fight and lost. I had a good laugh when I walked back into the coffee shop! I couldn't help myself. I thought to myself, *what in the world was I thinking, going out with that fool and being so in love with a dude that doesn't have any class. I should slap myself in the face for being such an idiot.* I laughed again and said to myself, *Breana the Brave, yeah okay, I should call myself Breana the idiot for being his fool.* Oh well, I dusted myself off and said to myself, *not my shit, not my problem anymore.*

Tony said, "Bree, what's so funny?" I was tickled when I said, "I'm laughing at myself for being a damn fool and an idiot." Tony started to laugh, "Yeah, been there and done that shit. Not ever again." Leeann, Sage and I stared at Tony because he was about to get started. He looked at us and said, "Oh, okay, here y'all go." We laughed. Leeann said, "Ugh. No. Here you go." Tony said, "What? I am lost?!" Sage retorted, "As you should be." We all started laughing. My supervisor Marie walked in as I said, "My ex is out there with his girlfriend." I was about to say something else, but everyone stopped what they were doing to take a peek. My supervisor said, "Oh my sweet honeycomb, God bless her soul, that child doesn't know any better. It's freezing outside and that child came out the house naked." Tony laughed so hard and said, "She must think she's Olaf from *Frozen.*" We all looked at him and said, "What?" Tony said, "Never mind. Look at the movie and you guys will understand." Leeann said, "Why didn't her man tell her she looks like pure trash? He must be blind, or maybe he just doesn't care?" Sage was putting her hair in a hairnet. As she put a string of purple hair in the net she said, "She knows she's cold." Sage tied up her black boots and said, "They are stupid. They came here because they know Bree works here. If they're coming here to start some shit, I am going to stomp both of them with my boots." We looked at Sage and busted out laughing. I said, "I do not think it will come down to that. If it did, I wouldn't let you do that." Sage looked at her black fingernail polish as she washed her hands. She dried them, put gloves on and prepared to make the next order and said, "Just because I'm a brunette, they better not get it twisted, they are not coming up in here starting shit." As she got the croissants off the shelf she said, "I got your back, Bree." Tony said, "Wait. They are getting up. It looks like they are about to come inside." I looked at them and said, "I wouldn't be surprised because they want to either give me a hard time or show off their toxic relationship. It's all good, though. I'm good. Shoot, as Lil Wayne says, "No love lost, no love found."

I clocked out to take my break. Since my daddy had dropped me off, I sat in my supervisor's office and called Chloe. I told her Brian and Angel were at my place of work. Chloe said, "Yin, no way in hell." I said, "Well...Hell must have opened the door because they are here." Chloe said, "Yin, do you want me to come up there because you know they are up there to start some senseless shit. Brian never came up there to your job—all of a sudden, he wants to show up. He is such a virus." I laughed! Chloe said, "Bree, I am serious, he knows you are getting over him and he wants to get the best of you and flirt with Angel around you. What makes matters worse, she is so clueless. She doesn't know she is being used." I was about to comment on what Chloe said, but she continued and said, "You sure you're good? If you want me to come up there, I will." I said, "Thank you, Yang, but I am good. I am not paying attention to Brian." Chloe said, "You know you haven't talked about that dude who came up to your job. What is his name?" I replied, "Oh... Eli. Girl, he isn't any good. He didn't know I saw him at the park with some girl when I was playing soccer with Summer. He was all hugged up on her, touching her butt and kissing all over her." Chloe paused and said, "What! Damn, Bree, what an ass. These dudes ain't shit. They just want some fast ass. We are not the ones. With that being said, he needs to keep it moving." I laughed and said, "You know it. Shoot, he kept calling and texting me. After I saw him with that girl I never answer any of his calls or responded to his text messages. Ugh, been there, done that, and most definitely not going back." Chloe said, "Yin, I hear you. My ex keeps calling me. Girl, he really thinks I am going to take his ass back. Nope. A person has one time to screw me over. One time and one time only." I laughed again, "Your ex. You are not going to say his name." Chloe said, "Hell no, he is not worth it. I was just telling you because we have to keep each other on a straight path." She continued, "I am about to get ready to go to my meeting. One day you have to come. You know I started a club that helps young girls work on their self-esteem." "Look at you, Chloe! I am so proud of you!" I said with excitement. I continued, "I am going to come soon." Chloe said, "Thank you. I know you are busy, but you have to be a special guest. I want you to talk about yourself because Yin, you are so smart. A lot of us do not have parents that are still together in a loving, healthy, marriage or a relationship for that matter. I would like for you to talk about your parents too." I replied, "I got you! I always make time for my girl!"

Brian and Angel came and sat near the entertainment stage where a guy was setting up for karaoke night. Brian came up to the counter and asked if I could make his jerk chicken sandwich over. He said it was cold. Angel came to the counter as well and asked me if I could make her tuna sandwich over too. She said it was cold too. Clearly, she's a dumbass, tuna is supposed to be cold—because she didn't ask for a tuna melt. My supervisor said, "That is not Breana's job. I will be more than happy to make your sandwiches over." She added, "Do you all want your bread to be toasted? Cheese? Wheat or white bread? Both of them said it didn't matter. I stood there shaking my head because they knew there wasn't anything wrong with their sandwiches. They thought I was going to be the one who had to make them over and wait on them hand and foot. Boy, were they wrong!

As time passed, karaoke started. There were couples dancing and having a good old time. There were people on the floor having a ball. Most of the people singing couldn't follow the words. It was too funny because the words were up front and center for them to read. Brian and Angel were still here. He was feeding Angel with his fingers. I was like, hello, the fork and spoon are next to your plate. He kept looking at me and from time to time I kept looking at him too without him knowing. Not because I wanted to be with him. More so, because he looked disgusting.

Leeann said, "Breana you have company." I thought it was Eli since he knew it was karaoke night. However, it was T'eo. He walked up to me and said, "Hey, Breana the Brave." I gently tapped him on his chest, smiled and said, "Stop." Since he's taller than me he looked down at me and said, "Well, it's the truth." He asked, "Is it karaoke night? I smiled and said, "Why are you asking? It's not like you can sing." He busted out laughing and said, "Breana the comedian. You are not funny." He had a suspicious look on his face as he raised his eyebrows and smirked. He added, "You didn't tell me it was karaoke night." I laughed and said, "Don't even think about it." T'eo said, "Come on, Breana. What are you scared of? You danced all night at the pizza joint." I laughed and said, "T'eo, that was dancing, this is singing. I can't sing." He pulled my arm gently and said, "Come on, girl, that's why the words are on the screen for us to follow along as we sing the song."

Brian was looking like he had fire boiling in his eyes. He kept looking; I'm more than sure he wondered who T'eo was to me. T'eo ran onto the stage and looked on the computer to find a song. He was smiling as he said, "Oh yeah, this is perfect!" He looked at me as the song started to play. It was *Can I take You*

Out Tonight by Luther Vandross. He looked over at me, pointed and said, "This song is dedicated to Breana the Brave. One of the first songs we danced to. I might add we danced the night away and I enjoyed every step!" He attached the mic to his shirt and started to sing. "Yeeeaaahhh... Here is it..." His voice was cracking. People were looking like, *is he serious?* I covered my face for a second. I walked up to the stage and rocked from side to side with the beat. He knows I love me some Luther! I couldn't help but smile, laugh and blush because I loved how he took a chance of not caring if he embarrassed himself for me. He was walking across the stage singing,

"*She caught me by surprise, I must say 'Cause I never have seen such a pretty face With such a warm and beautiful smile It wasn't hard for me to notice her style I was fascinated surely She took my heart and held it for me I wouldn't let her get away Not until she heard me say...*

T'eo jumped off the stage as he continued to sing, He touched my hand, put my hand on his chest, and then he put my hand in his hand as the song continued. He said, "Breana, I have a question for you." He then sang the chorus part) [Chorus]

Can I take you out tonight? To a movie, to the park I'll have you home, before it's dark So let me know Can I take you out tonight?

My eyes teared up, T'eo is such a sweet guy. He put his hands on my hips and pulled me closer. He looked me in the eyes and he began to sing the second verse. *Don't care if I get rejected At least then I won't regret Regret the fact I missed the chance for romance, at least I'll walk away knowing, I tried my best and I'm going I'm going on with my day 'Cause at least she heard me say...*

As the song continued to play, he jumped on stage, lowered the volume and said, "Breana, I have a question for you." I smiled and put my hand over my mouth as I laughed. He smiled and said, "I think that is so cute when you put your hand over your mouth when you laugh. You are too precious, Breana. Well... Breana Anderson, I have so much love for you. I know we've been out as (he put up the quotation marks with his fingers) "friends". I would like to know; can I take you out tonight? To the movies, to the park, wherever you want to go, and we can do whatever you want to do. As long as I am in your presence, (he was smiling from ear to ear) my world is perfect!"

I put my index finger on my bottom lip and said, "Hmmm, let me think about it."

T'eo smiled and started to sing a Capella,

"Don't care if I get rejected At least then I won't regret Regret the fact I missed the chance for romance, at least I'll walk away knowing, I tried my best and I'm going I'm going on with my day 'Cause at least Bree heard me say..."

I busted out laughing and said, "Boy you are too much, how can I say no?" T'eo smiled and said, "So, Breana the Brave, is that a yes? Are we finally going out on a real date?" I walked up to him as I smiled and said, "Hmmm, it's something like that."

A guy walked up with black-blue jeans on, a white t-shirt, a baseball cap on and asked T'eo for the mic. He said, "These lovebirds are going to fly away tonight and produce butterflies." He pulled out a sheet of paper and said, "I would like to share my poem. Lovebirds fly away. Enter her cocoon and produce butterflies." He cleared his throat and said, "That's all I have for now."

Everyone was looking like, Ohhh, Okaaay! That was odd and strange on so many levels. T'eo walked on stage and said, "Everyone, give this man a round of applause!" He looked at the guy and said, "When you finish the poem, I'm sure it will have meaning that only people with a wide imagination will understand." I looked at T'eo because he always has a huge heart for everyone.

I called my daddy and asked him would it be okay if T'eo could bring me home tonight after a movie. He said that would be fine.

Leeann pulled me to the side and said, "Girl, you should have seen Brian's face. I believe he and his girlfriend got into an argument. She hit his arm hard a couple of times because girl, he was looking at you. He knows he fucked up." I said, "Girl, I forgot he was here." I got off the subject and said, "T'eo is such a good guy. I am so scared. How about he turns out to be like Brian?" Leeann replied, "How about he doesn't." I looked at T'eo from a distance and said, "He is too good to be true. Maybe he's hiding the real him. Maybe his true colors going to come out sooner or later. Maybe..." Leeann cut me off, "Bree, stop with all the maybe's, stop trying to find something wrong. He is not Brian the asshole. Enjoy the moment and make the best of it." I looked at Leeann, gave her a hug and said, "You know what? You are right. I am going to enjoy the present and make the best of it. Thanks, girl."

I clocked out. I was about to walk over to T'eo but I paused because Brian was talking to him. I walked up to T'eo and said, "Can you take me home tonight? He smiled and said, "Hmmm, let me think about it." I laughed and said, "You silly." He laughed. I put wrapped my arm around his and asked, "Are you ready?" As T'eo was about to answer, Brian said, "Bree, you are not going to introduce us?" I looked at Brian and said, "I figured you two formally introduced yourselves since you all are talking." T'eo said, "Well... he came up to me asking me how do I know you, and then you walked over. Since his name is Brian, I just put two and two together. He's your ex. Right?" With an emphasis on the 'ex', I said, "Exactly. Ex. Such as, there's nothing to talk about, he's the past and we are going to leave it there. I can only say thanks for the experience, our time has expired, now please exit my life." I looked at T'eo and asked, "Are you ready?" He looked at me, "Yep, if you are, I am."

As we were walking towards the door, Brian yelled my name and said, "Bree, can we talk? Bree! Bree!" I told T'eo to not look back as we walked out the door.

T'eo opened the car door for me and as he cranked the car, he looked concerned and said, "Breana, are you okay?" I looked at T'eo, smiled and said, "I am, thanks for asking. I am better than okay, I am filled with happiness and joy all because of you." I looked down as I played with my fingers, and then I looked up and said, "Thank you T'eo." He kissed my forehead and said, "You're welcome, Bree."

"Where do you want to go?" T'eo asked. I said, "It's chilly, but let's go to the park." I called my daddy to ask him if that was it okay if T'eo and I went to the park instead of the movies. He was fine with that. As we walked in the park, the air was crisp and the breeze was a breath of fresh air. We sat on the swings as we enjoyed the city lights, with the stars and the full moon shining down on us. I laid my head on his shoulder as he wrapped his arms around me to keep me warm. We didn't talk, we just enjoyed each other's silence as the leaves on the trees played us a tune as they moved from side to side.

We only stayed at the park for about an hour because the temperature was dropping. We walked hand in hand back to the car. When he dropped me off at home, he walked me to the front door. He said, "Breana the Brave." I smiled. As it got colder the wind began to blow. He gently pushed my hair out of my face and said, "You are cold. Wait." He ran to his car and got his coat and put it over me. He said, "Breana, I enjoyed today. To be honest, it was one of the best days of my life. Thank you for your time." All of a sudden, I became shy. My hair blew back in my face, I pulled it behind my ears as I looked down for a second, then blushed as I looked T'eo in the eyes and said, "You're more than welcome. I really enjoyed myself too. Thank you for your grand invitation, the way you asked me out, that was very different and I loved it. Thank you for your time as well." I brushed my hair back again, and said, "Thank you for being the bigger person in the café." T'eo smiled and said, "Bree, he's irrelevant, but you're welcome."

T'eo came closer and said, "Bree, I always wanted to know what your lips taste like." My heart started to beat faster. I had butterflies in my stomach. I kept saying to myself, *Bree, get it together. This is T'eo.* I took stepped closer and said, "T'eo, I'm scared." He said, "Of what? Love? Being treated with respect? Being treated like a lady? What are you scared of?" I stepped back, "No, I am not scared of love or being treated right. I am scared of getting my heart broken." I took another step back and said, "This cannot be real. Is this real? Was tonight real or am I dreaming?" T'eo stepped towards me and said, "Breana Anderson, your eyes are not playing tricks on you. This is real." I closed my eyes, his lips touched mine, and we kissed. He kissed my lips so softly, I had never been kissed like that. He brushed my hair back as he gently touched the back of my head. He looked me in the eyes and said, "Most definitely, this is real." He kissed me softly again. As we came up for air, he said, "Wow... That's how your lips taste! They are so soft and perfect." I smiled, "Your lips aren't too bad." I smiled and kissed him again and said, "Your lips are perfect too."

As I pulled my keys out of my purse T'eo said, "Breana the Brave, you are changing my life for the better—and I am loving it!" I smiled, kissed him again, opened the door and said, "I'm

loving it too. Thank you for a beautiful evening, Goodnight T'eo."
He blew me a kiss and said, "Goodnight, Breana the Brave."

I watched him as he got in his car. I waved as he pulled out of the driveway. I closed the door and laid back against it, as my breath was taken away. I smiled and said, "Goodness, he is some type of man." My daddy said, "What?" I jumped and said, "Daddy, you scared me!" He smiled, "My apologies, baby girl. I see you had a good night." I was blushing as I said, "It was perfect." I told him about what happened and how T'eo asked me out, about Brian being there and about T'eo and my first date. My daddy was smiling as he said, "I love to see you happy. See, I told you there are good men out there like me, and better." I laid my head on his arm and said, "I have never been treated with so much respect. It was natural, too. I'm scared, Daddy because this is too good to be true."

He kissed my cheek and said, "You sound like your mother. She said the same thing. She thought I was too good to be true. One thing's for sure, baby, when a man loves a woman, he will make sure he to do anything to make her happy, and nothing less. I love your mother and I knew I never ever wanted to lose her. I try my best to make her happy in any and every way possible. I want my girls to know there are good men out there, that is why I lead by example. I want my son to see how he should talk and treat a woman. Again, that is why I lead by example." I sat up as I looked at him and said, "Daddy, you are doing a phenomenal job! Because of you, I know how I should be treated as a young lady and as I grow into a woman. Thank you, Daddy. I am blessed to have a Daddy like you!" I hugged him tightly, kissed him on the cheek and said, "I love you, Daddy, good night!"

After I got out of the shower, I read a text from T'eo telling me he made it home. I called him and we talked all night long.

207

CHAPTER SIXTEEN

16

EVERY SINGLE DAY T'EO AND I HAVE ENJOYED EACH OTHER'S company over the Christmas break. The other day, he came over to have breakfast with me and my family. After breakfast, he helped my brother Luke and Daddy with the yard. They bonded over chopping and gathering some wood for the cold weather ahead. I was surprised that he and my mother have been getting along so well, to the point that my mother helped T'eo understand some concepts he didn't understand in some of his classes. My bother and T'eo have been hanging out a lot as well. A week ago, they went to get their hair cut and went out to brunch. Even Summer has gravitated to T'eo! A couple of days ago he came by to spend time with me but ended up playing soccer with Summer. My family and I are really enjoying his presence.

* * *

    Bright and early Summer is running through the house screaming, "It's Christmas!" She jumped on my bed yelling with excitement, "Get up Bree! Get up!" I rolled over and said, "Summer, give me five more minutes." Summer started jumping on my bed and said, "No! It's Christmas! Let's open our gifts!" I looked at the clock. It was six thirteen in the morning. As I rubbed my eyes I said, "Goodness, Summer it's still dark outside." My brother was leaning on my door, laughing. I sat up on my bed and said, "Shut up, Luke." Luke ran, jumped on my bed, and started to tickle me. I was laughing so hysterically. Summer started to tickle me too as I tried to catch my breath. I said, "Okay. Okay. I'm getting up." My parents stood by the door, smiling and laughing. Daddy said, "Vanessa, look at our beautiful children."

    We all had our pajamas on as we walked downstairs to open our gifts. Since Summer is the youngest, she opened her presents first. She got everything she wanted; a new bike, skates, soccer gear, clothes, and shoes. She was happy, and thanked Mother and Daddy. Daddy said, "Summer, you forgot to open a gift." Summer said, "No I didn't, Daddy, I opened all of them." My daddy pulled out a box and read it, "To Summer, from Mommy and Daddy with love!" Summer said, "Well... What is it?" My mother laughed and said, "Well... Open it." Summer took the wrapping paper off and it was a large plain brown box. She looked and said, "Hmmm, the box is naked." We laughed and said, "Naked?" She said, "Yes, normally a box has a picture or something on it." She ripped the tape off the box and opened it. She pulled a smaller box out of the big box and started to scream at the top of her lungs as she said, "No way! Oh, my gosh! The microscope set!" She ran in place for a minute and took off running around the house. My daddy had tears in his eyes as he said, "I love to see my family happy!" My mother caught sight of his tears and said, "Me too, honey, me too." Summer ran back into the family room as she ran and dove into my parents' arms and gave them a huge hug. She jumped for joy with gratitude, saying over and over again, "Thank you so much, Mommy and Daddy!"

My brother and I got some clothes and shoes. We both got a $200 Visa gift card and $500 BP gift card for gas. We thanked our parents as well because Lord knows, I needed the BP gas card! My mother got Daddy some tools for his yard supplies collection. She also got him a new lawn mower and a new tool belt. He was so happy! He got my mother a diamond pink rose necklace and bracelet set, some earrings, and a $600 gift certificate to her favorite salon and a $200 gift certificate to her favorite place to get her manicure and pedicure. My mother hugged and kissed him. One thing's for sure, my mother faithfully gets her hair done every two weeks and once a month she gets her toes and nails done.

My parents opened my gift. It was a 120-minute full body couples' massage, a 30-minute foot massage and a 30-minute sauna to their favorite spa. They were very happy! My daddy looked at my gift, smiled, and said, "Uh oh, baby you already know what time it is!" My mother started blushing as if she was a schoolgirl. I smiled because I always think my mother and daddy are so cute. My brother Luke said, "Really, Pops? Really? Come on, not in front of the kids!" Summer said, "What? What time is it, Daddy?" He replied, "7:34 a.m." We all started laughing. My parents gave me a hug and said, "Thank you." My brother gave my parents a jewelry cleaner set. Luke said, "Since you're always going to get your wedding bands and jewelry cleaned, now you can save time and clean it at home." My mother said, "Luke Senior, that will most definitely save us a lot of time." My daddy agreed and said, "Yeah, it is because I do not like walking around without my ring on in public when it's being cleaned. I want the world to know I am taken!" My mother smiled from ear to ear. My mother and daddy are so adorable.

* * *

Later that evening T'eo and his mother came by for dinner. She is such a pretty lady. She looked as though she was a native Indian with high cheekbones and straight black silky hair that touched her bottom. Her teeth were pearly white and her smile was so beautiful! As T'eo's mother and my parents talked while preparing dinner, T'eo and I exchanged gifts. He looked at me as he said, "This is for the most beautiful girl in the world." I smiled and said, "Thank you." I opened the box and it was a diamond heart necklace with a matching promise ring. I touched my heart and said, "Oh my, T'eo, this is beyond beautiful! Thank you!" T'eo looked me in the eyes and said, "With this ring, Breana Anderson, I promise not to break your heart. I promise to listen to your concerns and I will do my best to make you happy. I always want to fill your heart with joy, and your mind with peace, because I love you so much. Believe it or not, when I first saw you on campus you didn't know I existed, but when I saw you I said to myself, Wow! She's gorgeous! One day, she will be my lady. Bree, would you do me the honor of being my lady? I promise, Bree, I will not fail you." I looked T'eo in the eyes as well and said, "Yes, I would be more than happy to be your lady. I wouldn't have it any other way." He kissed me and said, "Bree, I love you with all my being."

I gave T'eo my gifts. He opened the first one. It was a letter. I told him to read it later. He opened the box and it was an outfit that he wanted. Weeks ago, we went to the mall and he saw this outfit that he really wanted, but he couldn't afford it because he used his money to help his mother with her bills and to buy a plane ticket for her to come see him. I saw in his eyes how badly he wanted the outfit. So I went back to get it. It was a pair of Old Navy dark rinse slim jeans, with a cute light blue long-sleeve shirt and a short sleeve dark blue polo shirt, and a leather belt. I got him a pink polo shirt too because I love to see him in pink. I also got him a gift card to Foot Locker so he could buy some shoes to go with his outfit. T'eo said, "Breana, no. I cannot take all of this." I looked at him, "Yes, you can. You worked so hard in school. You're always helping your mother out, and still, somehow, you keep your head above water. I wanted to do this for you. You deserve it." He teared up and said, "Wow... I never had anyone who would go out of their way like this for me." I smiled. I had tears in my eyes too. He said, "You really paid attention to what I was looking at in the store. Wow... that means a lot to me." He looked at the size and said with excitement, "Wait! You got the sizes right too!" I laughed and said, "I sure did." He hugged me and we kissed.

* * *

Time passed and we all sat at the table and ate Christmas dinner. It was lovely. My mother and Rosa, T'eo's mother, laughed and had a good conversation. Daddy, Luke, and T'eo were having a good conversation too. I looked at Summer and she was getting down to the nitty-gritty, eating. It was so wonderful to see everyone getting along. It brought so much love and joy into my heart.

* * *

After everyone pitched in and cleaned the dishes, kitchen, and dining room, we were stuffed as we all gathered in the family room to watch a movie. My mother asked Ms. Rosa and T'eo if they would like to stay to watch the movie with us. Summer, Luke and I gathered some blankets, while Mother and Ms. Rosa made hot cocoa for everyone. As for me, I preferred chamomile tea. My phone rang and it was Chloe. She said, "Open the door, we are getting out of the car." Chloe and her mother always watch Christmas movies with us every Christmas after dinner. It's been a tradition since we were in elementary school. Chloe had her pink blanket and matching pillow. Summer said, "Gosh, Confident Chloe! Are you moving in?" I laughed because she looked like she had more than a blanket and a pillow. My brother Luke asked, "Chloe, do you need help with your suitcase?" As she struggled, she said, "No I have it, thanks." As Summer arched her eyebrows she said, "Are you sure, because you are knocking stuff over." Luke got up off the couch and helped Chloe with her things. Chloe's mother greeted everyone and walked into the kitchen to help my mother and Ms. Rosa get the hot cocoa together.

I walked with Chloe as she went upstairs to my room. After she threw all her stuff on my bed, I laughed and asked, "How many nights are you staying?" Chloe fell on my bed and said, "I have no idea." I reached for my pillow and lay on the bed beside her. We both looked at the ceiling. I broke the silence and said, "What's been going on with you?" She turned her head and said, "Nothing much. I've been thinking a lot lately about if I should have enrolled in the Early College Program. I didn't want to do the extra work, but now I see that it would have been worth it." I said, "Chloe, in tenth grade, I begged you to enroll with me so we could start together in eleventh grade." Chloe said, "Yep, Bree, you sure did. You begged me and I said nope. Wish I would have listened." I sat up and said, "It is not the end of the world. You have good grades and we will apply for some scholarships together." Chloe said, "Bree, you are already busy,

I can't ask you to do that. You already have more than enough on your plate." She laid her head on my shoulder. I said, "Chloe, we are Yin and Yang, we stick together and help each other out. There is no such thing as being too busy for my best friend." Chloe gave me a hug and said, "Thank you, my Yin." I hugged her back and said, "You're welcome, my Yang." Chloe said, "I see Mr. Charm is downstairs. He must have come over for the movie?" I started to blush. "Nope. T'eo and his mother joined us for dinner. They are staying to watch the movie." Chloe jumped on the bed and said, "His mother's here?" I was still blushing as I replied, "Yep." Chloe said, "Damn, Bree. Are you-all a couple?" I smiled from ear to ear and said, "Yep!" Chloe screamed, "What! When were you going to tell me?" I said, "You didn't give me time. We just became a couple today. He gave me a promise ring and necklace. I bought him an outfit and gift card." Chloe said, "You got him the outfit you were telling me about that he couldn't afford because he wanted to fly his mother here for Christmas?" I nodded my head. "Yep." Chloe said, "Wow. Bree. That was nice of you. He knows you are a keeper!" My mother yelled and said, "Girls, come on down. We have to vote on which movie we are going to watch."

Chloe and I gathered our blankets and pillows and walked down the stairs. Ms. Rosa, Chloe's mother, and my mother passed out the hot cocoa. My mother handed me my tea as I walked into the family room. Before anyone could say anything, Summer said, "Can we watch The Polar Express? It's a family movie and everybody will stay awake." Ms. Rosa smiled and said, "How sweet. That's fine with me." My mother said, "Well, does every-one want to watch The Polar Express?" We all agreed. I sat in the middle between T'eo and Chloe. My mother and Daddy cuddled together as they sat on the couch. Summer lay on an air mattress. Luke was in his space, lying on the floor near Chloe.

Ms. Rosa made herself comfortable, she sat in the recliner and made herself at home. Chloe's mother sat on the loveseat as she cuddled up with a blanket. As the movie started, my daddy said, "Everyone better behave themselves." I cried, "Daddy!" He said, "I am serious. Make sure you two keep your hands to yourselves." T'eo said, "Most definitely, sir." I said, "Daddy, I am a good girl." He winked his eye at me and dimmed the lights.

* * *

Chloe and I slept in because we stayed up all night talking. T'eo and his mother left around midnight. When I walked down to the kitchen to make some tea, Summer was still sleeping in the family room. Luke was outside on the porch talking on the phone. My mother walked into the kitchen and said, "Good morning, baby." I gave her a hug and said, "Good morning, Mommy. How did you sleep?" She said, "I slept good, thanks for asking. How about you?" I looked at my mother, saying to myself *are you kidding me*? I said, "I do not know why Chloe never wants to sleep in the guestroom. She always takes over my bed. Every time I volunteer to sleep in the guestroom she always says, "I'm coming too." So, I just stay put. My mother smiled and said, "Well, it always been that way since you two were babies." Summer walked into the kitchen, rubbing her eyes and said, "Confident Chloe is afraid of the bogey man. That's why she wants to sleep in your bed with you." My mother and I laughed. Chloe crept up behind Summer, tickled her, and said, "I am not scared of the bogey man." Summer said, "Well... prove it and sleep in the guestroom." Chloe said, "Oh goodness, Summer." Summer shrugged her shoulders and said, "See...Confident Chloe. Well... Scary Chloe is afraid of the bogey man."

* * *

Chloe stayed for the entire weekend. I talked to T'eo a couple of times, but not for long because he wanted to spend as much time with his mother before she left. That gave me enough time to spend with Chloe. Chloe and I enjoyed each other's company. We stayed in the house watched movies, baked, cooked, we went to a couple of her meetings she put together for the girls and applied for as many scholarships as possible.

* * *

Today is New Year's Eve and I cannot believe the year is about to be over. It went by so fast! I had a lot of ups and downs, more downs than ups, but I look at each downfall as a stepping stone and a lesson learned. Luke was going to a New Year's Eve party. My parents were hanging out with their friends, and tonight, Summer and I were staying home. I wanted T'eo to come over, but I know my daddy isn't going to leave T'eo, Summer and me alone, so I didn't bother to ask. He always says, "Ask, and you will either get a yes or a no." I know for a fact I will get a no. I asked Chloe to come over, but she decided to go to a New Year's Eve party with Luke. You know, they have really been acting strange around me when they are together. I wonder if... Nah... can't be... but I wonder... do they have feelings for each other, or are they going out without telling me? I wandered around the house, trying to put two and two together. Luke never asked Chloe if she needed help but the other day, he asked her did she need help with her suitcase. Just last week, he sat with her at the dinner table and lay beside her as we watched the Christmas movie. I yelled Summer's name, maybe I need to ask her because she knows all the gossip. Summer walked in my room saying, "Gosh, Bree, what is it? Is the house on fire? Did someone break in the house?" I looked at her, rolled my eyes and said, "You know my room isn't on fire." Summer put her hand on her hip and said, "Well, you're yelling like the house is on fire and as if someone robbing the place." I said, "Anyway... look... have you noticed Chloe and Luke acting strange?" Summer sat on my bed and said, "Yes! He opened the door for her the other day, and you know Luke never goes out his way for Chloe. He asked her during Thanksgiving dinner did she want a refill on sweet tea. He refilled her cup. I was looking at them like, what is really going on?" I put my hand on my chin and said, "Summer, that is a good question. What is really going on? You know Chloe and Luke are going out to a party tonight." Summer yelled, "Together?" I looked at Summer, "Yes, Summer, together." Summer said, "Bree, there is something going on, and you know what? I am going to find out!"

* * *

Thirty more minutes before the New Year arrives. My phone rang, and it was Brian. I looked at it but I didn't answer. He sent a text saying, "Breana. I wanted to say Happy New Year. Can we talk please?" I didn't reply, I deleted it. I texted T'eo to see what he was doing. He called me. We talked until the New Year came in. We wished each other an abundant and prosperous 2019. We made a plan to make dinner at his house before his mother leaves to go back home. I was happy we made plans because the break is almost over and we have hardly spent time together. Summer was already sleep. After T'eo and I got off the phone I went to sleep as well.

CHAPTER SEVENTEEN

17

AS I OPENED MY EYES, I SMILED BECAUSE IT'S A NEW YEAR and a new me. I have a pep in my step because in a couple months I am optimistic that I will be graduating from BSU and high school. I have a lot of work cut out for me—but I am up for the challenge like always.

I hopped out of bed, looked at myself in the mirror and said to myself, *Breana Anderson, it is 2019, and this is your year!* As I looked in the mirror, I asked myself, *Breana are you happy?* I smiled as I replied, yes, because Breana's happiness starts from within. I washed my face, brushed my teeth and walked into my meditation room to meditate before I started my day.

* * *

T'eo picked me up today as we headed out to the store to pick up some groceries to cook dinner before his mother leaves to go back home. I noticed he was extremely quiet. I looked at him and his eyes were focused on the road—as it should be—but he didn't say a word or make a sound. That is not like T'eo. "Are you okay?" I asked. He nodded his head yeah. I looked out the window and didn't say anything. When we arrived at the store he said, "We are going to make an Italian dish called Orecchiette Cime di Rapa." I said, "That sounds yummy! What's in it?" Very quickly and dryly, he said, "It's pasta. The best thing about these noodles is they are perfect for holding whatever sauce we wish to add. We mix it with broccoli florets, chili flakes, anchovies, spinach, cheese, garlic, and of course, olive oil, and Parmesan to give it a creamy texture and flavor. We are going to make pesto from fresh basil, toasted pine nuts, garlic, Parmesan cheese, and spread it on focaccia bread which we are going to make from scratch as well," he said quickly, as if he didn't really want to explain it all to me, and I was really turned off because I felt like he didn't want to be bothered. I said, "Oh, okay." We walked silently around the store as we gathered the ingredients. As we put the groceries in the car, I couldn't take it anymore; I had to break the silence. I looked at T'eo and said, "What is wrong? Do not tell me that you are okay and everything is good, either. Do you not want to be bothered today? I am not going to walk around all day with you acting bitter and having a nasty attitude. At least tell me what is the problem. If you say everything is okay, then cool, take me home, because I am not feeling your "okay" energy. I did not sign up for this today."

T'eo rolled his eyes and sucked his teeth as we drove off. I unbelted my seatbelt, put my purse on my shoulder and said, "Pull over and let me out. I am not up for this shit today." T'eo said, "Bree. You are talking crazy." I said, "Maybe, because you are not saying anything at all. Pull over and I will call my daddy or brother to pick me up." He kept driving. I yelled and said, "T'eo, pull the car over!" T'eo pulled the car over. I unlocked the door and reached for the handle and opened the door. T'eo reached for the handle as he tried to close the door said, "Breana, chill out." I looked at him and said, "I am not up for the silent treatment today, especially knowing I didn't do anything to deserve this shit. I asked you a couple times what's wrong, and you want to act like a complete ass." T'eo cut me off and said, "Bree, my father called me today for the first time in fourteen years." I was in shock as I put my hand over my mouth and said, slowly, "Are you serious? Oh, my gosh, are you okay?" T'eo gripped the steering wheel and squeezed it tightly and said, "He had the nerve to asked me how am I doing. I asked him, what does he want? He said, I want to know how you are doing, son. I heard that you are in college. I am proud of you. I asked him, who told you that? And what do you mean, you are proud of me? None of my achievements are thanks to you. You left my mother and me, remember? You should be asking how my mother's doing? You left us without a pot to pee in. You left us with one piece of bread to share while my mother starved as she fed me. He tried to explain himself, Bree, but I told him. I don't want to hear his senseless excuses. Bree, he had the nerve to say, I did not call to hear about your mother. I called to see how you are doing and to hear your voice. Bree, I was filled with rage. I told him he is fourteen years too late, and if he doesn't care about my mother, how could he care about me? Before I hung up, I told him he should thank my mother and be honored that she raised a man alone. After that, I hung up and blocked his number."

I didn't know what to say. I could only say, "T'eo, I'm sorry. You deserve so much better, and your mother as well." T'eo didn't say anything, he just hugged me as he cried and said, "Bree, I always wondered why wasn't I good enough for my father. I always wondered why he didn't help my mother take care of me. Why... Bree? Why now...? Why does he want to come back into my life after the hard work is done? If I wasn't in school, he probably wouldn't have called me. I am not letting him back into my life. He is not wanted or welcome."

I held T'eo in my arms as he lay on my chest. I wiped his tears and said softly, "It's going to be okay. One thing's for sure, you cannot run from this. You are entitled to feel pain, hurt, and you most definitely need to get it off your chest and tell your father how you feel. It is not for him, T'eo it is for you. That way, you can let go without a heavy heart. You will be able to live your life knowing your father knows exactly how you feel." He cried and cried as he said, "Bree, I do not want to see him. He is dead to me." I didn't know what to say. He continued, "Bree, I am so sorry I took it out on you. I am sorry." I rubbed his head and said, "No apology needed. It's okay. I understand. Know you can always talk to me about anything." T'eo asked me if I could drive back to his house while he got himself together because he didn't want his mother to see him upset. As I took over the wheel, he said, "Bree, you are amazing." I smiled and said, "Look who's talking, you are beyond amazing, you are strong-willed, a good son to your mother, a good friend, and a man to me." I reached over, touched his hand as he interlocked our fingers. He kissed my hand and said, "I am truly blessed." I smiled as I kept my eyes on the road and said, "I am truly blessed too."

* * *

Ms. Rosa hugged me as I set foot in the door. She said, "Hola! Breana! It is so nice to see you again." I replied, "Thank you kindly! It's so nice to see you too!" She kissed me on the cheek and said, "You are such a beautiful girl." I smiled and said, "Thank you." As T'eo walked in the door he said, "Well, I know for a fact I am getting a great workout, going up and down these steps with all these groceries." I laughed and said, "Look on the bright side, at least it will count towards your 10,000 steps." He looked at me as he put the bags on the counter and said, "Bree has an answer for everything." I made a funny face and replied, "You better know it." I continued and asked, "Do you need any help?" T'eo looked at me with a smirk and said, "Really? People are a trip, they watch you do all the work, and then want to ask do you need help when you are almost done so they can take the credit. People nowadays…" I walked over and hugged him and said, "Well, sweetie, you shouldn't complain about doing the work if you don't want assistance after someone offered to help you. It's not about if you're almost done with the task or not, it's about allowing someone to help if you need an extra hand." T'eo said, "Um, Bree, excuse me." I laughed and said, "My pleasure. You cannot say I didn't offer my assistance."

Ms. Rosa started to sing as she took the food out of the bag. I closed my eyes and listened to the melody and asked her, "Ms. Rosa, what are you singing?" She humbly smiled as she said, "You are my Sunshine." When I was carrying my T'eo I used to sing that to him. After he was born, I sang that to him as well. I also sing it to him as a grown man. It brings me great joy in my heart." She started back singing, "You are my sunshine, my only sunshine." T'eo walked in and he heard his mother singing, he started to sing as he took her hand and danced with her, "Please don't take my sunshine away." That was a beautiful sight to see.

We prepped the food and started to cook. I looked at the pasta and said, "They look like ears." Ms. Rosa started to laugh and said happily, "Si, they do! I love them because they store the sauce. Just wait and see! Your taste buds are going to be so grateful!" I smiled and said, "I can't wait. My mouth is watering." I took the garlic out the bag, washed them and cut them up so they would be ready when we make the pesto. T'eo washed off the broccoli and spinach, cut them up and put them the pan. As they started to steam, the aroma smelled so good! Ms. Rosa put some herbs in the pan as she stirred the vegetables. T'eo started to make the dough for the bread. I walked over and offered my assistance. He looked at me, smirked, and said, "You don't know anything about making homemade bread." I told him, "Nope. I don't. I am here to learn." Our fingers were playing together in the dough. I was getting all warm inside and goosebumps because he looked so sexy. As we seasoned the dough, Ms. Rosa flipped the dough, saying, "We have to show the dough some love." She flipped the dough as if we were about to make some pizza. T'eo started to make the pesto. He asked me to get the food processor as he washed the fresh basil. It smelled so good. He said, "Bree, I am going to let you make the pesto." I said in a panic, "No... No... I will burn it. No... I do not want to burn the food." Ms. Rosa and T'eo laughed so hard as they said, "You cannot burn pesto in the food processor." I looked relieved. T'eo stood behind me and said, "First things first, put in the basil." He then slid his hands gently down my arms and said, "We are going to measure the pine nuts and pour them into the food processor." I was blushing as I said, "T'eo, your mother is in here. We can't be doing all of this." He kissed my cheeks and said, "It's better to show love than to show hate. Don't you agree?" I continued to blush, "Yeah, but your mother is in here." I looked over, and his mother wasn't in the kitchen. T'eo said, "See, Ms. Anderson, you worry too much. Just go with the flow and relax." He reached for the olive oil and garlic. I took hold of the olive oil and T'eo put his hand on top of mine as he said, "We can freely pour the oil in and add the garlic." I was in a daze for a minute. He said loudly, "Bree! Wait! You are pouring too much oil." I said, "Well... you said we can pour the oil freely." T'eo replied, "Bree, you were being too generous." As he put in the Parmesan, he put a little in his mouth and said, "This cheese is so fresh." We started the food processor. Afterwards, T'eo took a spoon, scooped a little of the sauce and fed it to me. It was so delicious! I returned the favor and he said, "I am loving this!" I laughed, "You love everything I do!" He replied, "I sure do... I don't see any harm in that." Ms. Rosa ran back in the kitchen in a rush saying over and over again, "El pan. El pan." T'eo told her, "Mother, it's not burnt." He pulled it out of the oven, kissed his mother on the cheek and said, "See. Es perfecto!" Ms. Rosa said, "Breana, I have a good chico. He is so loving and patient." I smiled and agreed.

It was time to eat, and the food smelled so good! We sat at the table and talked about whatever came to mind. When I tasted the pasta "ears" the sauce melted in my mouth as it smoothly massaged my taste buds. As I covered my mouth I said, "Ms. Rosa, oh my goodness the sauce is perfect! I see what you mean when you said the noodles savor the taste. It is delicious!" I had seconds and made a to-go box to take home.

Later that evening we all cleaned up and sat outside near the fire pit in T'eo's apartment complex and looked at the stars in the sky. It was a perfect day!

CHAPTER EIGHTEEN

18

SCHOOL IS BACK IN SESSION! I AM SO READY TO GET THIS SEMESTER out of the way. I have everything jotted down on my calendar and everything is in order. All of my classes are on Monday and Wednesday from 9 a.m. through 5 p.m. The best part is that they are all back to back and I do not have to wait around campus for my next class to start. It's kind of a Catch 22 because I do not have a break in between classes. I will take advantage of the ten-minute break as I switch classes in order to eat something. Tuesday and Thursday will be my study days. Since soccer season will be starting soon, I will study when I take Summer to soccer practice. I cut my hours at work so I will only work on Saturdays. Sunday is my rest day. I cannot afford to fail any classes. This semester is make it or break it. I cannot afford to be distracted. My main goal is to graduate with an Associate Degree. I've outweighed my options with the credits I've earned—when I complete my classes this semester, I will be able to obtain an Associate of Science degree.

I called T'eo on my way to school to see if he was on campus. His first class starts at 11 a.m. I told him to have a wonderful and productive day and I will text him in between classes. As I walked into Anatomy II my professor, Dr. Robinson, was wearing casual blue jeans, a blue sweater, and he had on white tennis shoes. He had a fade and a thick mustache, sideburns and his skin was the color of dark chocolate. He greeted me and said, "Welcome, Ms. Anderson." I smiled, waved, and said, "Hello, Dr. Robinson." Everyone in the class was looking at me as if I was a celebrity. There was a dude with pimples all over his face, and his teeth look gross—he looked like he had a nasty yuck mouth. He said something about me to another dude with pimples on his face that look liked he had traced the puzzle from a kid's menu on his face, "I thought she would have transferred schools." They both laughed. I tried to ignore him, but he kept running his yuck mouth. I turned around and said, "Dude, I am right here. If you have something to say, say it to me." He and his friend laughed. I laughed back and said, "What the hell have you been doing? Chewing on rocks? You need to brush your teeth with your nasty yuck mouth." The class started laughing at him. He stopped laughing and said, "Dr. Robinson, did you hear that?" His friend said, "Yeah, Dr. Robinson." I looked at them as I arched my eyebrows and said, "You and your friend who has connected the dots on his face are little punks. You can dish it out, but you can't take it when someone retaliates. The both of you need to grow up." I turned back around and said, "For your information, I am not going anywhere. If you don't want to see my face then I suggest that you transfer. If not, get used to seeing me around." I opened my notebook and said, "Dr. Robinson, I apologize for being rude and interrupting your class. I had to set a couple of people straight, the ones who said something and the ones who didn't have the balls to say anything at all." Dr. Robinson smiled and said, "Well, Ms. Anderson, no apology is needed. To be honest, I would have taken the same route you took. Sometimes people need to be put in their place the first time around. That way, they know exactly where you stand." I nodded my head and said, "I agree, sir."

What a coincidence, the two ass holes were in my 11 o'clock Anatomy II lab. Dr. Robinson walked in, smirked a little and said, "We all meet again." I was looking like, ugh, this is going to be a long semester. I got myself together and said to myself, *you know why you are 0here—to graduate with an Associate in Science.* Dr. Robinson pulled out two human brains and a pail filled with sheep brains. He said, "Welcome to Anatomy II lab. Normally, some professor goes over the syllabus, but as for me, just like in our lectures, I am going to get right down to business. As we discussed the anatomy of the human brain in our first Anatomy II lecture, we are going to identify the structure of the brain, and we will dissect the sheep brain. Next week you will have your first lab exam and it will be about the sheep and the human brain." As he passed out a thick package he said, "This package is information on the brain. Do not get used to me handing out packages. It is going to be your job to do your own research. This is a one-time thing just to give you all a head start." After he walked around and passed out the last package he said, "Okay, let's get started." As time went by, I was engaged in my lab and lecture, however, my brain was fried.

As I walked out of the lab, I thought to myself, *will this be too much? Maybe I shouldn't have taken classes back to back. Am I putting the cart before the horse?* All kinds of negative thoughts were running through my mind. I walked into the ladies' room to wash my face because I was overwhelmed and it was the first day of school. "Hey, Breana," said a girl who had about twenty earrings in her ears. I said, "Hello." She said "I know you do not know me. My name is Ruby. I want you to know you are brave and strong. I might be older than you, but I want to be like you when I grow up. I am working on speaking up. You have given me strength. I want to say thank you." I really didn't know what to say, because from looking at her she seemed like she would stomp someone in the ground if they came at her wrong. I guess it is true that looks are deceiving. As I pulled some paper towels out, I said, "You are more than welcome. I really don't know what to say, but I do know that once you speak up, your soul will feel lighter and at peace." She looked in the mirror and said, "Peace sounds good. Setting my soul free sounds good as well." I knew I had to get to class but I couldn't leave her in the bathroom, talking like she was going to commit suicide.

I called Chloe. "Hey, Yin! You called me just in time. Since it's an early day for me I was about to put my car in drive and head home. I've been practicing not texting and driving." She said as she chewed the hell out a piece of gum. "Hey, Yang," I said, sounding concerned. She said, "Bree, are you okay?" "I am fine," I replied. I continued, "I am in the bathroom with someone I just met. Her name is Ruby. I was calling to get information on the classes you started to help girls that are..." Chloe cut me off and said, "Put me on speaker." I put her on speaker. Chloe said, "Hi, Ruby? Are you okay? Do you need any assistance or help? Do you need for someone to call 911?" I was looking like wow... this is Chloe talking? Ruby started crying and said, "No, I do not need anyone to call 911. I am tired of being mistreated and taken advantage of. Nobody believes me." Chloe said gently, "Ruby, I believe you." I looked at Ruby and said, "Ruby, I believe you too. What's going on?" She said, "Dr. Wright touched me too." I hugged her and said, "Ruby, trust me when I say you are not alone. I believe you." Chloe said, "Ruby you are more than welcome to come to our meeting, it's on Tuesday at 7 p.m." Chloe asked Ruby for her number and sent her the information. I said, "Thank you, Chloe, I will call you later. Love you." Chloe said, "Love you too."

I asked Ruby for her number and I called my lawyer. Ruby gave me her information to give to my lawyer. As Ruby and I walked down the hallway, Ruby said, "It's awful how people judge a person because of how they look or what they have on. It shouldn't matter. We all are human." I agreed with Ruby. I told her she should attend the meeting. I gave her my lawyer's number and I reassured her that she wasn't alone.

I was late for calculus. As I walked in, my professor, Dr. Gilbert, was writing on the dry board as she said, "I do not accept tardiness. Next time you decide you want to walk in my class late. Don't." I said, "Yes, ma'am. My apologies." Dr. Gilbert looked over and said with excitement, "Good afternoon, Breana!" I waved my hand and said, "Hello, Dr. Gilbert. I apologize again for walking into class late." She said, "Oh, do not worry about it, if you walked in late, there must be a good reason." I said, "Yes, ma'am, there was." She looked at me and waited for an explanation. I looked at her and said, "Dr. Gilbert, it's personal." She said, "Okay. Well... I hope your personal matters are worked out." I didn't say anything, I just walked up the steps and took a seat. I was playing catch-up because she had two boards filled with notes and she started on the third dry board. My fingers were numb, but I had to keep writing. After Dr. Gilbert dismissed class, I was still writing math problems in my notes. I knew I was going to be late to Economics as well, but I had to finish writing down my notes.

When I walked into my econ class, it was empty. I walked back out and looked at the room number. It said 511. I looked at my schedule to make sure I was in the right place. I looked on the door and it was a note saying, *Class is canceled for today.* Thank goodness! I was relieved. I sat in the empty classroom with my head on the table to collect my thoughts. I then gathered my things and headed home.

When I walked in the door I said hello to my daddy. He said, "Baby girl, how was your day?" I said, "Daddy, you don't want to know." He replied, "Yes, I do." I took off my shoes and told him, "It was long. I had to put two boys in their place. It's the first day of school and I have so much work to study. I am grateful that Econ was canceled. A girl name Ruby said Dr. Wright touched her too. Ugh. I had a lot going on today." My mother walked out of her office and said, "Gosh, sweetie, you had a long rough day. Is that young lady okay?" I took a breather and said, "I guess so. I called Chloe and she was a pro—she handled the situation very well because I didn't know what to do. Chloe invited her to the self-help group she came up with. I called our lawyer and hopefully, they talked." My daddy said, "I am waiting to hear about you putting the boys in their place. I didn't want to cut your mother off because it seems like you took care of the problem but I want to know what happened with those boys." I was tired as I said, "Daddy, it's not important, and yes, I took care of them. One boy said he thought I would have left the school. But I came back with fire and shut him up." He asked, "So you are okay?" I walked over and hugged him and said, "I am more than fine, Daddy. Thanks for asking. I am about to go to my room and study. I have an exam next week."

Summer came into my room and said, "I heard you had a rough day. Do you need me to do anything for you?" I had a pencil in my mouth and a black pen in my hand as I was writing notes and said, "No, I don't need anything, thanks for asking." Summer started to walk out of my room as she said, "Okay.

You're welcome." Her ponytail was swinging from side to side as she picked up the pace. I asked, "Hey Summer, how was your day?" Summer replied, "Bree, I see that you are studying. I don't want to bother you." I stood up and said, "I need to stretch my legs and body anyway. What's going on?" Summer said, "Nothing." I hit her on her leg softly and said, "Hey, this isn't like you. Talk to me." I opened my closet and got two PINK blankets out and said, "Come on, let's sit on the swing outside in the back near the fire pit and talk." As we went down the stairs I walked into my mother's office and asked her if she didn't mind making Summer and I some tea because we were going to have a little talk in the backyard. My mother was more than happy to make us some tea.

Summer and I cuddled up together to keep each other warm. She laid her head on my shoulder and said, "Some of the girls that didn't have boobs last year all of a sudden have boobs. I have a flat chest and all of the boys says I have a chalkboard chest." I looked at Summer and said, "They are lame." I continued, "Your boobs are going to grow before you know it. You already have 'mosquito bites'. Look on the bright side, at least you do not have to worry about your breasts moving all over the place when you are playing soccer." Summer made a face and said, "Oh my gosh, I didn't think about that. If my boobs grow, they are going to get in my way." I laughed, "Well...you'll have to wear a sports bra to keep them in place." Summer said, "I feel so much better because I do not want anything to get in the way of my playing soccer." Mother brought some tea and asked us what we were talking about. Summer told her. Mother smiled and said, "Aww, honey, you know what? Your breasts will form sooner and faster than you know it." Daddy heard the conversation and said, "Those boys are mad because you be tearing their butts up in soccer. Do not let them get in your head."

Summer smiled like the Grinch and said, "You're right, Daddy, they know I am better than them, and they will find any excuse to try to distract me. I am bringing the storm like I always do!" He replied, "Yeah, see baby, that's my kind of thinking." Summer said, "I love my family. Thank you." She looked up at me and said, "Bree, thank you for making time for me even though you were studying." I hugged her, "Anything for my baby sister." Summer cuddled on me, and our parents decided to join us. We all talked about our day and later that evening, called it a night.

CHAPTER NINETEEN

T'EO ISN'T HAPPY WITH ME. HE'S BEEN TRYING TO HANG OUT FOR A couple weeks but I haven't had the time. I called off at work two weekends straight. I've been studying nonstop. I am overwhelmed with so many assignments that are due. I do not have time to take a break. If I do, I will lose track of time and fall behind. He's in college, so he should understand.

I had books all over my bed when my daddy knocked on my door and said, "Bree, you have company." I didn't look up, I had a yellow highlighter in my right hand, an orange highlighter in my left hand and a red pen in my mouth. He repeated, "Bree. You have company." I spit the pen out of my mouth as I continued to study my notes and said, "Daddy, tell them to come back another day. I cannot hang out right now."

He leaned on my door and said, "Bree, look at me." I slowly looked up and said, "Yes, Daddy." He said, "I know you have goals, and that's great, baby girl, but for weeks you've been penned up in your room studying. You got to give yourself a break." I didn't say anything. I just looked at him as I blinked my eyes. He said, "Bree, I am serious. You are going to stress yourself out with all work and no play. Give yourself a break. Just for a couple hours." I said, "Daddy, who's downstairs?" He looked at me as he folded his arms and said, "T'eo." I said, "Daddy." He said, "I do not want to hear it, Bree. This young man's been calling the landline day and night and calling Luke, trying to get in touch with you. What you are doing isn't right. It's not right at all." I said, "But Daddy…" He said, "Remember this…we all make time for who and what we want too." I closed my books and notebooks and said, "Okay, let me freshen up. I will be downstairs in a couple of minutes."

T'eo was sitting on the couch, looking out the window, deep in thought. I put my hands in my purple sweat pants. I then took them out and put my hands in my PINK hoodie. I cleared my throat and he looked up. I said, "Hi." He replied, "Hello, stranger." I felt guilty, but I said, "How am I a stranger? You act like you haven't heard from me in years." T'eo said with a straight face, "I've heard from you by text 80% of the time. When we talk on the phone the conversation is extremely short, and we haven't spent quality time with each since we cooked dinner for my mother." I said, "But… we have seen each other." T'eo looked at me as if he was saying, Bree, are you serious. He said, "Breana, the only time we've seen each other is when we are passing by each other going to go to class. Yes, we speak here and there, but Breana, I'm sure you know just as well as I know, that is not quality time."

I looked down at the floor as I begin to swing my foot from side to side and said, "T'eo, I apologize. This might sound cold-hearted, but I have to graduate with an Associate degree. I've worked so hard through high school to complete all my high school classes in tenth grade. I also worked hard for two years, including going to summer school, to earn enough credits to graduate from college as well. That way, my credit will transfer over and I will have two years left to get my Bachelor's degree. I want to graduate with my Masters at the age of twenty-two so I can start my career or go to medical school. I would think you would understand how important school is to me."

T'eo sounded frustrated when he replied, "Of course I understand how important school is to both of us. However, Bree, I would think you would have made a little time for me." I didn't say anything because I was saying to myself, *he just doesn't get it.* He said, "Well. Maybe I should let you get back to studying. I just wanted to stop by to make sure you were still alive and well." I reached out to give him a hug, but he said, "Bree, you don't know how much I want to hug you right now, but I'd rather pass. I refuse to ease your guilty conscience." I threw my hands in the air and said, "Okay, T'eo. Really? I think you are in your feelings and taking this way too far." T'eo was walking towards the door. He turned around and said, "You think I am taking it way too far? I think Breana Anderson needs to look in the mirror. If you decide to look in the mirror, you need to tell yourself to get used to being lonely with your books, career and being by yourself. I love you, Bree, but I see you don't know how to handle being in a relationship and school at the same time." I didn't say anything. I looked at T'eo as he stepped one foot out the door and said, "I think we should break up because this isn't what I signed up for." He closed the door and I didn't go after him. Maybe he's right, I am not ready for a relationship—school comes first. I walked upstairs and started where I left off in my Anatomy book.

* * *

The semester is going by extremely fast and I am trying to keep my head above water. Every now and then, I run into T'eo. I'll speak and try to hold a conversation, but he always says he is too busy to talk and he has to get to his next class. I miss talking to him. I miss being in his presence too. I believe I messed up a good thing, but I wish he would understand how much my future means to me. I've worked hard to prosper, not to fail. I couldn't stress over T'eo because I had an exam in all my classes today. I was struggling the first couple of weeks in all of my classes. I pencil in my schedule to take advantage of tutorial sessions on Tuesdays and Thursdays. They've helped me out a lot. Now, I am on a straight path—I have all A's and one B in calculus.

* * *

Sundays are supposed to be a relaxing day. I never followed the rules for Sunday, because I am always studying. My mother walked into my room and said, "Bree the science kid! When are you going to take a break? Ever since school started you haven't hung out with anyone. I haven't seen Chloe or T'eo." I kept my head in the books and I said, "Mommy, I talked to Chloe this morning and yesterday. I talk to her every day. We haven't been out in a while because we've both been pretty busy, but we talk faithfully every single day." I reached for my highlighter and said with excitement, "Here is the answer! Darn it, it took me hours to find this answer." I looked at my mother and said, "You know, professors always say read this chapter or that chapter, but the answers are not in the chapters they ask us to read. I found the answer I've been looking for in Chapter 46."

My mother didn't say anything. I looked up to see if she was still there, and she was shaking her head as she sat in the chair with her legs crossed. I looked at her, my face confused, and asked, "Did I say something wrong?" She smiled and said,

"No, honey, you didn't say anything wrong. We are so proud of you. So proud. But you have been cooped up in this room as if you are held hostage in a dungeon." As I flipped the pages in my Econ book I said, "Mommy, my room isn't a dungeon—I have a lot of natural light shining in. My room is peaceful, Mom. I know what you are getting at. T'eo, right?" I put a bookmark on the page I was reading, closed my book and said, "Mommy, Daddy and I already had this talk. I really like T'eo. He is a good guy, but Mommy, it seems like nobody understands how hard I've worked to get here. I am almost at the finish line. I have to finish, Mom. I have to. I am doing this for me. If I do not do this for myself and fail, I am going to resent everyone who pushed me to do something that distracted me from my goal. It just feels like you all do not understand. I feel like you are all pushing me on T'eo. I know he exists. I know he's a good guy and he has a lot going on for himself, but I have a lot going on for myself too. It's already hard for women in the world today. I just want to make my mark and look back from time to time to admire my accomplishments. I just wish everyone would understand me."

My mother looked at me and said with great concern, "Honey, we understand you've worked so hard and we will not ever take that from you. Yes, you are almost at the finish line but remember, you didn't get there by yourself. You had help from your family and friends. We all are rooting for you. We are all your number one fans and we all want nothing but the best for you. We are not pushing you on T'eo. No, not at all. We do know he is a good young man who wants the best for you too. Although you haven't spoken to him, he calls us to see how you are doing on a daily basis."

I said, "What? When I talk to him in school, he acts like he doesn't want to talk to me. So, I take the bitter with the sweet. I am respectful and keep it moving." My mother walked over to my bed, rubbed my back and said, "He cares. When someone puts your needs and wants before theirs and respects your feelings, they care. He honored what you asked him to do—he gave you space while you focused on your studies." My face was confused and I looked at her and said, "Oh, okay. He is playing the innocent role." I threw my hands in the air and said, "He was the one who broke up with me." My mother said, "I know, honey, he was hurt, and he gave you what you asked for." I was upset and I responded, "Well... maybe I should send him a thank you letter. I'm over this. May I please get back to studying? I've wasted more than enough time talking about T'eo." My mother kissed me on the forehead and said, "Yes you may get back to studying. Dinner will be ready within an hour or so."

* * *

For days T'eo had been on my mind. I missed hearing his voice. I missed spending time with him. I took a break from studying as I ran down the steps, I asked my parents was it okay if I went to Chloe's self-improvement meetings. My daddy was reading the papers and my mother was doing something on her laptop as they said in a shocked tone, "Sure." My daddy looked at my mother as if his eyes were going to pop out his head. She looked at him and smiled. I said, "Come on guys, give me a break." Summer was lying on the floor doing her homework. She kept her eyes on her paper as she said, "The hermit came out of her cave." I laughed and said, "Come on guys. Cut it out. Gosh, is it a crime to study? Is it a crime to have a plan? It is a crime to..." Summer cut me off and said, "Please, Bree. Please... yes, it's a crime if you are not enjoying life. Life is supposed to be lived, not holding yourself hostage in a room filled with books. You're robbing yourself of happiness, Bree." I said, "Summer. Ms. Know-It-All." Summer answered, "No, I am Summer who has the common sense to not put a shield over my life. I share my love with the people I love. Bree, you share what you want to share when it is a good time for you. That's called being selfish." My daddy looked at me and didn't say a word. My mother smiled. I said, "Oh, okay, I know where this conversation is headed." I gave everyone a hug and said, "Well, let me get my selfish butt out of here."

I'd passed the place about a million times. It was in a cute little white church. I'd always thought the church was abandoned. As I walked in, I put my hair up in a bow and straightened out my shirt. I heard people talking but I couldn't find the room. I walked down a hallway that turned into a small eating area. Voices begin to become clearer as I walked past three small rooms. They were in a huge cafeteria in the back. When I walked in it was so bright, and I instantly felt the love because of the energy that was in the room. Instead of sitting in a circle, they used their chairs to form a heart; which was too cute.

Chloe was leading the discussion. She said, "Repeat after me; I am important. I am healthy. I am smart. I am in love with myself." She looked up and said as her voice changed and filled with joy as she saw me, "I am loved." She walked over to me with her arms spread wide as she embraced me with a hug. I hugged her back and she said, "Everyone, this is Breana. She is my sister, my best friend, and the Yin to my Yang." Everyone said, "Hello." A couple of people said, "That is Brenna the Brave." A girl walked up to me. She had to be around Summer's age. She had on what looked like an extra-large shirt, baggy jeans, and shoes that looked as if they were extremely too small. She had beautiful hair, but it was all over the place. Her skin was pale and she had a sandwich in her hand as she said, "How are you doing, Breana the Brave?" I smiled and replied, "I am fine, thank you. How are you doing?" She had the cutest smile and said, "I am fine, better than ever, thank you." I said, "That sounds awesome. What is your name?" She said, "My name is Katie." As I shook her hand I said, "Well... hello, Katie." I smiled and walked over to take a seat.

Chloe said, "We are about to touch bases on what we are thankful for." This one lady with long beautiful hair and a couple of teeth missing in her mouth said, "I am thankful to be alive." There was another lady who had on a black suit with a white blouse she said, "I am thankful for my job." The little girl Katie said, "I am thankful and happy to see Breana the Brave." I smiled. I looked over and saw Ruby, who looked at me and said, "I am thankful that people make time for others. I hope they realize they are blessings and angels walking on earth." Chloe said, "I am thankful for my family, friends, and for everyone in this meeting." It was my turn. I said, "I am thankful that I am loved by my family and friends. I am thankful for my journey. I am thankful to be healthy and alive. I am most definitely thankful for those who never gave up on me."

As the meeting proceeded, it was time for a light snack. There were tuna fish sandwiches, mixed fruits, bottles of water, and mixed nuts. I walked over to Ruby and told her she looked so refreshed. She said, "Thank you. I feel good. I was on my last legs and I just didn't have the strength to live anymore until you walked into my life at the right time. Chloe has been such a blessing. I talked to your lawyer, well... our lawyer. If I have to take the stand, I am going to speak my truth. Thank you for not being afraid to talk to me. Most people judge me and think I am a freak but you really gave me a second chance at life. ...and I am loving it." I said, "No problem. Us ladies have to stick together."

After the meeting, Chloe and I talked for hours. It was wonderful to see my bestie. I said, "I didn't know you had all of this going on. I didn't know it was this deep and heartfelt. That is wonderful, Chloe! You are changing so many people's lives." Chloe said, "This is my dream. I know my calling. I am going to start a non-profit for young girls and women. You gave me the name of it when you said to Ruby, us women have to stick together. How does that sound? I told her, "That sounds perfect!" Chloe said, "I started off at zero. I used to be in this big room waiting for people to come in. As the weeks went by I had maybe one person. Now I have eight people and it is going to grow." I smiled, "Wow, Chloe that is amazing!" Chloe said, "Yin, I am going to school to be a psychiatrist so I can help women. We as women go through a lot, and most of the time it is ignored. Not on my watch. I am going to do something about it." I replied, "I believe in you, Confident Chloe!"

I asked Chloe about Katie and she said, "Katie resides in a children's program down the street. I just so happened to see her at the church all the time and I asked her caregiver if it would be okay if she attended the meeting. She agreed."

I said, "Oh, wow."

Chloe said, "Yeah, I know what you are thinking. Just like you, that little girl is going places in life." I responded, "Correction, just like us she's going places in life." After Chloe locked the church up, we went to get something to eat. It felt so good talking to my best friend. I'd missed our long conversations.

I called Chloe to let her know I made it home. We continued the conversation we had during dinner. I talked to her about T'eo. Chloe reminded me to keep it straightforward and that T'eo isn't Brian. I had to reassure her that I am not putting up a wall, I just have goals that I've set and have to accomplish. I also told her what Summer had said. Chloe laughed, "Leave it up to Summer to speak the truth. She's going to do it!" I laughed. My face looked serious when I said, "Summer was right. I've been selfish and mean towards the people I love and who love me."

Chloe made sure I understood that I shouldn't shut people out and I have to learn how to juggle the things I need to do for myself, family and friends. I told Chloe how much I missed T'eo and she said, "Well... call him." I told her that was so much easier said than done. She replied, "Maybe, but you are going to miss out on a winner because of how much time you put into crying over spilled milk. That isn't fair. It is time for you to own up to what you've been doing." I agreed with Chloe, "Yeah, you, my mom, brother, sister, and T'eo are right. I am going to reach out to T'eo and hope he will talk to me." Chloe laughed, "Girl, please. He is miserable and waiting on your call." I told her, "I am doing to do something special." Chloe said, "Ugh, it better not be something I wouldn't do." I laughed again, "Ugh, Hell, no. I am not talking about that kind of special." I continued, "Speaking of you, what's been going on with you?" Chloe replied, "For the first time I have no drama and nothing to tell. I want to start the non-profit, go to school and take it from there." She continued, "Wow. We are seniors. Our life is just beginning." I laid on my bed and said, "Yeah, can you believe it? I remember when we were in grade school—time goes by so fast." Chloe agreed. "It sure does. That is why we cannot waste time because life is too short." She continued, "Well, Yin, I am tired and beat. I am about to shower and call it a day. It was good seeing you. I enjoyed spending time with you." I smiled and said, "It was wonderful seeing you too. I enjoyed our talk. My Yang, you are the best and I thank you for everything." We said goodnight and that we loved each other, and called it a day.

CHAPTER TWENTY 20

I HAD AN APPOINTMENT WITH MY HIGH SCHOOL COUNSELOR today so we could talk about where I am and what I have to do to get where I need to be. As I walked through the halls, I must say I do not miss this place. I noticed all the red, white and pink balloons and realized that it was Valentine's Day.

There were a few people in the hallway saying hello and waving. Of course, I spoke and waved back. I looked at the time as I hurried to Mrs. Morgan's office. I didn't want to run into any-one, since classes were still in session. I was told by the secretary that Mrs. Morgan had an emergency and she had to leave work early today, but she'd left me a package to look over.

As I walked quickly down the hallway, rushing to get out the school building, you would never believe who ran into me. Ugh, Right. Brian. He said, "Bree, I am glad to see you here." I kept walking and I threw a hand in the air and said in a dry tone, "Hi, Brian." He was trying to keep up with my fast pace as he said, "Dang, hold up, Bree." I kept on walking. He asked a dude with dreads if he could have two of the roses that were in a vase, and could he have one of his heart-shaped balloons? The guy said, "Man, no, these are for my girl." Brian said, "Give her the rest of the roses in the vase, and man, you have more than enough balloons. She wouldn't know two roses and a balloon are missing."

As I walked out of the office from signing out. Brian ran up to me and said, "Bree. I got these for you. See, you are still on my mind, day in and day out. I miss you, Bree. Remember, we were B&B? Brian and Breana." I looked at Brian as I shook my head and said, "You just took those roses and balloons from that dude over there. You should be ashamed of yourself." I laughed as I opened the door and said, "Some people will never change." Brian yelled my name and said, "Bree, don't think you are better than me! You ain't shit!" As I walked down the stairs I laughed because him breaking up with me is the best thing he ever did!

* * *

I went to the mall to get a couple of things for T'eo for Valentine's Day. I know he might not take them, but I do not care—I wanted to make this day special with the hope I can get him back. I went to Build-A-Bear Workshop to put a rush on an order for him. I did the same for a couple of things I bought from Things Remembered as well. While they were getting my purchases together I went to the Farmers Market to get him a plate and something for me to eat too. I went to Publix to get a small heart-shaped cake for us to share.

I texted T'eo and asked him, if he didn't mind, could he make time for me so we could talk? I waited around a little longer than I intended for the things I ordered, but since they were at the last minute and a rush order, I was patient. I didn't have anything to lose because I kept looking at my phone, but T'eo didn't text me back. I was disappointed, but I decided not to cancel the orders because I bought them out of the kindness of my heart.

As I walked around the mall there were dudes all over the place ordering chocolate candy, cookie cakes, carrying bouquets of roses and dozens of red, white and pink balloons. There were some balloons that had teddy bears in them—I thought that was too cute. I looked at my phone again, and no answer from T'eo. As I waited for a call or text from Build-A-Bear or Things Remembered, I decided to pull out a piece of paper from my purse and write T'eo a letter. I finally got the call to pick up my items. After I picked them up, I decided to take the long way home with hopes that T'eo would text me back.

On my way home, I pulled into a favorite park and sat there for a while and cried. I began to talk out loud to my higher self and said, "Maybe I was being selfish, but I wanted to stay focused. I have a lot to lose and I want people to understand that."

I sat back in my seat and said, "Bree, yes, you were wrong for pushing T'eo away because he is a good guy. However, you also have to look out for yourself because it is easy to lose yourself in a person and let your hard work slip away—not knowing it is slipping through your hands until it slipped so far to the point it's too late to redeem yourself."

I looked in the mirror as I wiped my eyes and said to myself, *they are right, I do not know how to be in a relationship anymore and be all about me too. I am scared. I do not want to lose myself. I do not want to set myself up for failure all because it didn't work out. I am so focused on completing the task I started because the finish line is right in front of me.*

I turned on the radio and one of my favorite songs was playing, *You Gotta Be* by Des'ree. My spirit was lifted as I started to sing out loud! This song was meant for me and came on at the right time. After the song ended, I turned off my radio. Sat there for a minute, smiled and said to myself, *well Bree, you can always go home and study. You cannot go wrong with getting a little studying in.*

I pulled up my seat, programmed my Bluetooth to my radio, buckled up my seatbelt, put the car in drive and headed home. As I pulled in the driveway, I cut the car off and was about to gather up my things. I got a text message from T'eo saying, I was busy, but if you have time you are more than welcome to stop by. I smiled and said to myself, *yeah right, his ass wasn't busy, he is trying to prove a point, that's why he stalls up time. I am going to let him think I believed he was busy.* I spoke into the voice text and said, "Okay Google, text T'eo and say, Okay, I am on my way."

It began to rain as I pulled up at T'eo's apartment. I blew my horn to give T'eo a heads-up that I was outside. I hurried out of the car and ran to the door. I knocked, and he took forever to come to the door. When I was about to run back to my car the doorknob turned as he opened the door. Teo said, "Were you about to leave?" I answered, "Yes, you took forever and a day to come to the door. The hoodie on my coat is getting soaked and I cannot afford to catch a cold. What were you doing in there?" He looked at me and said, "I didn't hear a knock on the door." I said, "Well you need to invest in a doorbell. I think that would help."

He was leaning on the door. I arched my eyebrows and said, "Well... are you going to invite me in, or what?" He held out his hand, smirked and said, "I guess you can come in. ...but if you're going to break my heart again then I'm going to have to say no." I stepped one foot in the door and he asked, "Are you coming here to break my heart?" I looked at T'eo and said, "T'eo, I apologize if I broke your heart. I think we both need to talk so we can have an understanding about both of our goals and our relationship. It was never my intention to break your heart. I would never want to break your heart. Ever."

T'eo said, "I forgive you, Breana the Brave. You are getting drenched out there. Come on in." I softly punched him in the chest and said, "Leave it up to you, you were going to let me stay out there in the pouring rain." T'eo looked at me, laughed and said, "No, that was your choice to stay outside and talk in the rain. I asked, are you going to break my heart again? You could have said no as you stepped in the house. You were the one rambling in the rain."

I softly punched him again, this time in the arm, as I said, "So you took what I said as me running my mouth." He reached for my coat as he took it off and replied, "No. I believe everything you said. What I am saying is, you were the one who kept talking in the rain." I started to shake my head and said, "Okay, this is going to be an agree to disagree conversation."

I looked around, sat on the couch and said, "I see you changed a couple of things around." He replied from his room, "Bree, you notice everything. What did I change?" I laughed and said, "Whatever. Well... since you asked. Once before when I walked in the house you had the black stallion picture on the left side of the wall. Now you've put it on the right, so now when you close the front door and sit on the couch the picture entertains your guest. You changed the loveseat. Before, it was on the right side against the wall. Now it's on the left side of the room near the window and the sofa took its place. You blew up your mother's picture and put it on the wall above your TV. T'eo, she's so beautiful!"

He was doing something in his room and said, "Yep, you are right. I changed it around a little just to see something different. And thank you, my mother said you are beautiful too." I sat back on the couch and said, "T'eo, what are you doing in there?" He walked out and said, "I had to find you another coat because that was one was soaked. I found you a hoodie, sweat pants and socks that you might like. That way you can take off those wet clothes." I couldn't help but blush when I asked, "That's what you were doing in there the whole time?" He smiled as he handed me the clothes and said, "Yep." I reached for them and said, "Well... thank you. I appreciate it. Before I change clothes, I have to run out to the car to get a couple of things." As he walked to the door he put on his coat and said, "Don't worry about it, I will get them. Are your things in the front or back seat?" "They are in the backseat on the driver's side. They are the only bags that are back there." T'eo opened the door and said, "Okay, you go change in the bathroom and I'll get the bags."

I hurried up and changed my clothes before T'eo made it back in the house. He walked in and said, "Dang, Superwoman, you changed clothes fast!" I was sitting on the loveseat in his gray Nike sweat suit, which was really comfortable. He sat the bags down by the TV and said, "Okay, we have to talk." He walked over and sat beside me. As I folded up my legs together on the side, rested my hand on the side of my face with the couch supporting my elbow, I said, "I agree. We have to talk." T'eo said, "You look very pretty in my sweatsuit." I blushed and said, "Thank you."

T'eo scooted a little closer and said, "Breana, I apologize if you didn't think I took your studies seriously. I know you set goals for yourself. That is one reason why I admire you so much. You know I have goals too. I came from barely anything because my mother worked so hard to make a living for us. I want to be counted and do something with my life. I want to make my mother happy so she can see that her hard work wasn't in vain. I also want to get her out of poverty. She has an education, but only a high school education. A little college, but she gave it up when my father moved her to the States. That is when she got pregnant with me and she didn't fulfill her dreams because she made sure she gave me her everything and all. So, Breana, I value education. Just like you, I want to be successful."

I touched his hand and said, "T'eo it wasn't you—it was me. You don't have to apologize for anything. I accept your apology and I apologize too because I honestly gave up on us after school started. I know I say the word "I" a lot, it's because I worked hard to get here. I am the one who put in the time, the effort, and set my mind to accomplish my goals and challenges. I know my parents and friends have helped me along the way, and I appreciate that, but I am the one who put everything in motion. I just want to successfully finish what I've started. However, I might add, it would be great knowing I have someone on the road to success with me. We can share each other's journey along the way. How does that sound?"

T'eo smiled and said, "Bree, I accept your apology as well." He continued, "I would love for us to share each other's journey. That sounds perfect!" He kissed me and said, "So will you be my lady again?" I rolled my eyes and said, "Um… let me think about it."

I told him to close his eyes. T'eo is so silly, he put his hands over his eyes. He spread his fingers as he was curious to see what I was going to do. I looked at him, laughed and said, "Stop peeking! You're cheating!" He said, "What you mean." He kept peeking and I said, "Never mind, take your hands down, cheater." He laughed. I got up and put the bags in front of him and said, "Happy Valentine's Day!" T'eo was in a state of shock and asked with excitement, "These bags are for me?" His facial expression touched my heart. I smiled and laughed at the same time and said, "Yes, they are."

He opened the Build-A-Bear box and had a good laugh! He said, "This bear is supposed to be me?" We both were laughing as I said, "Yep, you all day!" He looked at the bear and was going to town having a good laugh he said, "This bear has on a plain t-shirt, cut up pants and flip-flops!" He was tickled with joy as he said, "Ha! Yep, this is me all day! You have a sense of humor, Bree!" He admired the bear and said, "I love it, Bree! Thank you!" I gently smiled and said, "You're more than welcome, Mr. Flip Flop man of all four seasons." He laughed, "Sometimes I cannot find my shoes and it is easier to just slip on some comfy shoes." I started to shake my head and said, "Lazy. Just Lazy."

I loved to see him happy. I said, "I have another bag for you." He said excitedly, as his voice cracked a little, "No way! Are you kidding me!" I nodded my head as I said, "Nope!" He reached for the bag and opened it. He took out three boxes. The first small silver box had a cream bow on top. T'eo opened it and saw a keychain engraved with his name on it. He freaked out and said, "Oh wow! This is so perfect! I love this!" He got off the couch and walked to the kitchen to get his keys. As he was putting his keys on the keychain he looked at it, smiled and said, "Bree, I really love it!"

I smiled, and said with excitement, "Open the other boxes!" He opened a smaller box and inside was an engraved money clip. He was happy when he said, "Breana, this is exactly what I needed! Thank you so much!" He looked at it as he read his name so softly, "T'eo".

He opened another box and asked, "I wonder what this is?" As he opened it, he saw it was a leather wallet with his name engraved on it. He jumped up and said, "Breana, how did you know I needed a wallet? Thank you so much! You didn't know how badly I needed it." I smiled and said, "I noticed every time you took out your money that you always crumpled it in your front pocket." T'eo had tears in his eyes as he said, "You noticed that." I nodded my head yes. I caught his tears with my thumbs, wiped them away and asked, "Why are you crying?" T'eo said as he rested his hands on my wrist, "You are too good to me, I do not deserve someone like you. You pay attention to the smallest things and the smallest things are what count."

I started to tear up and said, "T'eo, you always deserve the best. If I could give you more, I would." He sniffled and said, "Breana, you have given me more than enough." I said, "I have two more gifts." I asked him to look in the Things Remembered bag, and he pulled out the card. I said, "That's one gift." As I reached in my purse I said, "Read the card later." I pulled out a silver box and it had a red bow on it. I said, "Let's untie the bow together." I touched his hands gently as we untied the bow. We took the lid off the box together. T'eo said, "You are filled with all kinds of surprises today." Inside there were two puzzle pendant necklaces. One puzzle piece had his name on it and the other puzzle piece had my name on it. I took out the puzzle piece that had my name engraved on it and put it around his neck and said, "Yes, I would like to be your lady again." His was smile wider than it would ever be as he put his puzzle piece around my neck and said, "I wouldn't have it another way." We kissed. And I said, "Wait. Look in the Publix bag." T'eo paused and said, "No way, something else!" He opened the bag and pulled out the heart cake and food. We ate our Valentine's Day dinner and dessert as we enjoyed each other's presence.

He said quickly, "Wait... Wait... I got you something too. What time is it?" He looked at his watch and said, "Oh shoot, we have thirty minutes to get there!" I was looking lost as I said,

"What?" He said in a rush, "Bree, I'll tell you later." He put on his coat and put one of his coats on me. He ran in his room and got two knitted hats his mother had made before she left, and a huge umbrella. I said, "Where did you get this umbrella?" As he opened the door, he asked, "Really, Bree?" I said, "Yeah, I've never seen that umbrella in here before." T'eo smiled, "You do not miss a beat. Like I said earlier, you noticed everything."

As he opened the car door he said, "I bought this umbrella just for this occasion. The forecast said it was going to rain today. I had to make sure I was prepared." I said, "Oh, well… where are we going?" T'eo started to drive and said, "You will see when we get there." We arrived at our destination. We were at Sky View, Atlanta's Ferris wheel. We got into one of the pods that was tinted black. I said, "I didn't know you had to make a reservation." T'eo said, "You don't, but I knew they were closing soon and I knew they were going to be busy today. A friend of mine returned a favor." I looked puzzled as I said, "Returned the favor…" T'eo started to shake his head, "Bree, I tutored a friend and helped with math class in return for this favor. I didn't want to wait in line and I wanted to have a pod with tinted windows." I smiled and hugged him and said, "Aww you did that for me?" He smiled, "Although I was ignoring you I still was going to do something for you on Valentine's Day." I blushed, "Aww, you are so sweet. That is why you are my sweet honey bun!" As the Farris wheel started to turn the city view was beautiful! We cuddled up together and it was a perfect, cold, cozy rainy evening.

Fifteen minutes later after we got off, he asked, "Are you warm?" I said, "Yes." As he held me close, he said, "Great!" He pointed to a white Cinderella carriage with white horses. It was breathtaking. I said, "Look at that! It looks like a fairy tale. Wow, it's so beautiful! The rain puddles and the wet streets complement the city lights and show its reflection. The horses are so beautiful!"

The horses and carriage stopped in front of us. I stepped back and said, "I wish we could get on the carriage and ride around the city." The coachman opened the door. He wore white gloves, a white tux, a fancy white hat, and he said, "Welcome aboard, young lady." As I looked around, I saw a couple of people looking like they were waiting in line to get on the carriage. I said, "Thank you sir, but this ride isn't for us." T'eo took my hand and said, "Let me help you." I screamed with excitement as I put my hand to my mouth and said, "T'eo! No! Are you serious?" He kissed my forehead and said, "You looked so beautiful when you put your hand over your mouth." He laughed, "This is not a fairy tale. This is reality; and this is for you, my love." I said, "T'eo, we are not dressed the part. We're wearing sweat suits!" He smiled and said, "Who said we have to be dressed a certain way to enjoy the one we love?"

I stepped into the carriage. Oh, my gosh, it was beautiful! There were pink roses and Mumba's (my favorite candy) on the red cotton seats. I laughed, and T'eo said, "Instead of chocolate, I wanted to give you your favorite candy." I started to cry and couldn't stop as I said over and over again, "T'eo, this is beautiful!" As the carriage started to move, I asked, "When did you do all of this? How did you know you were going to see me on Valentine's Day?" T'eo replied, "Well... I knew I couldn't afford it all. I only had half. I told your parents what I wanted to do and they helped me out with the rest." He laughed and said, "Even Summer wanted to chip in but I didn't take her money." I was crying and laughing at the same time and said happily, "What! Are you serious?" With tears in his eyes, T'eo said, "Yep. I wanted to make it special for you. I knew I was going to see you because I had faith and I had a plan." He looked at me as he smirked, arched his left eyebrow and said, "I learned from the best that having a plan is a good thing. Therefore, I had faith and followed my plan."

As we rode around the city, we talked as I laid my head on his shoulder and enjoyed the city lights. I never imagined someone would go out of their way to do something so special for me. After the ride, I asked the coachman what the horses' names were. He said their names were Bonnie and Clyde. I walked over to Bonnie and Clyde, I patted them and rubbed their faces and said, "Thank you!" They both nodded their heads as if they were saying, "You're welcome." The coach said, "Normally, they do not like when people touch them." I smiled and said, "We share the same high vibration and our frequencies are balanced." The coachman didn't get it.

As T'eo and I crossed the street it started to rain again. T'eo opened his huge umbrella as we took a stroll in Centennial Park. It was perfect! The rain soothed our souls and we realized we were surely the missing pieces to each other's puzzle. I put my arm through and softly asked, "T'eo, would you like to take me to the prom?" He stopped walking. He kissed me and said, "I would love to take you to your senior prom." As we walked through the park, we talked about what colors we were going to wear, our ride to the prom, and so much more. We walked around the park until it closed. This day was one of the best days of my life! It was more than perfect!

CHAPTER TWENTY-ONE

21

T'EO'S AND MY RELATIONSHIP IS BETTER THAN EVER! MOST OF OUR dates are at the coffee shop as we study together, at the park if the weather allows, the library, at his place or mine, and sometimes we sit in the Farmer's Market as we make a plate and sit in the eating area and study. I took everyone's advice that it isn't all about work and no play. We've taken time out to go skating, to the movies, and bowling, and to T'eo's favorite place, Dave & Buster's. I 'll admit they were right. When I was studying all the time it felt like a job nonstop and I put so much pressure on myself. When I learned to let go, study, and play, my life became more balanced than ever. I feel more alive, free and a lot happier. What tops it off is, my grades are amazing! I have straight A's! If you're wondering, I didn't quit my job, I told my supervisor that I have to focus on my studies this term but every now and then I clock in just stay in the loop with my crew. I love them, and we have so much fun when we work together. Overall, I am glad my supervisor understands and supports me 100%.

* * *

Midterms are tomorrow! I cannot believe how much time has passed by. I am ready and I know that I am going to execute them! It's funny how I was taking classes back-to-back on Mondays, Wednesdays, and Fridays and got the hang of them all. When I was taking a midterm for each class. I literally walked right in and right back out. They were a breeze. In between my breaks, I met up with T'eo to have lunch. He was worried about two of his exams. I told him he is too blessed to be stressed. Let it go and it will work itself out. I am working with T'eo on letting things be when he has put his best foot forward and to have faith that the Great Divine has taken care of the rest. He's doing better, but he has more work to do. T'eo has been working with me about not always having a schedule for everything. He tells me to go with the flow. Honestly, I am working on it, but it is hard because I wonder how people get things done without a schedule or plan. I admit I am a work in progress. I looked at the time and said, "It is time for my next final." T'eo said, "You got this, babe! Knock it out!" I kissed him on the cheek, rubbed his hair for luck and said, "Thanks! Don't you worry about your exams because I know you blew them out of the water!" I bit a piece off his sandwich and made my way through the crowded cafeteria.

* * *

I learned that waiting until the last minute to buy a prom dress is a huge no-no! I didn't think finding a prom dress would be so difficult. I guess people take prom more seriously than I thought. My mother, Summer, Chloe and I walked into (it felt like) thousands of stores and tried on millions of dresses but nothing cut it. I was very frustrated. I looked at Chloe and said, "It's not that serious. I can find something in my closet." Chloe touched my forehead as she asked, "Are you feeling okay?" I playfully slapped her hand away and said, "What? Girl, I am fine. I don't think finding a dress is a big deal. This is such a waste of valuable time." My mother said, "Bree, no it isn't. Prom is a special moment in your life." As I was struggling to take off one of the dresses that didn't fit, I said, "Really? Walking in and out of stores trying on one dress after another for one night to impress people who you see every day—and really don't care about? I don't think that is special. Graduation is a special moment because your hard work has paid off and you are moving on in life to conquer your next journey."

As I stepped out of the dress, I continued, "Some of the students who are going to prom aren't even graduating. I don't see how they can enjoy themselves on prom night as opposed to the day that really counts. And that day is graduation." Summer walked out of the dressing room wearing an ugly orange glittered different color beaded gown. She rolled her eyes and said as she looked in the mirror, "Ugh. Bree. Give us a break. Gosh, you're really spoiling the moment. Go shopping in your closet then, that way we all can be doing something else." I looked at Summer, as I was about to say something, but my mother said, "Come on, you two, stop it. We are going to find the right dress, and no, Breana you are not going shopping in your closet." Chloe laughed and said, "Sometimes I am glad I am an only child." Summer looked at Chloe as she put her hand on her hip and said, "Oh really? You are glad you're an only child? I can't tell. It seems like my parents have adopted you because you be at our house day in and day out." We all laughed and said, 'True." We were cutting it close. However, I lucked out because in the last week of March my mother, Summer, and Chloe helped me find the perfect dress.

* * *

Today I took Summer to her soccer camp. As Summer ran out the door with her soccer gear on, she was talking to someone. I walked outside, and it was T'eo. I smiled and asked, "What are you doing here?" He was about to speak, but Summer said, "I invited him to come to soccer camp with us." I told her, "That's the best idea you've had all day!"

When we arrived at Summer's camp, T'eo and I walked into the building (since the camp was indoors), and there were so many children bouncing balls everywhere. T'eo warmed Summer up before the training started. One of the coaches walked by and ask T'eo if he wanted to help with the camp. He agreed because he is really good at soccer. T'eo and Summer are always in the backyard, kicking the ball around and learning new tricks. The same coach walked over to me and said, "If you don't mind, will you sit on the bench with the other parents, guardians, etc.?" I was kind of offended. Summer and T'eo started to laugh. I said, "Coach, I can help out as well." The coach replied, "No thanks. I have all the help I need." Summer laughed, "Coach knows you cannot play, that's why he said no." I was like okay, well. Whatever. It was pretty cool seeing Summer and T'eo playing together. I said to myself, *I can get used to this.*

After camp, we all went to Fresh 2 Order to get something to eat. I ordered a tofu and veggie entrée. Summer and T'eo ordered the grilled salmon entrée. We all sat down, ate in silence until Summer said, "T'eo, I am so glad Bree didn't mess up a good thing with you." I was about to choke on my food as I tried to speak. I asked, "Summer, how do you know what a good thing is?" She looked at me, took another bite of her food and she said, "I know what a good thing is because I see it every day." I cut up my tofu and said, "Really, you see it every day? Where?" Summer cleared her throat and said with confidence, "I see it at home." Summer sipped some of her drink. T'eo started laughing. I said, "T'eo, please do not entertain her today." He continued to laugh. I rolled my eyes and said, "Ugh. Give me a break." Summer finished her juice and said, "Bree, it's important to know where I know about a good thing... but I'd rather talk about the word, who." I paused and said in a dry tone, "Who, Summer? Who?" Summer tilted her head to the side and paused. Then she slid out of her seat and said, "I am going to get a refill." She walked backwards and said, "Well, before I do that, let me give you something, or I should say, some people, to think about." She formed a quotation mark with her fingers and said, "Mommy and Daddy. That is how I know what a good thing is. Mommy and Daddy show us every single day. The love they have for each other is what I want. The love they have for each other is what you have sitting right beside you." Summer looked at her cup as she tried to sip the last bit of juice out and said, "Think about that while I refill my drink."

* * *

It was chilly outside. You would think in April it would be warm. The sun is out, but the temperature is still in the high 50's and low 60's. For the past couple of years, the weather does what it wants to do. That is why I keep clothes in my car for all seasons. Chloe, T'eo and I went to Home Depot to buy some organic seeds and dirt to start growing our garden.

As we walked around, T'eo said, "Wait a minute. I've noticed in the past month and a half you've taken my style." I was focused on finding an almond tree and said, "What do you mean, I stole your style? You have the worst style ever." I looked at the price for the Aloe Vera plant I passed and continued, "Well... you look cute when you dress casual. Other than that, your style is horrible." T'eo smiled and said, "Oh really? My style is horrible, huh?" As I kept looking for the almond tree I said, "Yep, and you know it too." T'eo laughed, "Well... if my style is horrible that means you are now a horrible dresser too. All of a sudden you wear my sweat pants, and my shirts, I might add." I turned around, looked at him and said, "Oh, whatever. I'll let you have that one." T'eo asked, "Is that so?" I replied, "Yep." He said, "Well, why all of a sudden you don't wear shoes? Huh?"

I was talking to him as I walked along a different aisle and said, "I wear shoes, you silly man." T'eo laughed, "Oh, I'm a silly man now?" I laughed but didn't say anything. Then he said, "You're wearing your silly man's flip flops too. I had so many pairs of flip-flops and all of a sudden I have to fumble around to find a pair that matches because the rest of them are at your house." I laughed. He asked, "How did they get over there?" I laughed again, "When I visit you, I want to be comfy, so I borrow your flip flops." He laughed so hard and said, "Yeah, I know because all of your tennis shoes, boots and dress shoes are at my house."

I walked over to the aisle he was on, walked up to him, kissed him and asked, "Are you complaining, or do you like it?" He put his arms around my shoulder and said, "No, I don't like it. I love it!"

Chloe said, "Lovebirds, please." I smiled at her and hugged on to T'eo arms and kissed him on the cheek as we continue to look for the things we needed.

* * *

Just when I was getting my life back on track, I forgot that today is the first day for Dr. Wright's trial. Before we got the car, there were people standing outside the courtroom with signs, yelling and screaming, Justice for Women! There were some people who were wearing *Breana the Brave: Unapologetic for my Flaws and All* t-shirts, long sleeves and tank tops.

As I stepped out of the car, people started to clap and scream my name. I heard someone say, "Breana the Brave is fearless!" The crowd shouted my name. I didn't know whether to wave or not. My lawyer walked in front of me. I kept my head straight as I said to myself, *Breana, you got this.* My mother asked me if I was nervous. I told her no, I am ready to get this over with. My daddy held my hand and said, "I know you are." T'eo was walking behind my parents and me. Chloe and Summer were holding hands as we walked in the courtroom.

As I put one foot in front of the other, I looked left and there were so many women waving at me with half-smiles of hurt. There were some who nodded their heads as if they were saying to themselves, *we all are in this together.* I saw Dr. Gilbert, Dr. Robinson, and the President of Brubaker State University.

I looked over to my left, and Dr. Wright was sitting at the table, wearing a black suit. He looked as though he had been beaten up; you could tell they tried to cover the bruises with makeup. I didn't feel bad for him if he got his ass beat in jail, he deserved it. For what he had done to us girls, that ass-beating wasn't enough. My facial expression began to turn sour. I tried not to be filled with rage, but looking at his disgusting face made me want to beat the shit out of him too. My brother touched my shoulder and said, "Bree. Do not look that way." I turned my head and looked straight ahead.

We've been the courtroom for hours. There were so many women who testified against Dr. Wright. He sexually assaulted and harassed so many women for years before I was even born. There were only twenty-one counts but to my surprise, it turned out to be sixty-six women and thirteen men. It should have been more, but some of his victims were deceased, therefore, they couldn't speak for themselves. Dr. Wright should be ashamed of himself. He started victimizing people when he was in his twenties.

One woman took the stand, she had to be in her early thirties. She told the jury, Dr. Wright (who was Mr. Wright at that time) followed her into the ladies' room. She explained it was a single restroom. He walked in after her and locked the door. He put his hands over her mouth, ripped off her clothes and raped her. She said she screamed but nobody heard her. He threatened her and said if she said a word, he was going to tell her husband that she cheated on him, and he'd have his way with her (at the time) sixteen-year-old daughter. Therefore, she never said a word.

I took the stand on the final day of the trial, which was the sixth day. His lawyer asked me to point to the person who touched me in a sexual way. I looked Dr. Wright in the eyes without blinking and pointed to him. His lawyer asked me my age. I told him I turned eighteen years old on the first of December, 2018. He asked me if I was in college or high school. I said, "I attend Jackson-Miles High school. I participate in the dual-enrollment program at my high school and attend college at Brubaker State University."

His lawyer paused, took a breath and said firmly, "Okay... Okay..." twice. He then put his right hand on his face. His thumb was under his chin and his index finger was resting on his cheekbone as he asked, "Would you consider yourself to be an independent young lady?" I replied, "Yes." He smiled as if he'd caught me in the act, or as if he'd just won the case, as he said slowly, "Oh, an independent and grown woman." I stayed calm and said, "Pardon me?" He repeated himself and said, "You are an independent, grown woman." I asked him, "Are you asking me or telling me?" He didn't answer, he said to the jury, "She is legal and..." I cut him off and said angrily, "Legal? What does that have to do with anything? I didn't give Dr. Wright permission to touch me. None of us women or men gave him permission!"

His lawyer tried to talk over me. The judge said, "Counselor, let the young lady talk. I want to hear what she has to say." I gratefully said, "Thank you, Your Honor." I then looked at Dr. Wright's lawyer and said in a firm tone, "Legal? What does age have to do with this? You are a lawyer and I am more than sure you have common sense. With all due respect, which you are lacking right now. But my age doesn't have anything to do with what Dr. Wright did to me or to any of us. I don't care if we were sixteen or ninety-nine—we were touched by Dr. Wright in the most distasteful way possible. He disrespected us on so many levels. Our age shouldn't matter. I am not going to apologize for my age. I am not going to apologize for my sex. I am not going to apologize for my race. The women and men who were sexually assaulted and harassed shouldn't apologize either. If we chose to be bisexual, gay or homosexual or whatever, we shouldn't apologize. Everyone matters! What Dr. Wright did to all of us is not acceptable, not on my watch and not on any given day that The Great Divines bless us with. I will make a fight for justice; and justice will be served. Dr. Wright does not need to be in a psychiatric ward. He's not crazy, he knew better and he knew exactly what he was doing. He needs to suffer in prison for the rest of his life. He shouldn't be given any mercy or grace. He should sit in prison and think about his disgusting ways."

I looked at the jury and said, "Look at Dr. Wright. If he touched your babies, your loved one, how would you feel? You wouldn't think about their age. You would think about the hurt, scars and pain your loved one endured. You would think about the stress and depression it caused. You would think about how

Dr. Wright took away their innocence. You all would think about how hard it is for your loved one to trust and love again. You would think about the burden your loved one had to carry over the course of the years or decades. You would think about the precious time Dr. Wright took away from your loved ones their happy, well-lived and joyful lives. Would you want justice to be served? Do the right thing."

I looked at the judge and said, "Thank you for letting me speak my piece." He looked at me and said, "You're welcome." I looked at Dr. Wright's lawyer and said, "Do you have any more questions?" He said, "No." I looked at my lawyer and he said, "I do not have any questions." I stood up, dusted off my shirt and stepped off the stand with poise, strength, and confidence.

The judge said, "Ms. Breana Anderson," I turned around and answered, "Yes, Your Honor." He said, "You said you attend Brubaker State University and Jackson-Miles High school, correct?" I replied, "Correct." He asked me what was my major. I replied, "Biology and Pre-med." He said, "It's no surprise that you are a smart, determined, fearless young lady." He cracked a quick smile and said, "If you don't mind my advice, I think you should go to law school. We need someone with such fight, drive and fearless attitude in our system." I cracked a smile back and said, "I will think about it. Thank you."

There were others who took the stand after me. Their stories made me sick to my stomach. As time passed, we patiently waited for a verdict in the courtroom. As they asked us to stand for the judge's return, in my mind I was ready to celebrate. As the jury handed over the paper, the judge read over it. I was trying to read his facial expression but his expression was plain and straightforward. He said, "Dr. Wright, please stand." He continued, "I think the jury showed you a lot of mercy." My heart dropped as I said to myself really quickly, No. No. No. No. No.

No. No. No. My left leg began to shake even faster than I was saying no. I sat back as far as I could and squeezed my daddy's hand tightly. I looked over at Dr. Wright. He looked relieved, and his eyes had a certain kind of peace, as if he was going to hear he was acquitted of all charges. His lawyer was nervous, but he looked like he was thinking the sentence would be cut in half.

As I sat there waiting, I relaxed my body, silently cleared my chakras and asked the Great Divine for justice to be served. I let go of my daddy's hand because I knew the Great Divine wasn't going to let me down. I took a deep breath. The judge said, "Dr. Wright, you are charged with 43 counts of statutory rape, 36 counts of attempted rape, 79 counts of sexual assault and 79 counts of sexual harassment. In all, you will serve 43 years in prison." I did the math in my head, he would be released when he was 107 years old. The judge continued and said, "You will have to serve all 43 years. You will not be eligible for patrol." I looked over at Dr. Wright. The judge asked him if he had any-thing to say. Dr. Wright said, "No sir." The judge then asked, "Dr. Wright, do you understand your sentence?" Dr. Wright said, "Yes sir, I do." The judge said, "Great, now take him out of here."

I was happy, but my daddy said, "I agree with the judge, they showed him mercy." I looked at him and replied, "Maybe, but at least he will not walk away without being held account-able for his actions. He will be released when he's 107 years old. I am fine with that. He will not touch or hurt anyone else." I thanked the Great Divine for the grace and mercy that was shed for myself and others. T'eo hugged me and said, "Breana the Brave." My lawyer said, "It is done!" I hugged him and said, "Thank you!" Attorney Davis said, "You did the work, I need to cut you half of the check." I laughed and said, "If I did the work, they need to deposit the entire check in my account!" We had a good laugh. I hugged my mother, brother, sister, Chloe and T'eo.

As I walked out of the courthouse, there were so many people coming up to me, shaking my hand and screaming my name. I pumped my fist and screamed, "We did it! We are not apologizing for who we are. We accept our flaws and all. Justice was served!"

CHAPTER TWENTY-TWO

"STOP SLOUCHING, BREE," SUMMER SAID AS SHE BRUSHED makeup powder on my back to cover up the blemishes. My mother said, "Breana is tired and restless because she's been sitting in chairs all day." I huffed, puffed and took a deep breath as I said, "Yes. Getting ready for prom is draining, it makes me not want to go to prom. Girls have to go through a lot to get dolled up. That's why I am plain Bree. I do what's comfortable for me." My mother and Summer helped me put on my dress, a sparkly peach colored princess ball gown. It's not as wide and big as my Cinderella homecoming dress, but it has a slight wide fluffiness to it. Honestly, I love it! Summer took her job seriously as she continued to brush my back, arms, and upper chest with the makeup powder to make sure every single blemish was covered up. After being in the salon all day, my mother made sure my hairstyle was still in place and neat. It is parted in the middle and slightly twisted on each side and my hair is curled towards the back as it hangs down. In the middle is a cute peach sparkly circle comb to make my hair look elegant and fancy.

Summer put my mother's pearls around my neck. She also put my mother's platinum sparkly dangling earrings in my ears. "Ouch!" I said as Summer pierced my earlobe. "My bad, Bree. If you stop moving, I will be able to put the earrings in your ears." "I'm not moving. I am trying to stay still as much as possible," I replied. Summer said as she focused on putting the earrings in my ears, "Bree, pretend you're a manikin. That way we can get everything done."

A short moment later Summer slid on my silver heels and said, "Bree, why do you never put some type of color on your toes? French pedicure and manicure are played out." I shook my head. My mother said, "Bree, stay still." I said, "Okay, Mommy." I answered Summer's question and said, "Summer, that's my style and I like it." After my mother put the finishing touches on my makeup, I peeled myself out of the chair. I stood in from of my full-length mirror. As I turned sideways to see myself, I patted my hair a little, brushed off my dress slightly, and I teared up a little as I said, "Oh my goodness, I look so beautiful!" I walked over to give my mother a hug and said, "Thank you." My mother was crying as she said, "Baby, sweetheart, you are beautiful and you're more than welcome." The doorbell rang. Daddy and Luke yelled as if they were singing a tune, "T'eo is here!" Summer was standing beside my mother. I reached over and gave her a hug too and said, "Thank you, baby sis." She teared up and said, "You needed a lot of work, I'll bill you later. ...And you're welcome." I laughed as I tried to hold in my tears and said, "Yeah, okay. Aww, are you about to cry?" Summer couldn't hold in her tears any longer as she said, "I am crying because I see that miracles do happen. You are evidence of it." She hugged me tightly and said, "Big sis, you are beautiful inside; and thanks to me and Mommy, outside too. Have fun, do not lose your virginity, and most importantly, be safe."

As I prepared myself to walk down the stairs, T'eo caught my eye as I stood at the top. I admired his dove grey suit. He was wearing a white crisp shirt, his grey blazer was casting it sharp, his slim trousers were a perfect fit, his dusky peach tie and handkerchief complemented the peach rose boutonniere I'd prepared to put on his jacket. As I walked down the stairs, all eyes were on me, however, my eyes stayed on T'eo. I heard my daddy say, "Look at my angel." I turned my head as I looked at him and smiled. Luke smiled and said, "Breana, you look beyond beautiful." As I reached the bottom of the stairs, T'eo had tears flowing from his eyes as if I was walking down the aisle and we were getting married. I put my hands on his face, and as my thumbs wiped away the tears I said softly as I smiled, "You look so handsome tonight." He kissed me on my forehead and said, "I cannot stop looking at you because you look so amazing!" Summer skipped down the stairs and said as she was sniffing her nose from crying, "Okay, we need to take pictures so you two can make it to the prom on time and so Bree won't be late for curfew." Everyone was taking out their phones. My mother walked into her office to get her Canon camera. First, I took individual pictures with my mom, Daddy, Summer, and Luke. Then I took group pictures with my parents, siblings, and a family portrait together. Then T'eo and I took millions of pictures together. My parents had leased a cream Range Rover Sport—and it was gorgeous! I told my parents, "If you are wondering what to get me for my graduation gift, this is it! This is the car that I want!"

T'eo opened the door for me and off we went. We talked in the car as we headed to the Westin Hotel. "You know, I didn't tell you Bree, but this is my first time going to the prom. My mother couldn't afford it," T'eo said. I looked at him with sadness in my eyes. I didn't know what to say, I wanted to say something encouraging, so I said, "Well, I believe everything happens for a reason. The Great Divine knew you were supposed to go to the prom with me. I also believe that there's a first time for everything." He looked at me, smirked and said, "Bree always knows the right things to say." I blushed and replied, "Not always."

We pulled up to the hotel. Everyone's here tonight. T'eo said, "Here we go." He walked over and opened the door for me and said, "You look so amazingly beautiful tonight." I blushed and I fixed his tie, smiled and said, "Thank you, honey. You look amazingly handsome tonight as well."

We walked in the hotel, down a long hallway, and entered the prom room. The lights were blue, silver and white. They were dimmed and the decorations were so beautiful. People were dancing, there were some sitting in chairs, standing by the wall, and walking in and out of the room. I tried to find Chloe but there were a lot of people in the room, so I text her instead. She didn't reply. T'eo asked me if I wanted to dance. I said, "Sure." He gently pulled me out on the dance floor. I pulled my dress up a little and wrapped the circular strap at the bottom of my dress around my finger because it was slightly touching the floor. After I got that taken care of, we were getting down to, *Nice for What*, by Drake. Someone who I didn't know said, "Look at Queen of Jackson-Miles tearing up the floor! Get it, girl!" I put my hands in the air as I raised them up and down. I took T'eo's hand as he twirled me around. After Drake finished, one of my favorite songs came on, *Super Duper Love (Are You Diggin on Me)*, by Joss Stone. I had a ball! We slow danced and pop danced to this song. I was singing as I was dancing. T'eo said loudly, "This is one of the first songs we danced to at the pizza joint! I said, "Yep, sure is!" I was really enjoying myself!

I walked up to the DJ booth and requested *Shallow* by Lady Gaga and Bradly Cooper. We slow dance as I laid my head on T'eo chest. I held his hand tightly—it felt so good to be in his arms; I felt safe.

I lost track of time. I looked at my phone and realized Chloe hadn't texted me back. T'eo went to get us something to drink. Brian came over and said, "Hey, Bree." I was looking at my phone texting Chloe, and I said, "Hi Brian." He said, "Bree, you look good tonight." Still looking at my phone I said, "Thanks." "Bree, can I have the next dance?" Brian asked. I looked at him and said, "No." Brian said, "Damn it's like that now."

T'eo walked up and handed me my drink. I said, "Thanks, honey." Brian walked away. T'eo sat down beside me and said, "You're welcome. Was he bothering you? Are you okay?" I smiled as I kissed T'eo on the lips and said, "I am fine, babe. Thanks for asking." I continued, "You know what? I texted Chloe and she never texted me back. If she doesn't say anything in five minutes, I'm going to step out to call her." T'eo said, "I'm sure she's fine." I said, "How do you know?" He took a sip of his juice and stuttered and he said, "I mean, I think she's okay? I agree with you, if she doesn't respond in 5 minutes you should call her."

I gave my drink to T'eo to hold before I got out of my chair. Chloe crept up behind me and said, "Damn, Breana the American princess—you look flawless! You better not come out of that dress tonight." I gave her a tight hug and asked, "Where have you been?" Chloe replied, "Girl, I've been getting ready." Something didn't sound right. I smiled, looked at her dress and said, "Chloe you look extravagant tonight! If I am a princess, then from looking at you, America has two princesses!"

I looked at her and said, "Funny, Summer said the same thing as you. Please, I am not losing my virginity just because it's prom night." I looked around and said, "I know Ms. Chloe has a date. Who did you come to prom with?" Chloe smiled and said, "You know your Yang." I kept looking around, but nobody was with Chloe. I said, "Yep, I do. So, who's your date?" She said, "He's getting me a drink?" I looked confused and said, "Damn, you keeping secrets now?" Chloe smiled and said, "Bree, you will see." The room was dark, but someone was walking towards us. I was thinking to myself, *I know that person's frame but it can't be who I think it is—or is it?*

As the person walked up, I yelled, "I knew it! I knew it! Summer and I knew there was something going on between you two."

My brother said, "We're busted."

I said, "Wait. How long has this been going on?"

I turned and looked at T'eo and said, "T'eo knew all along, didn't you?" T'eo said, "I'm guilty, babe." I tapped him on the arm and asked, "So you're keeping secrets from me too?" T'eo said, "Oh, no. Never."

I looked at Chloe and Luke and asked again, "How long has this been going on?"

Chloe stood there smiling. Luke looked at Chloe and said, "We've been talking since October."

I screamed again and said, "What! October! So, you two were talking during homecoming?" Luke said, "Guilty again." He continued, "It all started when Chloe called me to get advice about Darius, and honestly, it took off from there. I was telling her she deserved better. I didn't know it was me at the time, but I started to like Chloe's and my conversation. One thing led to another and I got hooked. Funny, I never thought I would like my sister's best friend or a girl who I considered a sister."

Chloe looked at me and asked, "Bree, are you mad or upset that Luke and I are dating?" I walked over, gave her a

272

hug, and said with excitement, "Are you kidding me! No, I am not mad. I am happy for you both!"

I looked at my brother, smiled, and said, "Chloe, my daddy is an amazing loving man who loves hard; and the apple doesn't fall too far from the tree." I hugged my brother and I looked at Chloe and said, "You have a good man." I looked at my brother, "Luke, you two deserve and need each other. You've had your share of bad relationships, and I think you two complement each other." Luke said, "Thank you, baby sis!"

I started dancing and said, "Come on, brother, let's dance!" I danced with my brother. Later that evening, Chloe and I danced, and T'eo and I got a few more dances in. Before we left, we took a double date prom picture and then we all took our own prom pictures with our date. I hope to never forget my prom. It was one of the best nights ever! As T'eo and got in our last dance, I looked over at Chloe and Luke, they looked so happy together. Chloe looked over at me, we smiled. I read what she was saying as she moved her lips and said, "My Yin." I smiled as she read my lips as I said, "My Yang." We all danced the night away, headed home and called it a spectacular night!

CHAPTER TWENTY-THREE

I WALKED INTO MRS. MORGAN' OFFICE TO PICK UP MY CAP AND gown for my graduation. She handed me my cap and gown, my medals and ropes. Because of finals, I'd missed my high school award ceremony. Mrs. Morgan said, "BSU submitted their grades to us." I looked at her and said, "Really? Because they haven't posted on the board yet." She looked serious. I said, "Well, I know I passed my classes. Like always, math was challenging. Hit me with the news."

Mrs. Morgan began softly, but she raised her voice with excitement, "You passed all of your classes with A's!" I looked totally confused and said, "Wait, what? I had a low B in Cal II. I know I failed the final and it dropped my grade to a C." Mrs. Morgan said, "That could be very well true, but Dr. Gilbert said a lot of students failed the final. She sent me an email and said she dropped everyone's final exam grade who came to every lecture, tutorial and did the extra credit. Which brought your grade to a low 90." I screamed with so much excitement and said, "What! Oh my! Oh, my God!"

I didn't know what to do with myself. I had to sit down on the floor because I didn't believe what I was hearing. Mrs. Morgan said, "Breana, are you okay?" I looked at her and replied, "I am. My heart is racing with so much joy. I am speechless." She rubbed my back and said, "Wait right there." She walked back with what I thought were some clothes she'd picked up from the dry cleaners, but instead, she said calmly, "Breana, you've completed all of your credits to graduate with an Associate of Science degree. Here are your college cap and gown!" I didn't know what to do with myself. I ran into Mrs. Morgan's arms and gave her a long, rocking from side to side, hug! I was crying tears of joy as I said, "Believe me when I say it wasn't easy, not at all. Any and everything worth having is worth fighting and working hard for."

Mrs. Morgan said with excitement, "Breana, brace yourself for some more amazing news!" I looked at her with excitement and butterflies in my stomach as I waited for what she was going to say. I asked, "What? What is it? What is the news?" She said, as she jumped up and down, "Not only are you Jackson-Miles queen, but you are Jackson-Miles valedictorian as well!" I was surprised and yelled, "No way! Are you serious?" Mrs. Moran hugged me and said, "I am not joking. I am for real! You did it! You earned it and most definitely deserve it." I cried on her shoulder and said, "We did it. I didn't do any of this alone. I had a team. I had you, my family and friends in my corner." As we continued to hug each other I said softly, "Thank you. Thank you so much, Mrs. Morgan." She cradled me in her arms and said, "You're more than welcome."

* * *

Today is graduation day at Brubaker State University. I opened my eyes and lay in bed for a little while. I stretched and kicked the covers off. I ran over and looked at myself in the mirror. I asked myself, *Breana, are you happy?* I smiled at myself and said, "Yes, ma'am you better believe it! I conquered and executed my high school and my college goals. I had a couple of highs and a lot of lows, but every moment was a lesson learned. I am so proud of myself."

My mother knocked on my door and said, "Hello, Ms. College Grad." Her mouth trembled. I said, "Don't cry, Mommy." She hugged me and said, "I am happy! You conquered something that I would have never thought you could do. I am so proud of you." My daddy walked into my room and hugged my mother and me. Summer walked in, and then Luke. We all were emotional as we hugged each other. Luke said, "Wow, my baby sis is graduating college before me. Now I wish I would have taken advantage of Early College." I said, "Yeah, you are a sophomore and I am going into college as a junior." Reality hit and I said, "When I start college in the fall, I am going to be a junior! Oh, my goodness, I am going to be a junior!" I jumped up and down and said, "This is surreal!" Luke hugged me once again and said, "Dang, I didn't look at it like that! Wow, sis, you worked hard for it and you deserve it!" Luke continued, "If I went to Early College this coming fall, I would be a senior." My mother said, "Luke Junior, don't be too hard on yourself because you are exactly where you are supposed to be." I looked at my brother and said, "Look on the bright side—I learned from your mistakes, and Summer is going to learn from my mistakes. You are the oldest. You should be happy we look up to you." Luke said, "That is true and I am honored. ...and I am happy that you didn't make the same mistakes I made. I always want the best for my sisters."

Like always, my mother and Summer helped me get ready. Chloe met up at my house and rode with us. My parents took pictures before I left the house. My mother had on her black pants suit with a red blouse, and my daddy had on casual light brown slacks with a red dress shirt. Luke was dressed to impress! Chloe and Luke looked so cute together—they both were wearing the same colors, black and white. Summer had on a cute white spring dress. I didn't want to be late, and my parents wanted to get good parking. T'eo met us at the school.

I had on my black gown as I walked into the building, T'eo said, "Look at you!" I smiled, spun around and asked, "How do I look?" He kissed my forehead and said, "You look like a beautiful, smart, educated woman!" My parents asked T'eo and me to stand near the fountain as they took more pictures. Chloe and I took some 'funny face' pictures. Summer jumped in and took the funny face to the extreme. Luke was calm, cool, and collected with his hand in his pocket when we took pictures. A lady in an all-black outfit said, "All graduates need to head downstairs for line up!" I smiled at my family and T'eo. I put on my cap—my green and gold tassel dangled in my face as I said, "I will see you all soon!" I walked down the hallway and I looked back at my parents and waved. I was nervous, happy, and so excited. I said to myself, *the next time I hug my family, I will be a college grad.*

As we lined up and prepared to walk in the ceremony, I thanked the Great Divine for being with me every step of the way. I took a deep breath and smiled with each step I made. I looked for my family. I didn't have to look far because Summer's big mouth was loud. Chloe was cheering me on, and I heard her say, "My Yin!" I smiled and waved as I tried to hold in my tears, but they disobeyed me and fell freely on my cheeks.

As I walked to my seat, I picked up the program and couldn't believe my eyes—my name was in written in black italic letters on a fancy cream background with the title of my degree: (Brenna E. Anderson, Associate of Science). After everyone said what they needed to say, it was time for the graduates to stand. The girl in front me tripped badly as she was going up the steps. I was afraid that might happen to me—that's why I wore flip flops with a gown that wasn't too long or too short—it was perfect!

My name was called by a chubby lady who had a deep strong firm voice, "Breana Anderson." She paused and added, "As we call her at BSU, Breana the Brave!" The crowd was screaming my name saying, "Breana the Brave!" There were some people screaming, "Breana the Brave, we love you!" I smiled. It took a while for the crowd to stop yelling my name. There were so many people standing up and giving me a round of applause. I was very emotional. I smiled and cried at the same time. I tried to hold in my tears again, but they ran down my face.

I walked up the steps, gave her a handshake and said, "Thank you." She caught me off-guard when she gave me a hug and said, "You're welcome! ...and no, we all thank you. You made us, as women around campus, speak up and be unapologetic for our flaws and all. We thank you so much." I nodded my head and smiled. I walked a little further along the stage, reached to shake everyone's hand, and towards the end, I put my hand out to shake the President of BSU's hand. He too gave me a hug and said, "Congratulations, Breana Anderson. You are going to change the world!" I smiled and said, "Thank you, sir." He handed me my diploma cover. I looked at my family as I turned my tassel! I walked down the stairs and took my graduation picture. As I walked back to my chair, people were still calling my name. I smiled and waved in the humblest way possible. I laid my eyes on Summer and blew her a kiss.

After the ceremony, I took a couple of pictures with my professors and family. Mrs. Morgan squeezed into a couple of pictures! My family, extended family and I went to one of our favorite restaurants, Tacos and Tequilas. We talked over dinner and had a grand time! There were so many of us we took up an entire whole section. Chloe and Luke were so adorable. I cannot believe they are a couple but they are perfect for each other. T'eo and I were playing with each other's hands under the table. After dinner was over, I asked my parents if it was okay if I left with T'eo. They agreed and told me to be home before midnight. T'eo and I went to the park. We laid out a blanket as we enjoyed the city lights and stars. It was breathtaking as we gazed at the sky and talked about our future.

* * *

I finally stayed in the house for a couple days and I still was living in a surreal life! Luke, Chloe, T'eo and I had a double date. We all went to Atlanta Botanical Gardens. It was so beautiful! I love nature. As I walked hand and hand with T'eo, I closed my eyes and cleared my chakras as the breeze tickled my nose and massaged my toes. At the Cascades, the water falling from the hand of the Earth Goddess felt so peaceful. I'd left my hair hanging down my back, and T'eo enjoyed pulling it behind my ears as he kissed my lips. I looked over at Luke and Chloe – they were hugged all up on each other in their lovey-dovey moment. I took a couple of pictures without them knowing. We all walked across the bridge. It was so romantic because it seemed that the birds knew we all were in love; they were singing us a lullaby and blessing us on our path.

After we left the Botanical Gardens, we took a stroll in the park for a little while. Then we all rented bikes and rode around the park. T'eo and I rented our own bike. Luke and Chloe shared a bike. Chloe was acting so silly as they went down the hill; her arms and legs were stretched out as if she was going on a roller coaster ride. Sadly, Luke lost his balance and they both fell off the bike. T'eo and I asked if they were okay. Chloe lay on the ground, rolled over as she was being overdramatic, and answered, "Yes, we are fine." I couldn't hold in my laughter anymore. We all had a good laugh as they both dusted themselves off. I reached for Chloe's hand to help her up as she said, "It's not funny, Bree." I couldn't stop laughing, "What do you mean, it's not funny? I can't believe you Luke wanted to share a bike anyway." I was laughing so hard my stomach was hurting as I continued, "Then your ass wanted to act like you were at Six Flags over Georgia on the *Goliath*!" I couldn't help myself as I continued laughing, "Then your ass wanted to stop, drop and roll as if you were trying to get away from a house fire." I was laughing so hard tears started rolling down my face and I said, "Oh lordy, I can't." Chloe stood there, looking at me with a straight face as she told me, "I hope you laugh so hard that you pee on yourself." I laughed even harder. "Don't get mad at me because your ass was literally bouncing off a bike!" Chloe couldn't help but laugh. We hugged onto each other and laughed so hard as we fell on the ground together. Luke and T'eo were standing over us, shaking their heads. They didn't get it!

It was fun, and such a lovely day to spend with my boyfriend, brother, and best friend. After biking, we all sat near the pond and fed the ducks. Later, we sat on our private swing as we watched the sunset change the outline of the sky. We had so much fun together. I think we will double date more often!

Chloe Google Duo'd me early in the morning saying, "Hello, Prom Queen, Newly Grad twice, and Ms. Valedictorian at Jackson-Miles High!" I rubbed my eyes and said in a groggy tone, "I haven't even got up or brushed my teeth, Ms. 2019 Graduate of Jackson-Miles High." Chloe answered, "We are Class of 2019! Wow, we are about to graduate high school today. We are not kids anymore." Her voice changed as if she was nervous as she asked, "What are we going to do?" I smiled, "Yang, we are going to live life." I closed my eyes for a short second, "We will not ever be alone, because we will always have each other." Chloe said sadly, "Yeah, but you are leaving. You haven't told anyone what school you are going too." I stretched and said, "Nope, nobody knows. Only the school that I accepted their invite and scholarships." Chloe said, "Every school you applied to, you received a full ride." I said, "Maybe, but I am only one person and I can only attend one school. I will announce it later. What school did you decide on?" Chloe replied, "Brubaker State University, because they have a full academic scholarship. Oh, and I want to say, thank you so much for helping me apply for the scholarships. I have just enough money to live on campus and receive a refund check!" I said, "Cool! Look at you! I am so excited for you! No problem, Yang, that is what sisters are for! Did you know BSU has the best all-around for medicine, psychology, psychiatry, economics, and law?" Chloe sounded sad, "That could be very well true, but Luke is going back to Markie Orr State University and you are going who knows where. So, it can't be the best all-around since the best aren't staying." I told her, "Chloe, take a chill pill. You worry too much! Be excited that you got a full ride and you are truly blessed! Are you on your way so we can get ready together?" Chloe sounded sad as she said, "I am leaving the house in five minutes." I said, "Okay. T'eo is calling me. See you in a few."

I smiled as I answered the phone saying, "Hey, my honey bun!" He laughed, "I'll be whatever you want me to be." I asked, "Whatever? Are you sure?" He laughed and said, "Okay, maybe not whatever." I giggled, "That's what I thought." T'eo asked, "Are you getting ready?" I rolled over on my bed and said, "Not yet. I'm about too." He asked, "Do you have your speech down pat?" I replied, "Nope. I gave the principal something, but I am going to speak from my heart." T'eo said, "Ohhh, you're going to get in trouble." I balled up my pillow and laid on it and responded, "Ugh. I doubt it." T'eo said, "Well, I'm on my way, and I'll let you get ready." I blew him a kiss through the phone. He said, "I caught it and put it on my heart." He blew me one too and I told him, "I caught it and put it on my lips."

* * *

I got myself ready for graduation. I put on some slacks, a t-shirt and some flip-flops. My mother's face looked disgusted as she asked, "Are you wearing that?" I said, "Yep! I want to be comfortable." Chloe laughed, "Well at least I am not the only one." Chloe had on joggers and a PINK t-shirt with some flats. Summer said, "Eww, Chloe, you are so tacky." Chloe retorted, "Thanks, Summer. I love the compliment." Chloe's mother said in a funny way, "Our girls! Gotta love em!" T'eo walked in the door and said, "You all should be ready by now." We laughed. I told him, "We *are* ready. This is what we are wearing." T'eo laughed, "You've been hanging around me too long. I see I am a bad influence on your style." Summer walked between us and said, "Yeah, pretty much." We took tons of pictures! Chloe's mother was dressed up like she was going to church. She was excited because she's graduating from medical school tomorrow. Luke was dressed up like always, my parents were too, and we headed on our way.

* * *

All the lovebirds rode with Luke. Summer rode with my parents. T'eo and Chloe kept talking about fall semester. I rolled my eyes, "Come on, you two, enjoy the moment. Fall semester hasn't started yet. T'eo keeps saying he is going to miss me, and

Chloe agrees." I looked at Luke because he was not hearing the end of it either. Chloe was talking about how she hopes their long-distance relationship works. T'eo commented on Chloe's concerns; they are both rocking the same boat. Luke and I were trying to get off the subject by asking what they want to do after graduation. They kept talking and going on and on and on non-stop about how they are going to cope by having a long-distance relationship.

Thank God, we pulled up, and goodness, parking was crazy! Finding a parking space took forever. Chloe and I had to run to make the line. We made sure we were looking our best. Basically, we were each other's mirror since we hadn't had time to freshen up. She fixed my hair and I fixed hers. I fixed her cap and made sure her purple gown was on straight since we were running for dear life to make it, and she did the same. Since we weren't partners or sitting together, we hugged each other and said, "Okay Yin and Yang, let's do it." We both shed a few tears, wiped them off each other, and off we went.

I walked down the aisle first. I looked over at my family so they could get a good picture. As I was standing near my chair I waited to see if I could see Chloe. She was walking proudly, with confidence and strength! "Chloe!" I yelled excitedly. She looked over at her mother first, then Luke, then she started grinning as she looked at me.

All of the higher authorities, principal superintendent and everyone else said their speeches, and it was my turn, the vale-dictorian, to walk up to the podium to speak. I straightened my gown and with each step I took, I was filled with happiness, joy, and peace. I adjusted the mic, cleared my throat and said, "Congratulations, Class of 2019! First and foremost, I would like to thank the administration at Jackson-Miles High for giving me the opportunity to stand before you all today. When I was younger, and up until this day, I would ask myself, am I happy? Believe it or not, I asked myself the same question the other day. I would either make up an excuse to make myself feel better or the answer would be a flat out no because I had a lot of work to do. I had to work on me and let go of what didn't serve me.

Breana, are you happy? Yes, I am. I am free because I learned how to love me. Breana. I love myself during my toughest and hardest trials. I am proud of myself because I didn't give up. I loved myself through the roughest seasons because the roughness helped me create a thicker skin. There were some seasons when it was brutally dark, cutthroat and cold, but I loved myself enough to shed a little light of warmth. My pride was cut down in size, my heartache, and my mind was an emotional wreck. I needed to experience that to notice my core. I needed the heartache to heal me from the inside out. I was happy that the emotional rollercoaster finally wrecked because then I started to rebuild myself from the foundation up. I let other people's words have power over me; however, I used their words to sharpen my sword. When they threw their negative energy my way, they never took me down, because their words were empty—better yet, I used that energy to fuel my fire. I had a choice to listen to it and let it eat me alive—instead, I never gave them the satisfaction to fill their ego, therefore, I let them starve because I refused to give them a drop of water to drink or bread crumbs to eat. Life was waiting for me to start living for me.

However, my journey started when I started to love me. There were some seasons that were too hot. I was uncomfortable because my classes got the best of me, but I had to ask myself, Breana how badly do you want it? I wasn't sure, because I faced so much. I didn't know where I fitted in or where I wanted to be. I was lost because I had to find out who I was. Who is

Breana Elizabeth Anderson? Honestly, I didn't know. However, I was on a mission to find out.

Most days it was difficult. There were seasons when I had to find a way to embrace me for who I was; and who or what people wanted me to be. That is when I said, Breana, you have to do more than survive. You're working hard to live... And you are working hard to live for you and nobody else.

I transformed my words, my mind, my inner ability, because my roots run deep, deep in my core. I had to buckle up, stay conscious, and keep my eyes on the prize. Failure wasn't an option for me, because I didn't allow failure to exist in a negative way. Once upon a time I was afraid and feared failure; until I made failure a close friend. I rose from what I thought had failed because failure made me realize my wrongs so that I could make them right. Failure made me realize if I wanted it bad enough to not be afraid to get up and start over again. Failure became one of my closest friends because it gave me that extra push; it put fire in my eyes and it gave me great strength to execute my goals.

I worked hard and made a lot of sacrifices because that was a choice I made. It was my best choice thus far in life, and one that I wouldn't ever regret. With hard work, dedication, sacrifices, and concentration, I graduated from college before high school and earned an Associate of Science degree. (Everybody applauded!).

I was challenged in the most disrespectful way, but I wasn't going to let fear keep me quiet. I wasn't afraid to take a stand and if it took making me taller for people to hear my voice, well I'll be darned, I took it up a notch and stood on my tippy toes. I'm standing on my tippy toes as I speak—does everyone see me now? (The crowd started cheering and saying, Breana, we see you!).

I am a warrior, and Class of 2019, you all are warriors too. We are the future and we have to make our marks. We have to make everything we put our mind to, to count. Know your hard work isn't in vain, have a plan, execute it and make it happen. Don't be afraid to stand on your toes to be heard or seen. Don't be afraid to make sacrifices—remember—easy come, easy go. Through the madness and chaos, never give up! Never give in! Count every step and count every single step as joy, because when all is said and done, you are victorious. I love you, Daddy. Thank you, Daddy, for being my rock. Thank you, Mother, for being my strength. Mommy, I love you dearly. Summer, baby sister, you are my joy and thank you for always keeping it real—I love you to the moon and back. Luke, my older brother, thank you for being the role model that I needed. I look up to you. You are the best brother on the planet—my love for you is out of the universe. Chloe, my bestie, my Yang, my girl, we've been through some of everything together since elementary school. We've had our ups and downs. Good and bad. Happiness, sadness, laughter, and joy! We are sisters from another mother. You are the Yang to my Yin, and I love you so much! Say it with me, Class of 2019! You cannot shake my core! I am victorious!"

They yelled, "I am victorious!"

I said, "Say it one more time and mean it, "You cannot shake my core! I am victorious!"

They said it, loud and proud "You cannot shake my core! I am victorious!" They said it over and over again until the superintendent came to the mic and asked us to stand.

I heard people calling me "Breana the Brave" and I waved my hand and smiled as I walked down the stage to my seat. Taking a seat wasn't an option because the line started to move. I got behind the third person and waited on my name to be called. As the superintendent called my name "Breana Anderson" I heard roars from the audience. Some people were saying, "We are victorious." Some were saying, "Breana the Brave" Class of 2019 were saying, "You cannot shake my core! I am victorious!" I pumped my first and said, "You cannot shake my core! I am victorious!" The superintendent announced, "Breana Anderson has over $300k in scholarships and has been accepted to over thirty universities. As she mentioned, she holds an Associate of Science degree and maintained a 4.0 average in high school and college." I was very emotional because I had worked so hard for this day. It finally came. It's finally here. Hard work pays off. As other people's names were called, Chloe's name finally was called. I screamed, "My Yang! Get it, girl!" The superintendent said, "Chloe, Chloe, Chloe, you will be truly missed. I love your confident ways, sweet child. You are going far in life. Chloe has a full ride to Brubaker's State University!" She hugged Chloe and said, "Make us proud!" I screamed again, "Chloe! I love you! I know you are going to make us proud!"

We weren't supposed to change seats, but I asked the girl beside me, since they are not going to keep track of our names anymore, if she would switch seats with Chloe because I wanted to throw my cap in the air with her. She agreed. I texted Chloe and told her to come up here and switch places. As they said, "Class of 2019, turn your tassels around," Chloe and I looked at each other and turned each other's tassel. As they said, "You are officially graduates of 2019," Chloe and I looked at each other and threw our caps in the air, caught them, hugged each other tightly and said, "We did it together!" This is a memory I will always cherish and never forget!

* * *

After graduation and the celebration, we all met at my house. Luke and I had news for our family and partners. Luke looked at me and said, "Bree, you first." I looked at Luke, smiled, and said, "May I have everyone's attention?" Chloe put her drink down and said with a little sadness, "Bree is about to reveal the college of her choice." She walked up to me and said, "Bree, I am happy for you." I looked at Chloe, "Thank you, but ugh, I haven't told you yet." Chloe said, "I know, but I want to say, whatever college you chose I am happy for you and I will always be here for you—distance cannot tear us apart." I smiled and said, "You're darn right because I am staying at Brubaker's State University!"

Chloe screamed so loud as she ran and hopped into my arms. She almost fell but I wasn't going to let her fall. T'eo said, as his eyes watered, "Are you serious?" I walked up to him and said, "Yes. I am. I am lucky and you are too. We are in this together, honey bun!" Chloe was jumping for joy! She couldn't control herself. My parents were happy because I was going to be close to home, yet staying on campus. I need my freedom."

Luke said, "Hello! I have an announcement too." All eyes were on Luke. Luke said, "Well…" Summer groaned, "Oh my gosh, Luke, get to the point. Well… What?" Luke looked at Summer, laughed and said, "Gotta love this kid." He looked at Chloe and said, "Guess what?" Chloe asked calmly, "What?" Luke said, "I am transferring to BSU!" Chloe screamed as she started to cry and said, "Are you two pulling my leg?" She covered her mouth as she walked over and hugged Luke, and asked, "Why?" Luke said, "I belong here with you and my family. I miss out on too much, and I don't want to miss a thing." Chloe said, "Bree, all the schools you got into. You worked hard to get in those schools." I said, "These past couple of months have taught me, it's not all about me. I want to be with the people I love the most, and you all are right here." I said, "Group hug. We are all in this together!" We hugged each other and said, "We are all in this together!"

I pulled Summer in, "Summer, you are a part of us and you are in this together too." She smiled and said, "I love you, big sis!" She looked at Luke and said, "I love you, big bro. You and Bree are the best!" My parents were happy to know all of their children were at arm's length. I looked over at my parents and the smile on their face was priceless. I am blessed to have family and friends who love and care about me. We are one big happy family who has our ups and downs, and I wouldn't have it any other way.

* * *

I learned a lot and gave a lot. I know that I am loved and loving. I found my identity and that is... I am Breana Elizabeth Anderson. I am unapologetic for my flaws and all because I love me for me and nothing less.

INTRODUCTION FOR THE BOOK:
A Woman's Love Is Never Good Enough.

Love.

What is love? It is the essence of the unknown and will overwhelm you if you do not realize you are giving too much of yourself.

Love is an intense emotion that will take a toll on you mentally, emotionally and physically in an unselfish, yet bittersweet way that develops into a deep affection; and sometimes, an unknown outcome.

Love is filled with a lot of sacrifices and resentment and is underestimated in so many ways. It is something of a Catch-22 and an overwhelming source of empowerment. You might feel as though love didn't give you an answer to the questions that you asked. You've been waiting for days, even years; and perhaps you will never receive an answer at all. Maybe you've received an answer; however, it wasn't what you expected. The question is—did you accept the answer, or are you still searching for the answer you desire?

Love is a strange word. It can be misleading and confusing. It can break you down with tender grace and mercy, while at the same time building you up to become a powerful force—and after that, you will never be the same.

The ripple effects of love are beautiful and peaceful, yet can also be disturbing and ruthless. At times, love takes advantage of its powers; it causes you to suffer from loving someone too much and finding yourself lost, without hope and giving too much of yourself to the point that you suffer because you're neglecting yourself. It can cause you to lose faith. Its tremendous effect has a full impact as you find peace and happiness in your life.

Love will open your eyes to realize you are not the victim; instead you are victorious over the trials, battles, and challenges of life.

Love will show you that you do not have to search for it because it abides in you whole-heartedly. Love can be bitter-sweet but its grace is patience. Love is difficult but its mercy is tender. At times love might make you feel empty but you are never alone.

Love abounds against all odds. One thing about love is that it comes with many sacrifices. Its good intentions always reassure you that in order to love someone else, you must be willing to love yourself first.

* * *

ABOUT THE AUTHOR

Charlena Jackson, B.S., M.S., M.H.A. is a professor at a university in Georgia. She is a prolific writer and has published several books No Cross, No Crown: Trust God Through the Battle, Teachers Just Don't Understand Bullying Hurts, I'm Speaking Up but You're Not Listening, and, A Woman's Love Is Never Good Enough—her positive, dedicated and determined attitude has encouraged many people to put up a good fight for justice and to be treated with respect. She is currently working on her Ph.D. in Healthcare Administration. Charlena is a much-loved inspirational speaker. She loves to read, roller skate, cycle, write, and travel.